ARSON AT THE ASHMOLEAN

An Oxford Key Mystery

LYNN MORRISON

The Marketing Chair

Cover design by Emilie Yane Lopes

Published by

The Marketing Chair Press, Oxford, England

LynnMorrisonWriter.com

Paperback ISBN: 978-1-8380391-2-7

To Inga, she knows why.

Contents

Chapter One

It's seven in the evening on the night of the women's celebration at Barnard College. As the Head of Ceremonies, I've spent most of the day running around, making sure the celebration went off with no surprises. In something that has become a bit of a tradition, I invited my friends back to my flat for pizza afterwards. I was desperate for the cheesy goodness of my favourite pizzeria and for all of us to put our heads together about what we need to do next.

The trill of a mobile phone peals across the room, sending my friend Kate rushing over to grab it. After she says hello, she listens for a moment, her face draining of colour. Her normally steady voice tremors as she repeats the caller's words, almost as though she is praying that she misheard.

As her words ring out, I look around the room to find matching expressions of shock and horror on everyone's face. There's no doubt this call has once again thrown all of our plans into disarray.

I know I shouldn't be surprised. In the six months since I arrived at the University of Oxford, I've had to deal with magic, murder and mysteries. It is safe to say I didn't expect my dream job to come along with that kind of baggage. However, as one of the three prefects responsible for the upkeep of Oxford's magic, I didn't have any choice but to dive straight in.

After the events earlier this term at Barnard College — finding a dead body, discovering the existence of a secret chamber, learning about the origins of Oxford's connection to the magic, unmasking a murderer and even getting shot — I guess I shouldn't be caught out by much of anything anymore.

"What did you say?" I ask Kate as she disconnects the call.

"The Ashmolean is on fire," she repeats, her voice barely above a whisper. She shakes herself out of her near fugue state before she continues. "Not the museum proper, but the archives building a few doors down." She shoves her phone into her pocket, her gestures frantic with worry. "I've got to get over there. Right now!" She scans the room frantically, unable to decide what or who she needs to take with her.

I leap into action, rushing over to my front door to grab the handbag hanging on the back of it. I rustle around inside until I feel the cool touch of metal. "Here, Kate," I call out, catching her attention before tossing a set of keys. "Take my bicycle. It's locked up outside and will be faster than any car would be. We'll be right behind you."

"Thanks, Nat." She gives me a quick squeeze before gathering up her coat and handbag. She turns to the man standing beside her. Although he looks to be in his mid-thirties, his actual age is closer to a hundred.

Bartholomew Kingston, known to us as Bartie, was one of the first Eternals I met here at Oxford. After I used the key to unlock the magical properties of my bloodline, the magic and the existence of the Eternals was revealed. As the Head of Eternal Affairs at St Margaret College, he quickly became one of my favourite Eternals to turn to for guidance. Apparently, Kate saw something more in him. They've been dating for the last four months, proving just how strong a connection we prefects have to Oxford's magic.

"Bartie?" Kate looks around when she doesn't find him sitting next to her.

"I'm already at the door," he calls out, standing with his hat in hand. "I'll go straight there and have a quick look around so I can update you as soon as you arrive. It should only take you a few minutes on the bike."

I close the door after them and lean my back against it. My boyfriend Edward, the third prefect Mathilde, and our friend Harry are all rising from the sofa, their expressions heavy with worry. H, my wyvern companion and flatmate, is perched on the mantle near where my grandfather Alfred is standing.

Harry climbs to her feet and begins shooing us towards the door. "You all go on over to the Ashmolean. I'll stay behind and tidy up."

"Are you sure, Harry?" I ask, catching her eye as I wave my hands over the empty pizza boxes and a stack of dessert plates. "We can leave this all here. Edward and I can deal with it later."

Harry shakes her head. "There will be enough lookie-loos there as it is. I know you'll call or text me if there is anything urgent. I'll lock the door behind me when I leave."

As the long-time assistant to the Principal of St Margaret College, Harry has had plenty of experience keeping a cool head in times of stress. It is exactly why I was able to convince St Margaret's Eternals to throw all the magical rules and traditions out of the window, and to allow me to make their existence known to her. Harry, ever the professional, barely batted an eyelid and accepted the existence of magic as though it were perfectly normal.

"Mathilde," I call out. "Are you coming with us?"

I turn to find her already standing with her handbag in hand. "Of course, I'm coming along. All the rare books and manuscripts we found in Barnard's secret chamber are in storage in the Ash's archives. We moved them there a week ago. I can't bear to think about them burning."

I flinch at the thought of losing those materials. Mathilde, my grandfather and Barnard's Eternals spent long days combing through every page of spidery handwriting, searching for information on how Oxford's connection to the magic works and who might damage it. Although they've read everything, none of us would want to lose those pieces of history.

The Ashmolean is the oldest museum in England and it houses most of Oxford's collection of paintings, artefacts and sculptures. In the centre of Oxford, on the corner of two main roads, the building's bright yellow facade and Corinthian columns are highly visible to passersby.

Visitors feel like they are travelling around the ancient world as they view the Greek sculptures, Egyptian mummies, and Chinese pottery. Africa and the Americas are also represented, testaments to the reach of the British empire and the British explorers. From what Kate has told us, the public exhibits barely scratch the surface of the Ash's collection. Millions of pounds' worth of artwork and treasures are carefully stored in the basements and in the surrounding buildings.

One of those buildings is now host to a fire.

When Mathilde, Edward, H and I are all ready to leave, I look around to see what is taking my grandfather so long. In his younger years, he was also a prefect here at Oxford. After his retirement and before his death, he used to tell me stories about ghosts who walk the halls and a mischievous wyvern who was always causing shenanigans. Little did I know he was preparing me for my future as a prefect.

When he died, he somehow returned to Oxford as an Eternal. He stayed hidden from sight during my first term, when I was working here at St Margaret College. He wanted to give me time to settle in and find my feet.

Thankfully, his patience finally wore out, and he revealed himself to me earlier this term, when I first started working at Barnard College. His knowledge of Oxford and his experience as a prefect and now an Eternal, have made him the ideal mentor for me, Kate and Mathilde.

"Grandfather, aren't you coming?" I yell when I cannot find him.

He pokes his ghostly head through the wall. "Sorry, I was waiting in the hallway. Since the fire is in another building, I'm going to go straight to the Ashmolean proper and make sure everything there is as it should be. If this fire has anything to do with our problems with the magic, we may be in for more surprises this evening. I can get in and out with no people being the wiser," he explains.

"That is a great idea, Alfred." Edward pulls open the flat door and waves Mathilde and I into the hallway. "If you learn anything, or need any help, you'll know where to find us."

"I'll follow the smoke trail," my grandfather promises, grimacing, before he disappears from sight.

Outside in our small carpark, I ask H to fly up ahead and figure out exactly where the fire is located. I slip my hand through Edward's arm, pulling myself close against him as we make our way out of the carpark and onto the pavement. The Ashmolean may only be a ten-minute walk away, but the March air has turned chilly and there is enough moisture in the air to hint at a chance of rain. In other words, it is like most every night here in England: cold and somewhat wet.

Mathilde falls into step on my other side, burrowed up in a

scarf and coat. Kate is the oldest of our trio of prefects at forty. Mathilde is the youngest, a mere twenty-five, and I'm not much older than her at twenty-seven. Edward, a veritable prodigy, is a full professor at Oxford despite his relatively young age of thirty-five.

Mathilde's preference for jeans and t-shirts makes her look like a student, but she's actually a senior researcher at the Bodleian Library. She's forgotten more literature and history than I ever knew, and she loves nothing more than whiling away the hours chatting books with my grandfather. She is the perfect person to have the role of the bibliothecae praefectus, known to the layperson as the prefect responsible for books. I oversee the people and ceremonies while Kate has charge over the arts and sculptures.

"So much for having a plan," Mathilde huffs. "With everything that has gone on over the last six months, I am struggling to believe that a fire in the Ash could be unrelated to our problems with the magic."

We pause at the corner to let a car go by before crossing the street and continuing on our way. Already, I can smell a hint of smoke in the air.

"Let's not leap to conclusions just yet," Edward suggests from my other side. "The murderers at St Margaret and at Barnard ended up being ordinary humans. There may be a perfectly good explanation for the fire that has nothing to do with magic."

"That's true," I agree, "but I wouldn't be quick to discard the idea that it may be related to the magic, either. We know that someone has been breaking into the colleges and making off with valuables for at least six months now. Having St Margaret's missing candlestick turn up as the murder weapon at Barnard confirms the robberies are all connected. A fire would be a perfect cover for another burglary."

We fall quiet, each of us mulling over what a fire might mean for the future of the magic of Oxford. If it is indeed a cover for another theft, potentially a larger one, could the person behind this destabilise the magical boundaries enough to cause us to lose our connection? The idea makes me shiver, and Edward pulls me closer to his side.

Edward raises his voice to be heard over the sounds of passing traffic. "I don't know if any of you have properly taken me through the timeline of all the criminal activities — the magical ones, that is. I've picked up plenty from listening to all of you chat, but I could use the full picture. We've got a few blocks to go. Would you mind?"

I glance over at Mathilde and she nods for me to take the lead. "As best as we can tell, it all started shortly before my arrival. Items went missing, but the prefects and the Eternals thought it was Lillian's fault. Poor woman. She worried that her dementia diagnosis was to blame, and so she brought forward her retirement plans and hired me as her replacement."

"And that's when you stepped into my life," Edward says with a smile before leaning over to plant a kiss on my forehead.

"Yes, yes, you're very lovey dovey," Mathilde smirks, rolling her eyes.

"Back to my explanation..." I interject before she can say anything else. "If I were drawing this on a whiteboard, I'd make two lines. One would be for the thefts directly related to the magic, and there, we'd have Iffley College, St Margaret and Barnard on the list, in that order. The second line would be for the crimes which happened in part because the magic isn't working as it should."

"Those are the two murders, right?" asks Edward as we cross another intersection.

"Exactly." The smell of smoke increases as we get closer to the town centre, reminding me I need to hurry with my explanation for all the crimes. "Bartie explained it to me like this. Imagine you're on a call while riding on the train. For part of the time, you can hear everything perfectly. Then you go through a dead spot and you miss whatever the other person was saying. With the border stretched out of alignment, the magic has dead spots where the Eternals miss out on things which are happening."

"And that's why it is so important we figure out who is behind the problems with the magic," Mathilde adds.

Edward presses the button for the crosswalk. While we wait for the light to change, he looks over at us, confusion still etched on his face. "There's one thing I haven't understood. Why would the burglar carry St Margaret's candelabra into Barnard?"

A beeping noise alerts us to cross the street. I step out first, spinning around to walk backwards so I can explain to both Mathilde and Edward. "I think I know why. Remember how we used St Margaret's antiques as props for the Autumn Gala? If an Eternal holds onto the props, they can appear to be as solid as we are. If the person behind the thefts thought they might be caught in the library, the Eternal could have become visible and acted as a distraction so they could get away."

Mathilde stares at me with her eyes wide open. "I never thought about that, Nat, but I bet you are right. It makes perfect sense. They carried it in so they could be sure they had something which would work, right from the start. They probably set it down on the shelf when they went to open the secret chamber and then forgot to collect it before they left."

"And there it sat," I pick up, "until Master Finch-Byron grabbed it in his moment of need and used it to bash Ms Evans over the head."

"Wow," Edward says, looking stunned. "I would never have figured that out on my own."

"And that's why you need to stick with us prefects, Edward. We're practically magical." I give Mathilde a big wink and she snickers in response.

We pick up our speed as we pass in front of the Radcliffe Camera, the cloud of smoke clear on the horizon. The city lights illuminate the outline of a grey smudge swirling up into the sky. A black speck detaches from the cloud and grows larger, getting closer to us until I can see that it is H making his way back.

H glides towards our group, buzzing across the top of Edward's head, sending Edward ducking for cover.

I've got to do something about those two, I think to myself. They have been snapping at each other since the day Edward discovered H's true identity, and it is only getting worse. But now isn't the moment to worry about how to forge a peace treaty between my boyfriend and my wyvern.

H flips a somersault and comes to a stop hovering in front of us. "I spotted Kate and Bartie. There's a lot of smoke and it doesn't look good. Stop your yappin' and 'urry up. We need to get over there."

By unspoken agreement, we break into a quick jog, following behind H as he flies around a corner into a narrow side street. We pass in front of my favourite ice cream shop, continuing until we hit the entry to a courtyard.

A tiny park sits in the middle, its trees casting dark shadows on the pavement. We're forced to slow our pace when we hit cobblestones, knowing all too well how easy it is to slip on their smooth surface when they are wet. Smoke is heavy in the air, just shy of making us cough.

As we reach the far side of the courtyard, I can see a crowd gathered up ahead, all staring off in the same direction. The flashing red lights and sounds of water jets confirm we've arrived at the scene.

From the street view, you'd never know that the Edwardian

buildings around the Ashmolean have anything to do with the museum. University researchers and visiting scholars use the front rooms, giving passersby a view of casual office space and masking the true purpose of the buildings. That is part of the security system, keeping the average person from knowing that those buildings are warehouses for priceless works of art.

With H's help as our guide, we make our way to the front of the crowd to find Kate and Bartie staring off into the distance. Hose lines snake from a pair of bright red firetrucks and down an alley. The firefighters look like alien giants in their oversized protective gear as they make their way in and out of the narrow smoke-filled path between an Edwardian home and a boxy multi-story building. I realise that the people living in the high rise of flats must have spotted the fire out of their window, putting in the first call for help.

Standing in front of the police cordon, Bartie has Kate pulled tight against him, the flashing blue lights illuminating the tear tracks running down her cheeks. She looks ghostly pale.

"Oh Kate," I murmur as I come to a stop at her side. "How bad is it?"

Kate turns in my direction, surprised to see me standing there. "I didn't even hear you walk up, Nat." She dashes the tears from her face and forces herself to pull away from Bartie's embrace. "I don't know yet. I can't stop myself from imagining the worst."

Bartie gives us a nod of acknowledgement, looking relieved to see us arrive. "Kate, darling, now that the rest of us are here, I thought I might go into the building and see how things stand."

Kate's eyes go wide with concern. "Bartie, you can't! You'll get hurt."

"I'm part of Oxford's magic. No flame can damage me unless I will myself into solidity." Bartie gives her a last squeeze before stepping away. "I'll slip in and out and no harm will come to me."

We watch as he strides through the police tape cordon and

steps past a group of firefighters in mid-conversation before his ghostly form merges completely with the heavy smoke and disappears from view.

Kate continues to stare down the alley, her face forlorn. I decide a minor distraction might be in order. "Kate, has anyone said anything to you, or provided an update?"

Kate finally turns her head from the alley, taking a moment to process the words she heard but didn't really take in. "An update? Um, no. Not yet. There was only one fire truck here when I arrived, but then the second one pulled up. Everyone looks so busy that I hadn't wanted to interrupt them..." Her voice trails off as she refocuses her attention on the scene.

I tap her arm to attract her attention. "I know you don't want to get in the way, but you may know something which could be of use. Maybe something about the fire protection system or the layout of the interior?"

Kate blinks a few times. "Oh my, you're right, Nat. I didn't even think about that. Of course... but who do I tell?" Her gaze darts left and right, looking for someone who appears to be in charge.

"Edward?" I tug on his sleeve to get his attention. "Could you go find out who is in charge here? I don't want to send Kate off on her own."

"Of course," Edward says, and then he lifts the cordon tape and slides underneath it. We watch as he makes his way over to the nearest firefighter, a younger man wearing a t-shirt and bright yellow trousers held in place with black and yellow suspenders. His face is smeared with smoke. He reacts with surprise when Edward presents himself.

The two fall into conversation, both twisting to look at our small group, when Edward points in our direction. The firefighter frowns but then nods agreement, reaching for the walkie talkie hanging from his waistband. He raises it to his mouth and mutters something into it, waiting for a response. What comes back remains a mystery as he motions Edward to stand over to the side and wait rather than return to us.

Moments later, an older gentleman emerges from the alleyway, dressed in fire gear. His confident strides eat up the ground as he makes his way over to the younger firefighter, handing off his helmet, gloves and protective mask before crossing to Edward.

"That must be the fire chief." Mathilde shifts uncomfortably on my other side, nervous tension impeding her ability to stand still. "That's a good sign that he came so quickly. Hopefully Edward will get an update."

"Looks like we'll get one better than that," I murmur as the pair make their way over to us.

"Ms Underhill?" the older gentleman asks.

"That's me," Kate confirms, her voice sounding confident, even though I can see a slight tremble in her arm. "How is it inside? Are you close to having the fire out?"

"I'm Chief Albright. I'm in charge of the scene. It's taking longer than I would like," he replies with a grimace of frustration. "These old buildings are difficult to assess, and have so many hidden cubbies and small rooms. They are tricky to extinguish when they go up in flames."

Kate's tremor ticks up a notch, her hand visibly shaking. "The damage? How much? The works inside are priceless..." Her voice trails off as the magnitude of the risk overwhelms her.

Chief Albright reaches out a hand to her. "Steady up, Ms Underhill. It looks worse than it is, that I can confirm. The sprinkler system kicked in right away and should limit the spread of the flames. With any luck, they will protect most of the works stored inside."

Kate, Mathilde and I seem to exhale as one, letting loose some of the fear we were holding inside.

"Thank goodness! But if the fire is contained, and the spread is limited, why is it taking so long to put out?" Kate asks.

Chief Albright replies, "Although we'll need to wait for the fire investigators to confirm it, my professional guess is that the arsonist used an accelerant to start the fire. The fire spread straight up in a distinct line along a main corridor."

"Chief Albright!" a woman shouts from the alley. "We've got a Code Yellow situation. The paramedics are en route."

"Code yellow?" Edward voices the question we're all thinking.

Chief Albright spins back to Kate, his face carved from stone. "Ms Underhill, might anyone have been inside this late on a weekend?"

"Inside?" Kate's face pales. "Oh god, Andrei. Andrei Radu, our security guard. He makes a circuit of the buildings. He could have passed through as part of his normal routine." She sniffles as she pulls her phone out of her pocket. We all stand watch as she searches through her contacts and finally dials a number. "Come on, pick up, Andrei. Pick up!"

When the call goes unanswered, she presses the button to ring again. The second attempt also rings out, but Kate is undeterred. It is almost as though she fears giving up on the call means giving up and accepting that whoever the firefighters have found is the missing security guard.

She presses the call button a third time but gets distracted as the woman jogs back out of the alley with a phone in hand.

"Chief Albright, our Code Yellow... this phone keeps ringing," she calls out as she comes closer, a small black object in hand. Kate looks down and ends her call, and almost immediately, the phone stops ringing, inadvertently confirming the identity of the person they've found.

"Code Yellow?" Kate chokes, unable to get the words out.

Edward steps smoothly in, allowing her a moment to reset. "Is he dead?" he asks the chief, his voice void of all emotion. I glance at Edward, amazed at his transition from friend of the Director to professional investigator. His shuttered expression gives no hint of any emotion he must be feeling.

Kate, Mathilde and I wrap our arms around one another, in need of support as we wait to hear how the Chief will respond.

Chief Albright looks pained as he searches for the right words. "Code Yellow means there is a chance. I've got a couple of medics on the team and the ambulance with more paramedics and equipment are on their way."

The screeching sounds of the ambulance cut him off from having to say anything further. It swings in behind the fire truck, two medics jumping out of the driver and passenger doors, immediately prepared to take on their lifesaving task.

"I need to go," Chief Albright apologises. "I assume you're all staying?" We nod, determined to stay until we know the outcome. "I'll have one of my team update you as soon as I can." With that, he disappears down the alley, unknowingly passing by Bartie, who is on his way back to us.

Unlike Edward, Bartie's face broadcasts his emotional state. His brow is wrinkled, eyes filled with concern. "I found him. He was lying on the floor, soaked by the sprinkler system. I don't know... I hope it wasn't too late. I shouted at a firefighter to get his attention. I should have gone in sooner. They couldn't have known..." His babbling comes to a halt as Kate separates herself from me and Mathilde and pulls him into an embrace.

"Shh, it's okay, Bartie," Kate gently reassures both him and herself. "You did good. The Chief said there is a chance he'll live. You may have saved him."

Our group lapses into silence. We huddle together against the chill spring evening, the light rain eventually soaking through our coats and scarves. Firefighters scurry in and out of the alley, looking like ants on a mission. I check their faces and expressions as they walk past. They look tired and frustrated, but the looks of tension and stress gradually give away to signs of relief.

Eventually the smoke slows its billowing, lessening its grasp on the alley. The streetlights break through the gloom, their bright lights highlighting the ash still floating in the air. Firefighters return to their trucks, working soundlessly as they gather up their hoses and equipment.

Bartie and Kate lean against one another, trying to share what little strength they have. Edward tucks me against his side. H has his tail wrapped around Mathilde's legs, periodically sending plumes of steam upwards when she shakes from the cold.

My grandfather returns with the news that all is well inside the museum proper. It does little to perk up our group. We all know that the longer we stand there with no updates from the fire crew or the paramedics about their efforts to save the security guard, the higher the likelihood that no news is bad news.

A crunching sound of tires heralds another arrival, but our line of sight is blocked by the yellow and green striped ambulance. We hear a car door open and slam closed. Finally, a shape emerges from the side of the ambulance. The flashing lights reveal the identity of the new person on the scene, a man dressed in a suit and tie, with a mid-length winter coat swirling around his legs.

"Detective Chief Inspector Robinson," Edward confirms, loud enough for all of us to hear. "I don't think Andrei survived. If DCI Robinson is here, we're looking at a case of homicide."

Chapter Two

I wake up late on Sunday morning, my hair still smelling of smoke despite a late-night shower. When I close my eyes, I see the spinning red and blue lights of the fire engine. Thankfully, the fire didn't spread beyond the single archive building and the museum itself remained undamaged. However, Kate will no doubt need to spend the next few days assessing the extent of the destruction, what can be saved and what might be lost.

In the early afternoon, my mobile dings with the sound of an incoming message. The email confirms what Kate had announced over pizza the night before. My team has been assigned to the Ashmolean to help with the secret chamber exhibition, with a request to start immediately. Before I have time to wonder whether a delay might be in order, my phone signals another email, this time from Kate asking Mathilde and I to turn up on Monday morning as planned.

The next morning, my work week begins when I spy a familiar form striding up the steps in front of the Ashmolean. Raising my voice, I am just loud enough to be heard over the passing cars.

"Morning, Mathilde!"

Mathilde's head snaps up, a smile blossoming on her face

when she sees us waiting. She picks up her speed, jogging the last few steps to catch up with me and H where we wait at the front entrance to the museum. "Hiya, Nat and H."

She halts beside one of the enormous white concrete columns that line the front of the Ashmolean, shaking out her umbrella, last night's mist having turned into proper rain this morning. She's swapped her favourite trainers for a pair of worn leather boots, but otherwise looks the same as always in her jeans, a puffy coat, and with her long, blonde hair pulled up in a messy bun. When she spins around, I note a couple of pencils shoved haphazardly in there and I stifle a snicker.

Inside the museum there are no obvious ticket booths, as entrance is free, but off to the right I can see a raised counter offering self-guided audio tours and guidebooks to visitors as they arrive. I let Mathilde take the lead, H at her side. I follow a few steps behind, my head turning as I take in the first displays.

Off to my left is a long gallery, lined with grassy green carpet designed to draw the eye down its length. On either side of the walkway sit marble statues that appear to be ancient Greek or Roman in origin. Medusa stands tall with her twisting snakes coiled like curls about her head. Nearby is a headless man, his flowing toga carefully carved from the marble to look as though he is mid step. I say a silent prayer that he isn't one of the Ash's Eternals, not sure if I can carry on a conversation with a headless man.

"Nat?" Mathilde's voice echoes in the atrium further ahead, obviously wondering why I'm no longer behind her.

"Sorry! I'm here," I call back. "I got distracted by the statues in the gallery." My heels click across the creamy white tile floor as I pass around a glass case half-filled with pound notes and coins. The donations sign encourages visitors to support the museum's work, a narrow slit at the top offering space for them to drop in their spare change. I eye the case, dropping a few pound coins in, before moving deeper into the expansive building in search of Mathilde.

After passing through another wide doorway, I find her and H standing beside a young woman whose long, dark hair and silk scarf nearly hide the museum badge hanging from a lanyard around her neck.

"Nat, this is Francie Zhao, Kate's assistant," Mathilde introduces us as she passes me a lanyard of my own.

Now that I'm closer, I notice that Francie's swollen eyes and slightly red nose are a marked contrast to her smart skirt and blouse. She offers me her hand; her grasp firm as we shake. "Kate asked me to wait for you here. Her phone has been ringing off the hook this morning with questions from university leaders, major donors, and journalists. It's a rough morning for all of us."

"Nice to meet you, Francie. I was a bit surprised when Kate emailed us yesterday, asking us to come in today. Between the fire and the death of your security guard, I imagine this is a hard day for all of you. If it helps, we can come back tomorrow."

Francie sniffs into a tissue. "No, don't leave. I think we could all use a bit of a distraction today. That's why I'm here; I didn't want to sit home alone thinking about poor Andrei." She tears up again, taking a moment to breathe carefully as she fights for control.

I catch Mathilde's eye, but she looks as unsure as I am about what the right thing to do is at a moment like this. Francie blows her nose and gives us a weak smile.

"I'm sorry for your loss," I murmur. "I take it you knew Andrei well?"

"Better than most, but perhaps not as well as I thought," Francie replies cryptically. "But thank you for saying that. Now, I promised myself I wouldn't cry at work, and look at me." She brushes away the last of her tears, putting an end to any further conversation as she motions us to follow her up the nearby staircase.

As we wind through the galleries on the next level, crossing a glass-lined corridor, I look down to catch a last glimpse of the bright, light-filled atrium, with its winding staircase and primary-coloured pop-art murals on display. If Kate doesn't have a museum tour on my agenda for today, I'm definitely going to ask for one to be added.

I quickly lose my way as Francie leads us in and out of doorways, the displays taking us from the Middle East to Southeast Asia and back to Europe again. Finally, she pushes open a plain white door labelled *Staff Only*. She passes all the office doors until only one is left at the end of the hallway. After a sharp knock, she opens the door when a muffled voice replies from inside.

I had wondered what Kate's office would look like, imagining modern glass, metal furniture and abstract art on the wall, complete with floor-to-ceiling windows looking down onto the centre of Oxford. It would be the perfect space to entertain donors and artists alike.

I was partially right.

Her furniture is sparse and certainly much more modern and expensive than any of the college offices I've seen so far, and the oversized window floods the room with the soft lighting of a spring morning. However, the office is on the backside of the building, with a view of a small side street instead of Oxford's dreaming spires.

Kate sits behind her desk, absently tucking her straight brown hair behind her ear as she listens to the faint voice coming from the phone. She waves us into the visitor chairs in front of her desk and then pretends to sip from an imaginary teacup. Francie catches on, grabbing Kate's mug from her desk before asking Mathilde and I how we take our tea. H flaps his wings, reminding me to ask Francie to bring back a saucer of cream for my cat as well.

"We can't get inside to examine the artwork until the fire investigator and insurance adjuster arrive later this morning. I'll ring you back as soon as I know more. Bye." Kate settles the handset back into the base of her phone, massaging her earlobe. "I've been on the phone for the last hour and my ear is flaming." She flinches as her choice of words, moving her hand from her ear to massage her forehead. "It's been a long day, and it isn't even nine am."

"Did you get any rest yesterday?" Mathilde asks. Between the dark shadows under Kate's eyes and her wan complexion, my guess is no.

"I spent the day at home, but it wasn't particularly restful," she confirms. "Poor Andrei, I feel terrible." She shifts her laptop, turning it so we can see the display. She has her browser window open to show a screen from the university directory. Bold lettering identifies the individual as Andrei Radu, Security Officer at the Ashmolean Museum. His ID photo takes up a third of the screen. His strong masculine features, dark hair and steely green eyes make it look more like a headshot than the typical ID photo.

"He was only twenty-nine," Kate says with a sniffle. "They say it was smoke inhalation, but I can't understand how he got stuck inside. The building isn't that big and there were sprinklers and smoke detectors installed throughout. Such a tragedy."

Mathilde and I exchange glances, each unsure of what to say. Fortunately, the scrape of the door opening saves us. Francie backs her way inside, her arms loaded with a tray laden with four mugs of tea and a small bowl of what must be cream for H.

"There was a queue at the kettle," she explains as she carefully makes her way over to Kate's desk, settling the tray onto the corner. She quickly passes out the mugs, the laptop screen catching her eye when she turns to hand Kate her tea. Francie freezes in place, the tea sloshing over the top of the mug as her hand trembles.

Kate quickly closes the laptop, but it is too late to keep Francie from seeing what was on screen. The emotional damage is done. Before our eyes, Francie's professional, friendly demeanour crumbles, tears bursting from her eyes as a sob escapes her chest and she flees the room.

"Oh no," Kate says as she pushes back her chair. "I had heard a rumour that Francie and Andrei were involved, but as I hadn't seen any evidence of it myself, I didn't give it much credence. Looks like I was wrong." With that, Kate follows on Francie's heels, leaving Mathilde, H and I behind in her office.

After Kate returns from checking on Francie, she passes us both an activity schedule for the day. "I thought it would be useful to attend a series of introductory meetings with a few of our researchers, specifically the ones you will need to know for your work on the upcoming exhibition of the items we found in Barnard College's secret chamber. I had planned to go with you, but obviously I've had to rearrange my agenda for the day because of the fire."

I give the schedule a quick scan, noting that our first meeting starts shortly. "This all sounds brilliant, Kate. I still can't believe you didn't tell us about the plans to hold an exhibition."

For the first time this morning, Kate shows a smile. "I wanted the announcement about the exhibition to be a surprise. Honestly, seeing the look on both of your faces made it all worth it."

As Mathilde and I gather our things and head off to our first meeting of the morning, I turn back, catching Kate's eye. "I imagine your day is going to be pretty terrible, having to deal with the fire department, insurance and everyone else. But please try to take care of yourself, okay? We'll check back in on you later." Kate smiles in thanks, her ringing phone cutting off any further comment.

Poor H gets stuck tagging along with us and snores his way through discussion after discussion. He only wakes up long enough to join us for lunch in the underground cafe, scoffing a sausage roll and a cheese toastie while Mathilde and I opt for soup and salad.

By the time four in the afternoon rolls around, we're all dragging. "Are we done for the day?" I ask Mathilde. "We've been in so many meetings."

Mathilde shuffles through her notebook to check her copy of our schedule. She skims the list, our pace slow as we meander through the first-floor galleries in search of the hallway where Kate's office is located.

"One meeting left, but it doesn't say who it is with. I guess we'll have to ask Kate," Mathilde replies. "I can't imagine who is left to meet, and if I'm being honest, my brain is just about at capacity."

"I hear you," I agree. "I had no idea how much science and research went into dating and identifying all the painters and sculptors. And the coin collection! It is really incredible."

H keeps his thoughts to himself as he flies ahead of us and uses a talon to tap on Kate's office door. "Oi, Kate, we're ready for our next meetin'. What is it?"

The door swings open to show Kate still sitting behind her desk, her reading glasses perched on her nose. The desk is covered in stacks of papers. Kate is literally up to her elbows in work. Yet, her face lights up as she spots us coming in, perhaps seeing us as an excuse to set aside her current task for a moment.

"Ah, you're back. Don't sit down," she calls out, halting our progress towards her visitor's chairs. Kate points us back towards the hallway. "As you can see, I'm still trapped here, however I've found someone to fill in for me for your next meeting. You'll need to take the lift to the third-floor mezzanine. You're about to get an extra-special, behind-the-scenes look at the Ashmolean's magic, led by our most experienced tour guide... Xavier de la Tours."

The words are barely out of her mouth before H flaps up into the air and executes a celebratory backflip before flying out the door. "Xavvie! Yes!"

Kate stifles a laugh as Mathilde and I roll our eyes. "As you may have guessed from H's excitement, Xavvie is an Eternal. He was a major donor to the museum in the 1950s and 60s, and apparently he loved the Ash so much, he returned as an Eternal after his death in 1968."

"That sounds amazing," I gush with enthusiasm. "I had hoped to get a proper tour, but I got so caught up in our meetings that I forgot to ask."

Kate's smile broadens. "I knew you would. When Xavvie is finished, he will escort you upstairs."

"Upstairs?" I ask.

"I know we had a long night on Saturday, but we need a little pick-me-up after recent events. I've booked us a table at the rooftop restaurant and Edward and Bartie are both going to join us for dinner."

"That sounds fab, Kate. Thanks so much for organising all of this, particularly given how stressful your day must have been," Mathilde replies. "I can't wait to meet Xavvie and find out what secrets the Ash is hiding away."

After we say our goodbyes to Kate, Mathilde and I file behind him into the lift and wave our arms around to clear up the plume of excited smoke leaking out of his nostrils. I arch an eyebrow, but Mathilde seems just as lost as I am. "You haven't met the

Ashmolean's Eternals yet?" I ask as the lift bell signals a passing floor.

"When you say it that way, you make it sound weird," she quips back. "But I've only been in Oxford a couple of months longer than you have, and I have spent most of them either learning my way around the Bodleian or solving mysteries with you."

"Fair point," I admit as the lift bell dings, signalling our arrival at our destination. The doors slide open to reveal a man in a wheelchair waiting outside. I leap forwards, rushing to get my words out. "Sorry, sir. Were you waiting for the lift? I'll hold the doors open for you."

"Mais non!" he replies with a cheery grin and a twinkle in his eye. "After fifty years here, I can manage the stairs faster than you can!"

"Xavvie!" H cheers, pushing his way past me to land in the man's lap. "Lookin' good, mate. 'Ow 'ave you been?"

Mathilde takes me by the arm and pulls me the rest of the way out of the lift, allowing the doors to slide shut behind us. "You must be Xavier, I presume?"

"Xavier de la Tours, at your service, *mademoiselles*." Despite sitting in a wheelchair with a wyvern in his lap, he somehow executes an elegant bow. Both his thick hair and oiled moustache are salt and pepper grey, his cheeks ruddy and his bright blue eyes sparkle with merriment.

His appearance calls up a memory from the back of my mind. "Wait, my grandfather told me a story about you. Well, you and H. I had completely forgotten it, but seeing you made me remember. Something about popping wheelies in the galleries?"

"Like this?" he asks as he spins a full circle in front of us. I can't help but laugh at the sight of the pair of Eternals popping wheelies in the middle of the museum gallery.

"Exactly," I cry in delight. "I visited the Ash once when I was in secondary school. It was well after my grandfather's death, but I kept my eyes peeled for the entire day, searching for any sign of a man and a wyvern. I looked everywhere."

"I remember your visit well, my dear." Xavvie grins, his eyes sparkling. "While you were looking for us, your grandfather and I were keeping an eye on you."

"Really?" The surprise is evident in my voice.

"Really," he replies. "I recall your grandfather being at once both delighted and frustrated by your presence. He was so thrilled to see you again, and see how much you'd grown, and yet he had to keep his distance. It wasn't yet time for you to know the truth about Oxford's magic."

As I dash away a quick tear, my emotions getting the better of me, Xavvie turns his attention to Mathilde.

"You must be Mathilde, our library prefect. It is my pleasure to make your acquaintance." When Mathilde offers her hand, he takes it and places a small kiss upon it, much like a gentleman in the days of yore.

"Come along, you two," Xavvie spins his chair again with a laugh, sending H flying off his lap. "I promised Kate I'd show you how the magic of Oxford comes to life here at the Ashmolean."

Mathilde and I jog to catch up, falling into place on either side of Xavvie's chair. With H now perched on the top of the seat back, flapping his wings, Xavvie's chair rolls along at a sedate pace, leaving him free to point to the artwork surrounding us.

"Much of the magic of the Ashmolean is subtle," he explains as we enter a gallery of pre-Raphaelite paintings. "To the regular eye, the works of art are fixed moments in time. But for our prefects, the works come alive to offer you a glimpse into the mind of either the artist themselves or the subjects of the works."

We pause in front of a portrait of a young man. "This painting is a good example. Believe it or not, it is a self-portrait, and the artist was barely in his teens when he painted himself."

As we lean closer, the youth gives a small shake and comes to life, preening as he tilts his head left and right. I turn but stop when I catch him pulling a strange face. Artist or not, there is no denying he is also a precocious teen boy.

"Why doesn't he speak?" Mathilde asks, still staring at the portrait.

"Because 'e isn't an Eternal, Tildy," H replies from his perch. "Only Eternals can step out of their portraits and walk beside you."

Mathilde nods her head in understanding before moving on to admire a white marble statue of a man and woman standing together. Although she seems to have understood H's remark, I've still got questions.

"Wait a minute." I flag the others to a stop, circling around to stand in front of them. "What do you mean they aren't Eternals?"

Xavvie reflects for a moment before offering an explanation. "Yes, I can see why you specifically would be confused. Everyone you've met so far has been an Eternal. But there is so much more to the magic of Oxford. There are so many books, paintings and statues which also help our students and fellows succeed, but do so with a lighter touch than the Eternals."

He pushes his wheels, guiding us into the next gallery. "Eternals have a very specific, and very strong relationship with the university. We are either creatures, like our friend H here, or ghosts, like me. And there aren't very many of us."

"Right," I say as it becomes clearer. "H came from the Bodleian, and Bartie worked at St Margaret for years before he died. Lady Petronilla definitely had an everlasting connection to Barnard."

"And I provided the funding for one of our largest galleries," Xavvie adds.

"I guess we really haven't shown you how the magic impacts the books and art, even the buildings themselves," Mathilde marvels, her tone apologetic. "One more thing we should have done, but that has fallen by the wayside amid the craziness of the last six months."

I give her arm a quick squeeze of assurance. "Okay, so they aren't Eternals, but they are magic. How do you, um, work with them? Oversee them? I'm not sure what the right word is here."

"It's as Xavvie explained earlier," Mathilde replies. "When Kate or I, or any of the Eternals, work with the literature and art, we gain insight into the mind of the creator. For me, when I flip through a book, I can somehow sense how it is connected to others. I use those insights to guide the scholars who come to me for advice. The Eternals use it to nudge our students towards just the right book."

I raise my eyebrows, still trying to make sense of what she is saying.

Mathilde scrunches up her nose in frustration. "Ugh, this is harder to explain than I thought. Sorry, Nat. I guess it is like your magical touch when it comes to bringing events to life. That is a magic which is solely yours alone. Working with the books and the art is the same for me and Kate."

With that, my mind clicks into understanding. "I think I get it. I always wondered why you and Kate can't imagine events the same way that I do. I thought it was training, but now I can see that your minds and your magic are busy elsewhere."

"Excellent!" Xavvie cheers. "Now that we've sorted that out, let's continue on with our visit. There is still much yet for you two to see."

The closing announcements sound their warning halfway through our tour, but thanks to our staff badges, no one tries to usher us out of the building. By the time we make it back to the ground floor, our voices echo in the empty atrium, the glass and tile bouncing the sounds back to us.

I shout out Edward's name when I see his tall form staring off into the distance. He's waiting near the front entrance and seems to be as mesmerised by the Greek and Roman statues as I was when I arrived. I call again, but he still fails to hear me.

"That's odd," I remark to Mathilde. "I wonder what could have so captured his attention that he doesn't respond to his own name."

We move closer. Mathilde and I are well ahead of H and Xavvie. Those two are like long-lost best mates, more interested in trading stories of past antics than in getting to the front of the museum to meet the others.

Before we can reach him, Edward takes off into the statue gallery with a determined stride.

"Where is he going?" I ask, but Mathilde is as perplexed as I am. We speed up our steps. However, by the time we reach the doorway to the gallery, we're barely in time to see the back of his head as he moves further into the museum.

The statue hall is empty. And I don't mean of museum visitors. The pedestals and alcoves sit barren, no sign of the busts and sculptures which usually grace them. I exchange wide-eyed glances with Mathilde, both of us breaking into a speed walk to hurry after Edward.

"I thought Xavvie said that the Ashmolean's magic was subtle?" I huff my question out in between breaths.

"I think his exact words were *much of the magic*, not *all the magic*," Mathilde huffs back. Despite walking as fast as we can without resorting to jogging, we enter room after room just in time to see Edward moving off into the next one. I feel like a mouse in a maze, worrying I won't be able to find my way back to the front entrance again. When I hear Xavvie's wheelchair coming from behind, I exhale a small sigh of relief.

Finally, Edward comes to a halt at the top of a small set of stairs. Massive stone carvings flank the entryway to the next room, but don't offer many hints of what is inside. However, if what I can see of Edward's expression is any indication, it isn't your traditional museum display.

Edward splutters his words out, muttering to himself as he struggles to put his thoughts into a coherent sentence. "How? But did you? The magic? Shouldn't they be..." He shakes his head, taking a closer look to see if the scene has remained the same.

I take the steps two at a time to land by Edward, touching his arm to catch his attention. Then I look to see what is it that has him so discombobulated.

If I didn't know better, I'd swear the next room over was playing host to an ancient Roman Bacchanalia, complete with food, wine and dancing. However, it isn't people inside. The statues have grown ghostly arms, legs, heads, and even full bodies to fill in for the missing parts.

Bacchus himself reclines atop a marble lounger, his arms crossed behind his head as a nymph feeds him ghostly grapes. Ovid is on the other side of the room, his deep voice purring out the words to what I assume is one of his favourite poems as Venus and her cherubs look on with appreciation.

The sound of hooves clicking on the wooden floor grows closer until a centaur prances past me, clutching a woman in his muscular arms. Edward swings me out of the way in time to avoid being struck by the centaur's flank.

"We don't have anything like this at the Bodleian," Mathilde utters, her tone filled with wonder. I have to admit, I agree with her. My mind wanders off as I imagine how I could use them in a gala.

It takes Xavvie multiple attempts to pull our attention away from the scene and get us back on track to meet Kate and Bartie upstairs in the restaurant. We leave the statues to their revelries and exit the gallery to find the correct lift. After introducing Xavvie and Edward, we pepper Xavvie with questions about the scene we just witnessed.

He holds up a hand to halt our onslaught, explaining that those statues — after millennia of being worshipped, adored, and admired — have a magic all of their own. "They are most definitely not part of Oxford's Eternals. All our attempts to communicate with them have failed. The only interest they have is in reliving the glory days of civilisations which died out nearly two thousand years ago. Sorry, Nat. I don't think you can use them in one of your events."

After taking the lift to the top floor, the rooftop restaurant proves to be every bit as lush as Kate described it. The rich wooden floors and floor-to-ceiling windows elevate the space from casual dining into a favoured place to linger away an evening. Edward slips his hand in mine, leading me out onto the terrace. The last rays of the waning sunset bathe the nearby Randolph Hotel in a ruby glow.

As he pulls me into an embrace, I can't help but remember a different scene only a few months ago, when Edward invited me out for drinks here and I awkwardly bumbled my way through an acceptance. Little did we know that fate would intervene, with me being shot by Barnard's murdering Master on the day before our big date.

"I'm glad we finally made it here," I whisper quietly enough that only Edward can hear me. Instead of a reply, he gives me a light kiss of agreement.

"Come on, you lovebirds, I'm starvin'," H grumbles from a nearby table. True to her word, Kate has reserved a large outdoor table, with heat lamps at either end to keep us warm. The morning rain has pushed onward, leaving behind a clear sky and a fresh spring evening. Kate, Bartie, Mathilde, H and Xavvie are already sitting down.

Edward rolls his eyes at H's antics, but dutifully follows along as I work my way over to the remaining pair of empty seats. There's no menu to peruse, Kate having ordered a set dinner in advance. A waitress fills our wine glasses and leaves bread baskets and small bowls of olive oil on the table to take the edge off our hunger. Or H's hunger, I should say. By unspoken agreement, we pass both baskets to him to keep him occupied while we wait for the appetisers to arrive.

Over dinner, we fall into a familiar rhythm of chatting and laughing, taking turns poking fun at one another as only friends can do. It takes me a while to notice Kate isn't taking part. Normally, her biting wit would have us all in stitches, but tonight she's quiet, more often looking off into the distance than keeping up with the to-and-fro of the conversation.

I raise my eyebrows at Bartie when he catches my eye, silently asking if she is okay. He quirks an eyebrow up in response, no clearer than I am on her state of mind.

"If you don't mind excusing me, I need to pop to the loo," I say, pushing my chair back to rise to my feet. "Kate, Mathilde, do you want to join me?"

Mathilde looks confused for a moment, but when I nod my head towards Kate, she quickly catches on. "Sure."

None the wiser, Kate comes along, pointing us in the right direction. When we meet back up at the basins, I catch Kate rubbing her temples.

"Are you okay?" I ask, my eyes meeting hers in the mirror. "We can call it a night, skip dessert..."

"Am I that obvious?" she replies.

"Perhaps not to someone who doesn't know you as well..." I offer. "Somehow, I have the sense that this is more than simply being tired. What's going on?"

She twists around to stare at me and Mathilde. For a moment, I think she might brush off the question, but then her shoulders slump and she leans a hip against the countertop, covering her face with a hand.

"Kate, talk to us," Mathilde murmurs gently.

She moves her hand, but not before brushing away a wayward tear. "I feel so incredibly guilty. Poor Andrei. His death is all my fault. I asked him to do extra patrols and look at what happened. He was only there because I asked him to be, and it killed him."

Without thinking, I take two steps forward and wrap my arms around her, Mathilde circling around to pat Kate on the back. "This is not your fault, Kate. Or if it is, Mathilde and I bear some of the burden as well. We never meant for anything like this to happen."

"She's right, Kate," Mathilde adds. "None of us could have predicted this level of escalation. It was a terrible accident. You can't take the blame for that."

Kate takes a ragged breath in before straightening up again. "Whether or not we lit the match, we're the only ones who can figure out who is behind the theft of Oxford's magic and the cause of this weekend's fire in our archives. We've got to do everything we can to solve this. For our Eternals, and now for Andrei. Agreed?"

Mathilde and I don't hesitate. We both nod, committing ourselves to making this task our top priority. We will find out who is causing all our problems, and we will do whatever it takes, just like always.

Chapter Three

"**M**y head hurts," I moan to H as we trudge along the pavement towards the Ashmolean the next morning. "And does the sun have to be so bright?"

"I told you not to 'ave that third glass of wine last night at dinner, but no, you didn't want to listen to your old mate, H, did you?" he smirks back.

"I knew I shouldn't, but Kate was not her usual self; I thought if we lingered over drinks long enough, she might eventually cheer up."

"I don't think a glass of wine is going to solve 'er problem, Nat," H replies, leaning against my legs as we wait for the crosswalk sign to change. "But that was nice of you to try any 'ow."

I reach down to stroke the top of H's scaly head. "Thanks, mate. What are your plans for the day? I've got Will and Jill coming over to plan the exhibition's grand opening party. They are brilliant assistants, but they probably won't bring along any treats for you. I'm guessing you don't want to tag along to that meeting."

H huffs his reply, a plume of dark smoke indicating his

agreement with my assessment. "Don't worry about me, missie. I'll 'ave a look around, maybe find Xavvie and see what 'e is doin'..." His twinkling eyes set off alarm bells in my head.

We lapse into silence as I debate whether I need to set some ground rules for H and Xavvie. They're both old enough to know what is and is not acceptable... in theory. However, overnight, I remembered a few more of my grandfather's stories about the pair wheeling around the museum, creating bedlam just for the fun of it. As the ceremonial prefect, I'm sure I'd take the blame if they cause too much trouble.

I stick a foot out to halt H's progress before we go into the museum. "You're not going to cause any trouble for the staff or the visitors, are you? No steaming up anyone's ankles or causing small cyclones or playing parkour on the display cases."

H looks up at me, his face seemingly aghast at the mere suggestion. "Of course we won't cause any problems! We're Eternals, Nat. We're 'ere to 'elp people, not make messes!"

I narrow my gaze, not at all convinced by his batting eyelashes. "While I know the magic will automatically restore anything you damage, let's try to keep it to a minimum, okay?"

"Sure, Nat," H promises, before darting off into a crowd of entering visitors. Once inside, he stops briefly, flying up to hover above their heads as he calls back to me, "You won't even know we're 'ere. See you later, missie."

I follow the signs to the underground cafe, grabbing a large latte and a chocolate muffin in the hopes that the caffeine and sugar will help cure the last vestiges of my hangover. Upstairs, after only getting turned around twice, I use my museum badge to unlock the door to the small conference room Kate set aside for our use.

"Morning, team!" I force some cheer into my voice. "Did you have any trouble finding the room?"

Will and Jill beam at me from the opposite side of the table, their notebooks, pens, and mugs of coffee in perfect alignment. After nearly three years of working together, the two of them can pretty much finish each other's sentences. However, they couldn't look more different if they tried. Will is wearing his standard uniform of a plain polo shirt, its muted colour in sharp contrast to the vibrant swirls of jewel tones on Jill's African head wrap. I match their smiles with my own, pleased as always to have such a dependable and qualified team to work alongside me. Their most charming feature is their enthusiasm, which is of great help to me today.

"We got here early so we could poke around a bit before the museum opened. Kate's assistant Francie bumped into us and showed us how to get here," Will explains as he picks up his pen and prepares to make notes.

"Lucky for you! I don't know how anybody learns their way around here. There are offices and meeting rooms tucked away in every corner of the museum," I reply, pulling out a chair to settle across from them. "I hope you both enjoyed your day off yesterday. You certainly earned it with your hard work over the weekend."

They nod in unison, beaming smiles.

I double-check my notes before diving in. "Shall we start by talking first about any past events you've organised at the Ashmolean? I've got some initial ideas for the event, but I don't want to accidentally repeat something you did a year ago."

"We haven't done any events here, Nat." Jill shuffles through some printouts until she finds the right piece of paper. "I thought you might ask this question, so I pulled up the events list from the last ten years. The Ceremonies team hasn't done a single event at the Ashmolean in at least that long."

"Ten years?" I stare at them, trying to make sense of the words. "How can that be? The Ash has events multiple times per year."

"I glanced through last year's calendar to get a feel for what they do," Will interrupts. "Most of their events are informal evenings with guest speakers or artists. The few official events they host are always in concert with another museum, showcasing loaned artwork or a special visiting exhibition, and they use an internal team to oversee the coordination. This is the first time in a long while that an Oxford college is the co-host rather than an external entity."

"Right," I say, while opening my laptop. "We're all going to be newbies here, so I suggest we take the next few days to get the lay of the land."

Before long, I relax into my happy place of To Do lists and spreadsheets. With St Margaret's gala and children's Christmas party, plus Barnard's celebration of women under our belts, our team has learned which tasks we each prefer to do and where each other's strengths lie. When my stomach growls, we're well on our way to an event preparation plan.

I close my laptop, signalling a halt. "According to my stomach, it's time for lunch. Shall we have a wander around on our way down to the cafe, maybe see if we can find Mathilde as well? I'm sure she'll want to join us."

Both Jill and Will nod their agreement, the relief evident on their faces. That chocolate muffin must have tided me over more than I thought. "If you two are ever hungry or want to take a break, speak up. I tend to lose myself in the details and forget about important things like loo breaks and tea runs."

With that agreed, we lock our personal items in the conference room and return to the maze of interlinking galleries. We all stop to admire a suit of traditional Samurai armour, wondering how strong you'd have to be to hold up the intricate beaded chest-wrap and helmet. Jill bends over to read the card in front of the display. "It says here that this was a ceremonial suit and wasn't meant to be worn into battle. And those aren't beads, they're silk."

"Silk?" I lean closer, squinting my eyes to focus on the detail. "Too bad this wasn't tucked away in Barnard's secret chamber. It would have made an amazing centrepiece for the entire exhibition. Incredible, really."

A glassed-in walkway forms a bridge to the next gallery where ceramics fill the display cases. One of the signs catches my eye and draws me in for a closer look. "East meets West," I read aloud. "Discover how ceramics makers from the Far East influenced their counterparts in Europe."

Serving platters and large bowls sit side by side, their designs similar but not quite exact copies. Viewed individually, you'd easily overlook the relationship between the two, especially as one is from China and the other is from Italy. I realise that this sort of display is exactly what Xavvie meant when he explained how the magic works within the Ashmolean. The museum staff have found the perfect items to bring to life the historic trade routes between Europe and the Far East and to bridge the gap between countries which were thousands of miles and weeks of sailing apart. The display showcases a brotherhood of artists who forged a connection despite never meeting one another.

As my eyes skim over the items, I can feel the first hint of an event theme tickling in the back of my mind.

Before I can get the words out, I hear Mathilde's voice calling from behind me. "Nat? Is that you?"

I spin around to greet her. "Perfect! You found us. We were looking for you to see if you wanted to join us for lunch."

"Um, yeah." She bites her lip, her mirth evident. "I'd love to, but I need to borrow you for a minute before we go down to the cafe. There's something you've got to see."

"Just me?" I reconfirm. My curiosity sparks when she nods.

"We'll head on down and grab a table," Will offers.

"Great! We'll be there in few minutes," Mathilde replies.

Mathilde leads me to a spacious gallery at the back of the building, one that seems more suited to being a reception room in an English palace. The walls are papered with crimson silk embossed with an old-fashioned floral motif, adding a richness to the travertine wooden floors and the white and gold wainscotting.

Portraits of 18th century men, women and children gaze down from the walls, their pompadour hairstyles powdered into towering white confections. Busts of bishops and scholars are dotted in between, their cloaks, caps and crosses identifying their occupation as well as any sign would do.

My gaze skips around as I move through the room, admiring the heavily carved wooden side tables and the urns and sculptures that adorn them. In the middle of the room sits an oak harpsichord, the golden gleam of the wood calling me to come closer and tickle the ivories.

However, before I can take a single step in that direction, I hear Mathilde call out from my side, "Okay, mates. She's here."

The sound of wheels moving across the mezzanine above us sends a rumbling echo into the room. I try to see what is going on, but it is too high up to get a view. Whatever is rumbling around the mezzanine, their pace picks up as I listen to them move from one corner to the other. When my eyes land on the marble staircase in the far alcove, I get worried.

"Um, Mathilde?" I barely get the words out before she shushes me.

"Just wait, you won't be able to believe it." Her words tumble out in between excited giggles.

H's voice shouts from above, "Oi, Nat. Watch this!"

The staircase is angled so I can't see the top steps. However, I

can hear when H and Xavvie start their way down. With each
stair they bump, they screech with laughter.

I stare aghast at my first glimpse of H. He has the wheelchair
firmly in his claws and is swinging Xavvie around the first bend in
the stairs.

"Wheeee!" his voice roars, smoke billowing behind him.

The pair soon move further into view as they descend the
next section of the staircase. Xavvie leans left and right, looking
less like an older French gentleman and more like a beaming child
on a carnival ride. His hands grip the armrests, the look in his
twinkling eyes show he is thrilled with this game.

For his part, H is winding up for the grand finale. He flips over
Xavvie's head, landing on the back of the chair. His feet and claws
grip the seat as he throws his head back to straighten out its
trajectory. His wings flap like mad to keep the chair angled
enough to hold Xavvie safely in his chair. Their wild ride sends a
nearby vase on the window ledge teetering on its perch.

The two of them whoop and holler their way along the
remaining stairs, expertly navigating around the last bend and the
final few risers. They hit the wooden floor hard enough that I can
feel it shake beneath my feet.

H spreads his wings, popping them out like a set of emergency
flaps to halt Xavvie's wheelchair. For his part, Xavvie pulls on the
wheels of his chair with all his strength. The chair screeches to a
halt, sending the two of them lurching forward until they catch
themselves before tumbling to a heap at my feet.

My mouth drops open, but nothing comes out. I'm too
stunned to know what to say. Before I can figure out the correct
response, H and Xavvie thrust their arms into the air, waving in a
flourish and then taking a bow as the finale to their acrobatic act.

This pushes me right over the edge. I laugh until tears stream
out of my eyes, unable to stop myself while the pair of Eternals sit
before me, looking entirely too pleased with themselves.

Even Mathilde is overcome with laughter, the second viewing apparently no less hilarious than the first. Xavvie and H exchange high-fives, leaving us to laugh like loons.

After several minutes, our laughter tapers off into chuckles and finally a couple of deep breaths and heavy sighs as we slowly work our way back to normal.

"That was..." I start, searching for the right word to describe what I've just seen.

"Incredible?" offers Mathilde.

"Fantabulosa?" adds H.

"Magnifique?" Xavvie proposes in his heavy French accent.

I weigh their words but decide that another one is better suited. "Perfect!" I cheer as I give a soft clap of congratulations to H and Xavvie on the accomplishment of their incredible feat.

Back upstairs in our conference-room-turned-office, I send Will and Jill home at mid-afternoon, balancing out the long days they put in last week leading up to the women's celebration at Barnard over the weekend. So much has happened since then, between the fire in the archives, meeting Xavvie, and dinner at the rooftop restaurant. It feels like weeks have gone by instead of a couple of days.

The hush of the room weighs on me after a bit. After so many months of having either H or Will and Jill working close by, I'm not used to the quiet. A quick text to Mathilde resolves the problem. She turns up a few minutes later to join me, happy to make use of the near-empty conference room to catch up on her own work. We sit in a comfortable shared silence, the sounds of our fingers clacking on the keyboards keeping us from feeling alone.

"Knock, knock," Kate says as she raps on the edge of the half-open door. "I thought I might find you two here. I've finally finished meeting with the fire investigators and returning urgent phone calls. I could desperately use a cuppa and a quiet space."

"Come on in," I reply with a smile, happy to see Kate looking better than she did last night. She must have slept well, finally, as the bruises under her eyes have disappeared. "I'll make a tea run; you sit down and relax."

In the nearby tiny kitchen, I refill the electric kettle and busy myself with rinsing out teacups and selecting teabags. I return to the conference room with two cups of traditional English tea for myself and Mathilde, and a cup of Earl Grey for Kate.

Kate wraps her hands around her cup, warming them with its heat. "I know I said I wanted quiet, but I think what I really need is to discuss something other than the fire. How are you two getting along?"

Mathilde picks up her tea, leaving me to speak up first. "Good, I think. Will and Jill were here today; we started putting together a plan. Did you know that it's been over ten years since the Ceremonies department has helped the Ash with an event?"

"So long?" Kate asks, her voice surprised.

"Jill looked into our event records," I reply. "It's given us an extra incentive to make the exhibition's grand opening even more spectacular."

"Having seen your other events, I cannot imagine how you'll top them." Kate gives me a knowing look. "However, if anyone can do it, you can." She sips her tea. "What about you, Mathilde? Are you getting all the help you need to organise the books and journals for the exhibition?"

Mathilde gives a small laugh before responding. "You won't be surprised to hear that Xavvie is probably my best help. He knows everyone and everything within the walls of the museum and can often come up with an answer before I even think to ask the question."

"Xavvie was a lifesaver when I arrived," Kate agrees. "There had been an internal candidate for my role, and he did *not* take it well when the hiring committee awarded the job to me."

"Wait a minute," I interrupt. "Didn't you once tell me about getting into a physical fight with someone here? Was it the internal candidate?"

Kate looks at me with surprise. "I had forgotten I told you about that. To answer your question, yes, it was him. He attacked me near the front entrance, in front of a tour group, and I had to order him escorted from the building and banned for life. It was awful."

Mathilde and I give the appropriate murmurs of support and understanding.

"Thank goodness for Xavvie," Kate says with a twinkle in her eye. "He straightaway disabused me of any notion that the staff might resent a newcomer coming into the team. Nearly everyone was relieved that the hiring committee selected an outsider."

"He's so different from all the other Eternals I've met," I muse. "He's as knowledgeable as Lady Petronilla, yet he shares H's love for fun and adventure. If you've only got one Eternal, he is great to have by your side."

"Yes, he is," Kate agrees, her mobile interrupting her before she can say anything else. "Sorry, I need to grab this," she says as she swipes her finger across the screen.

Kate's call is brief, and the half we can hear doesn't give us many insights into the caller or the topic. "That was the front desk," she explains. "Chief Inspector Robinson just turned up and has asked to meet with me. I hope you don't mind that I asked them to escort him here. I figured you'd both want to hear what he has to say as much as I do."

Mathilde and I agree and jump into action, clearing up our papers and laptops from the table. By the time a sharp rap signals his arrival, the room is once again in order.

Kate opens the door and steps back to allow DCI Robinson inside. His deep brown eyes flash in surprise when he sees Mathilde and I sitting at the table. He knows us well enough from when we discovered Ms Evans body lying in the Barnard library. However, it doesn't appear that he knew of our connection to Kate.

"Hullo, Detective Chief Inspector Robinson. I'm Kate Underhill. It's a pleasure to meet you," Kate says, offering her hand to the officer. "I only wish it were under better circumstances."

"Yes, I get that a lot," he replies.

"I believe you know my colleagues here at the university, Mathilde and Natalie?" Kate motions across the table to where the two of us are sitting. "They are working with me on a new exhibition."

He gives us a nod, his expression flat. "Ms Payne, we meet again. Our third university death in six months. I don't know why I am surprised to see you here."

I can feel a blush fire up my cheeks. I explain, "We were all together when Kate got the call about the fire, and we came down to keep her company while she waited to find out about the damage."

DCI Robinson's eyes skip from me to Mathilde. I can't help but feel like he is weighing my words, particularly when his eyes narrow in suspicion. I paste a bright smile on my face to hide my nerves.

Kate coughs to recall his attention before she asks, "I heard you have some new information on the fire. Would you mind sharing it with us? I have no issue with discussing the matter in front of Nat and Mathilde."

"Yes..." he drags the words out as he pulls out a chair at the head of the table and opens his briefcase. He retrieves a notepad and a pen, holding them close to his chest as he sits down. "Let me start by thanking you for giving us access to the Ashmolean's Head of Security. It is a pleasant change from some of the other university institutions who prefer someone internal take the lead on investigations."

He gives me a hard look, leaving no doubt as to whom he means. Poor Edward. Master Finch-Byron's heavy-handed efforts to block the police from investigating Ms Evans' death at Barnard have clearly had an impact on DCI Robinson's relationship with Edward. He didn't appreciate Edward being put ahead of himself.

Kate lays her hands flat on the table and leans closer. "As soon as I heard the fire chief mention an accelerant, I knew this couldn't be an accident. I want whoever is behind the fire to face justice for their actions."

DCI Robinson gives her an appraising look before glancing down at his notepad. "Excellent. I have an update, and then if it is okay, I've got some questions for you."

Kate nods for him to begin.

"The fire inspector's report confirms the presence of an accelerant poured along the main aisle within the storage area and throughout the ground floor. Mr Radu was found in the far corner. Originally, we believed he died from smoke inhalation, but the autopsy revealed he fell from height first — perhaps a ladder or the shelves." He pauses again to look at his notepad. "Now, there are separate security feeds for the inside of the building and the back entrance. We were able to retrieve the exterior footage from the university system yesterday, but there is an issue with the interior footage. It was stored on a local hard drive and was damaged in the fire. Your Head of Security has contacted the university's computer science department to see if it can be recovered."

Kate shifts in her chair, her interest clear. "Did the exterior footage capture the arsonist?"

The Chief Inspector nods, but he doesn't answer her question in any greater detail. "Before I go into that, I'd like to ask my questions, if I may?"

Caught off guard by the sudden turn in the conversation, Kate sits back, looking wary. "Of course. I'll help however I can."

"How well did you know Mr Radu?" he asks. "Did you know anything about his life outside of work?"

"No," Kate shakes her head to punctuate her reply. "I joined the museum last summer and have been quite busy since I arrived. The museum has over two hundred staff members and nearly three hundred volunteers. Thus far, I've been focused on learning their names and job roles, and I know very few of them outside of the office."

"I see," the Chief Inspector replies, his voice unrevealing. "What about your HR policies? Are there any restrictions on relationships within the office?"

Kate quirks up an eyebrow, and I can't help but look over at Mathilde. "Inter-office relationships aren't encouraged, but like most businesses, our guidelines only restrict relationships between employees and their managers." Kate's tone changes, her confusion with this line of questions clear. "Where are you going with this, Chief Inspector?"

The detective's dark brown skin takes on a rosy tone as he flushes under her stare, but he holds firm in his position. He waits to see if Kate will reveal anything else, allowing the silence to stretch to uncomfortable lengths. For her part, Kate straightens, but remains mum. Neither Mathilde nor I dare to interrupt, not that we have anything to add, anyway.

"I'd like to interview some members of your staff," he says, finally breaking the silence.

"Of course," Kate responds as she settles back into her chair. "We can set up a conference room for your use, perhaps arrange for a rota so we can be efficient with everyone's time..."

"Thank you, but that won't be necessary." He cuts across her offer. "I'd prefer to take people down to the station."

Kate, Mathilde and I all sit up straighter at his words. Interviews at the station are certainly a step up from a few questions in a conference room.

DCI Robinson opens his briefcase and slides his notepad back inside before rising to his feet. Kate matches his movements, slipping out of her chair to approach the conference room door.

"Who can I help you find, Chief Inspector?" Kate asks, her friendly tone ringing somewhat false.

He gives her a hard look, once again taking her measure. Kate's smile doesn't slip. He reaches past her, placing his hand on the door handle. "Please call your assistant, Francie Zhao. I need her to accompany me to the station."

Chapter Four

"Francie?" Kate's friendly smile disappears from her face as she tries to process the Chief Inspector's words. "Our Francie?"

"She's on the security feed seen leaving the building only minutes before the start of the fire," he explains.

"Minutes before the fire?" Kate repeats his words, her eyes darting to mine as though I might offer some explanation for why this would be the case. However, I'm equally stunned by this turn of events.

Kate clears her throat and tries again. "Francie can't possibly have anything to do with the fire. It's inconceivable. She's as dedicated to the museum as I am. Why would she want to risk damaging the art stored in the archives?"

"That's what I'm hoping to find out, Ms Underhill." DCI Robinson motions towards the open door. "Now, if you wouldn't mind calling her, or escorting me to her desk, we can be on our way."

I watch as Kate's eyes shift left and right, certain she is searching for some explanation for this development. After all, we know the arsonist must be the person behind the problems with the magic. That couldn't possibly be Francie.

Is DCI Robinson on the wrong track, or are we the ones who are mistaken? Have we wrongly leapt to the conclusion that our suspected burglar is to blame, setting the fire to cover his or her tracks? Could there be a simpler explanation for the fire?

Kate must arrive at the same conclusion as I do. We have nothing to gain by standing in the way of DCI Robinson. She pastes a professional smile back on her lips, nodding her head before stepping out the door. When the pair is out of sight, I hear Kate ask the inspector to wait for a moment. Her footsteps grow louder on the wooden floor as she makes her way back and pokes her head around the door frame.

She whispers just barely loud enough to be heard, "Nat, would you mind phoning Edward while I escort DCI Robinson to Francie's work area?"

"On it," I reply, holding up my hand to show I've already got my phone out.

Mathilde scoots around the table to close the conference room door when Kate once again departs. She leans her back against its hard surface, looking bewildered. "I couldn't imagine where the Chief Inspector was going with his line of questioning, but not in a million years would I have guessed he'd ask to speak to Francie. *Francie!*"

I pause before hitting the call button. "Remember Saturday night, when we were talking as we walked over to the fire? Edward was the first to suggest that the arsonist might have nothing to do with the magical problems. Do you think maybe he was right?"

Mathilde shrugs, her expression uncertain. She motions for me to hurry up and get Edward on the phone.

"Hiya, it's me," I say when he answers the call. "Sorry to interrupt your research, but we've got an emergency here."

I rush to reassure him that everyone is fine and then move into a recap of our meeting with the DCI.

"We don't know what to think, Edward," I blurt into the phone. "Can you come over? We need the help of someone who understands how a police investigation works." I exhale as he promises to leave straightaway, making quick work of the ten-minute walk from his office at St Margaret to us. When we hang up, I send Kate a quick text to suggest she wait for him downstairs once DCI Robinson and Francie have left the building.

Mathilde and I spend the intervening minutes weighing up theories, but we can't make any further headway in figuring whether the fire is connected to the magic. It is a relief when we hear Kate and Edward's voices coming from the hallway.

Edward opens the door and steps inside to make his way over to my side of the table, squeezing my shoulder in greeting before pulling out the chair beside me. After ensuring the door is shut completely, Kate joins us at the table.

"I know I shouldn't leap to conclusions, but there is no way Francie started the fire," Kate says, her tone firm. "If you had seen her face when DCI Robinson asked her to come down to the station for questioning, she didn't look shifty or guilty. She looked lost, confused and upset."

"Let's work this through one step at a time, starting with what you know about Francie," Edward suggests gently. I lean over to grab a pen and paper as Kate settles into her chair.

"I hired Francie as my assistant around the time that you arrived, Nat," Kate begins. "Francie had read Art History here at Oxford and had joined the museum staff through our internship programme. When the assistant position became available, she submitted her CV to the hiring department and sent me a personal email explaining why she would be a great fit for the role. Despite being young and relatively inexperienced, Francie immediately impressed me, far more than some of the other candidates."

"So, you hired her," I interrupt. "How well do you know her?"

Kate pauses before answering, her pale cheeks flushing mildly. "I always make a point to get to know my immediate team, but I have to admit I've been remiss with Francie. I took her out to lunch twice before we closed for Christmas, but then we were all locked away inside Barnard's old library for two weeks. By the time I returned to my office here, my responsibilities were piled up and screaming for attention. Francie's told me a little about her background, but I didn't know she was seeing Andrei."

"When did you find out about Francie and Andrei?" Edward asks.

Kate thinks for a moment. "A couple of weeks ago. I overheard one of our volunteers commenting that the pair were cute together, but I thought nothing of it. Some of our older volunteers fancy themselves as matchmakers. I chalked it up to being another one of their efforts to pair off our younger staff members. I didn't remember it until Francie broke down into tears yesterday morning, when we were all in my office."

"That's right. I felt so bad. She was so clearly upset," Mathilde murmurs. "You went out to calm her down. Did she say anything then?"

Kate nods, saying, "She told me they had been seeing each other for close to a month. He hadn't wanted anyone at the museum to know, so they kept it quiet."

"Was it serious?" I ask as I make notes.

Shrugging, Kate replies, "Honestly, I'm not sure. Francie herself described it as a 'whirlwind romance'."

Edward leans back, mulling over the information. "Kate, can you think of any reason why Andrei would have wanted to keep the relationship a secret? Would it have caused any problems here at the museum?"

Kate shakes her head, looking uncertain. "DCI Robinson asked something similar. We have so many employees and volunteers here, plus the visiting researchers. It's inevitable that people will meet up and find a connection with one another. As long as the two people don't work for one another, I can't see why there would be a problem. In this case, I wouldn't have had any issue with Francie dating Andrei."

Edward taps his chin as he considers his next question, leaving me space to jump in with one of my own. "Tell us about Andrei, Kate. What was your perception of him?"

"He was very handsome with those sharp cheekbones and strong brow, and he was clearly fit." Kate looks up, lost in her thoughts. "He would strut around the galleries. I would say that he knew he was attractive, and he was happy to enjoy the attention of our female staff and visitors, but he never did anything which crossed a line. I'm not aware of any issues with his work. As far as I knew, he came in, did his job and then left."

Edward rises to his feet and walks over to stand near the window. Although you can't see the site of the fire from the museum itself, Edward stares off into the direction of where that archive building is located.

"So, we've got two people in the early days of a relationship. Both dedicated employees, with no problems at work. And as far as we know, no issues within their relationship, at least none which had been carried into the workplace." Edward turns back to look at us. "You said DCI Robinson mentioned Francie being on the security tapes. Have you seen them, Kate?"

"No..." Kate's face looks grim. "However, I think we need to remedy that. Give me a second to call Security and ask if they can email them to me. We can go over to my office and watch them on my laptop."

I stash my paper and pen in my bag, and Mathilde and I gather our things. Given the late hour of the afternoon, it is clear we aren't going to get any more work done here today. As a group, we leave the conference room and return to the maze of interconnecting museum galleries.

"Make yourselves at home," Kate offers as we go into her office.

"Shall I pull an extra chair over?" Edward asks, his arm resting on the back of a nearby seat.

"No need," Kate reassures him. "I've got a screen I can lower down." She searches through papers lying on her desk until she finds a small remote. "Here we go."

The small click of a long, narrow flap opening in the ceiling is followed by a whirring sound as a white fabric screen unrolls from its storage compartment. Edward looks like he has a serious case of office envy, his mouth slightly open in disbelief.

Glimpsing his face, Kate explains, "Sometimes, I have to hold meetings in here, particularly with donors who prefer to remain anonymous. No one can see into my office, so we videoconference them into meetings."

"That's convenient," I agree with a smile. "I was wondering how we were all going to gather around your laptop screen."

While Mathilde, Edward, and I rotate our chairs to face the screen, Kate sorts through her unread emails to find the one from Alan. True to his word, his email, the signature proclaiming his title as Head of Security, is near the top, with a video file attached. The message explains that he's sent over the relevant footage from the evening of the fire and there is no sound, only images.

Kate's double-click causes the right programme to open, and she quickly expands the image to fill the entire screen. "Let me know if you want me to pause it, or to go back."

"Let's watch it all the way through first," Edward suggests. "Then we can go through a second time to get a better look at the bits that catch our eye."

With that agreed, Kate presses the play button. At first, it appears the video has failed to start. The screen is split down the middle, one side showing a view of the front entrance, and the other showing the back alley where the rear entrance is located. Almost as one, we lean in closer, entirely focused on the footage.

Thanks to the lengthening spring day, there is plenty of daylight even though the display shows a time of seven in the evening. The camera on the front of the building pans and moves, following small groups of people as they make their way along the pavement. There doesn't seem to be any obvious rhyme or reason behind which people the camera tracks, sometimes following them for the full length of the visible pavement, and other times focusing on and off them. After a while, it stops moving, remaining fixed in one angle.

The other side of the screen is much more monotonous. It shows part of a concrete courtyard and a view of the alley leading back to the main street. The alley looks barely wide enough for a compact car to pass through, more likely originally built to provide access to a stable instead of a garage.

Without warning, Francie comes into view, first on the camera showing the front of the building. She appears happy enough, one arm swinging by her side while she holds a large carry-out bag in another. She pauses near the stairs up to the front entrance, but thinks better of it, turning around to continue towards the entrance to the alley. She disappears from one side of the screen and soon appears on the other, as she exits the alley into the back courtyard. We see her dig around through her purse, eventually pulling out a familiar-looking lanyard and badge and disappearing out of the frame.

"She must have gone inside the building," Kate explains.

We watch as the timer on the display ticks along. One minute, three minutes, five minutes. Then Francie comes stumbling back into the camera range. Her body language is so dramatically changed, I can almost convince myself this is a different girl. Her shoulders are slumped and one arm is wrapped around her own waist, as though she is in physical pain. She shambles over to a large waste bin, moving her arm up to throw open the top and sling the carry-out bag into it before slamming it shut again. She pauses with her hand on top of the lid, hunched over, her shoulders heaving. Slowly, she gathers herself back up, pushing off the bin to stagger her way into the alley.

We get a last glimpse of her when she exits the alley and reappears on the front feed, sobbing into her hands as she leaves. The video moves towards the end, eventually stopping shortly after smoke billows around the courtyard.

Edward is the first to break the quiet. "Okay, before we discuss what we've seen, I think it would be interesting to get your immediate opinion on Francie as a suspect. You three know as much as the police know, and you've seen what they saw. How many of you agree with their line of thinking about her potential guilt?"

Not a single one of us speaks.

"None of you? Really?" Edward asks, his voice thick with suspicion. "I have to be honest; I can somewhat see DCI Robinson's perspective here. What are you three seeing that we're missing?"

Kate, Mathilde and I swap gazes, each of us looking amused at Edward's predicament. Kate starts us off. "Francie did not look like an angry woman scorned. She started off looking happy-go-lucky, like a young woman in the first blush of love, and in the end, she looked like a woman who had just had her heart broken. She might have decided to set him on fire eventually, but less than ten minutes after he hurts her feelings? I don't buy it."

"Plus," Mathilde steps in, offering her thoughts next, "she threw the bag away in the bin right outside the door. She touched so many things! If she is a criminal, she is one of the worst. Her fingerprints must be all over the place."

Edward turns his head in my direction. "All right. Nat, is there anything else you want to add to the above?"

"Just one small thing," I reply with a cat-ate-the-canary smile. "Someone else left the building after she did."

My words land like a bomb in the room. Kate and Mathilde each look thoughtful, while poor Edward looks stunned.

He eyes me dubiously, but the smirk on my face convinces him I'm serious. He spins around to Kate and asks her to back up the video and replay the end.

We watch those final moments three times in a row. Francie leaves the building, goes over to the bins and then disappears. The camera moves position, focusing on the edge of the courtyard nearest the alley. Nothing happens, and then smoke billows from the courtyard.

After the third time through, Edward raises his hands and begs for an explanation. "All I see is an empty courtyard and then smoke. What are you seeing that I'm not?"

I give him a gentle smile to soften my words. "Don't feel bad, Edward. I'm pretty sure that the only reason I figured it out is because I've spent the last six months living with a smoke and fire-breathing wyvern. You sweep up enough ash and you notice how smoke moves around."

I rise to my feet and start across the room. "Kate, do you mind if I drive the video for a minute?"

"It's all yours," Kate replies, pushing back her chair to make space for me at the desk.

I slide the button to back up the video, and then carefully work it towards the end again so they can see the action in slow motion. "Do you see the smoke here when it first shows up on camera?"

All three nod, so I carry on further. "As you can see, the smoke is low to the ground, and quite minimal. Basically, it's what you would expect if the smoke was leaking under the bottom of a door or through a narrow opening in a window."

I drag the cursor again and then leave it, moving in front of the screen. "Look here at this plume of smoke. There is no way the smoke is going to suddenly increase in volume like it does here unless it finds another way outside."

"Such as someone opening the door," Mathilde states, her confusion clearing up.

"Right! Now hold that thought for a moment." I return to the screen and advance the image another thirty seconds. When I've got the image where I want it, I return to my position in front of the large screen. I wave my hand around, explaining, "Pay close attention to this area right here," and then I quickly return to the laptop. I move the slider left and right, slowly advancing and rewinding the scene until I'm sure everyone has seen it in detail.

I glance at Edward to see if he has caught on, but he is scratching his head, both figuratively and literally. Kate and Mathilde don't look like they are doing much better. Apparently, this is going to take some detailed explanation.

"I'll walk you through what I'm seeing. First, the smoke rolls out, which to me indicates that someone opened the door. If you're inside a building which is on fire, my guess is that you wouldn't open the door and then turn around and go back inside. That's why I expected to see someone else come into the frame."

"That makes perfect sense, Nat," Edward interjects, "but no one does."

"That's where you're mistaken, Edward. Watch!" I back the

video up once again and then press play before moving to stand up front. "Here is where the door presumably opens, then the smoke billows, and then it rolls across the courtyard. Except for right here…" I point in the direction of the smoking shelter. "If you look closely, you'll realise that the view of the shelter isn't blocked by smoke. It's blurry."

"Blurry?" Kate pipes up, not following.

Edward, however, has caught on. "Wait a minute. Do you mean blurry like the Barnard security tapes? Are you sure?"

"Exactly!" I beam at him in satisfaction. "At Barnard, we had a working theory that our burglar had figured out how to hide themselves behind an Eternal, so he or she could get past the security cameras without being caught on film. Kate, can you replay this part again for me?"

Kate rolls her chair back to her desk and does as I ask.

Standing beside the drop-down screen, I trace the action. "The smoke billows… now here comes the blur… see how the smoke moves to the side as the near-invisible people make their way out of the courtyard and into the alley? It looks exactly like when H flaps his wings to dissipate smoke after a sneeze. It may not be obvious, but I am positive that someone left the archives building after Francie stumbled off in tears. She isn't the arsonist."

Kate sits up straighter in her chair, her expression hopeful. "Well done, Nat. We never would have spotted any of that if you hadn't pointed it out. We've got to tell DCI Robinson."

"I agree," Edward chimes in. "This is a critical piece of information, but there are two problems. The first is that we don't know for sure that an Eternal could help someone sneak past a video camera. The second is that DCI Robinson doesn't know Eternals exist."

"We can resolve the first issue easily enough," Mathilde says. "I'm sure Bartie and Alfred would be happy to help. We could use St Margaret's security cameras after hours."

"Fair point," Edward concedes. "But what about the second problem?"

His words stump all of us for a long moment. My mind races as I consider the challenge. How have I dealt with this issue in the past? I clear my throat and offer a suggestion. "We don't need to tell DCI Robinson what we think happened. We have to plant a seed of doubt, one big enough that he will reach out to a fire expert and ask for a second review of the footage. If I can look at the smoke pattern and figure all of this out, an expert certainly could do it."

Edward weighs my words and then grimaces. He reaches into his pocket and pulls out his phone, scrolling through the contact list until he finds the name he needs. "It hasn't been long since they left. Hopefully, I can catch him before he questions Francie."

I return to my chair, scooting it closer so I can listen in on the conversation.

"Trevor? It's Edward Thomas. I'm glad I caught you. I'm here at the Ashmolean and we've got some new information we need to share with you." Edward picks his words carefully, recounting the anomalies I spotted in the footage. When he finishes, he lapses into silence, listening carefully to DCI Robinson's response.

Short of climbing into Edward's lap, I can't make out the words coming from the faint, tinny voice on the line. I'd ask Edward to put it on the speaker, but the conversation is awkward enough without making DCI Robinson feel as though he has an audience hanging on his every word.

Edward finally speaks again. "Yes, I can understand why you want to question her. But if there is a chance it is someone else, doesn't that warrant an additional review of the footage?"

I don't think Edward gets the answer we'd hoped for, as the conversation turns choppy.

"Yes... No, I'm not second-guessing or trying to impede your investigation... I do understand why you'd... You're right, I would do the same..." Edward sighs in frustration. "Very well, that is fair. I don't want to hold you up any longer. I appreciate you taking my call. Goodbye."

Edward's face is grim as he ends the call.

"What did he say?" Kate asks, her voice barely above a whisper.

Edward pulls his attention away from his phone, raising his head to meet Kate's eyes. "He seemed skeptical. Unconvinced. In the past, he probably would have listened to me, but after being shoved out of two murder investigations in the past six months, he didn't appear to have any patience for me getting involved in this one. He's found a likely suspect, and he intends to question her."

Edward flinches when Kate's face drops. "It wasn't all bad news, however. He said he has a warrant to search Francie's flat, but if the questioning and the search fail to turn up any evidence of her involvement, he'll take another look at the security footage."

Edward's words do little to erase the worry from Kate's face. I paste a smile on my own, standing back up to attract her attention away from Edward's words. "Let's not borrow trouble. None of us think Francie is the arsonist. If they question her and search her flat, maybe that is a good thing? The police can exonerate her and move their attention in the right direction. Right?"

Kate huffs out a breath. "Yes, you're right. I was being silly, hoping we could save Francie the experience of a police questioning. Even if she is innocent, she was there moments before the fire started. She may have spotted something out of place and not realised it. I'll clear my schedule tomorrow morning to make sure I can check in with her and see how she is doing."

Feeling relieved, I move my gaze over to Mathilde and

Edward. "While Kate is doing that, the rest of us need to get to work. I suggest we reconvene at my flat, together with H, Bartie, and my grandfather. We've got an arsonist to identify, and no one is better placed to figure out who that person could be than we are."

Chapter Five

"I never thought I'd look forward to dining hall food," I confess to Edward as we walk into the main building at St Margaret College. "But when Harry suggested we get a bunch of takeaway meals from here instead of ordering delivery, I leapt at the chance."

"Yes, the quality of the menu is certainly one of the top reasons I am still living in the college flat," Edward agrees. Our steps click and clack on the old wooden floors, halting only when we stop to say hello to Catherine Morgan. As usual, she is comfortably ensconced in her portrait near the college's main entrance, on the lookout for anything unusual or of interest. With nothing new to report, she quickly sends us on our way to the dining hall.

In short order, we retrace our steps, our arms laden with bags of steaming takeaway boxes, leaving a trail of delicious-smelling air in our wake. Back in the college gardens, I fall into step with Edward as we navigate our way along the garden pathways. My mind wanders through a highlight reel of my time here in Oxford so far. Though first I was at St Margaret and then at Barnard, the colleges had quickly moved from workplace to becoming more of a second home, and I took full advantage of their dining halls, residences and entertainment options. For all the stress of the last few days, the Ashmolean might be just the motivation I needed.

I heft a bag further up my arm, jostling Edward as I do so. "You know, I'm thinking that working out of the Ashmolean right now is a bit of a blessing in disguise."

Unaware of my train of thought, Edward glances over with a confused look on his face. "What do you mean?"

"I've got to move out of my flat here soon. If I were still working out of the office in this college, it would be a shock to the system to cut myself off from daily dining hall dinners and evening reading sessions in the Senior Common Room. The Ashmolean doesn't have that same homey feel. It is more like a regular workplace where you go during the day and willingly depart in the evening. It is almost easing me out of my dependency on the colleges, and that is probably a good thing right now."

"Why are you determined to leave St Margaret straight away?" Edward interjects, reviving the discussion I keep trying to avoid. "I've offered several times. You can move upstairs with me for a while, and then look for a place when things have settled down. Or not. We can see how it goes."

I could move upstairs, but even if it is only temporary, I'm worried about how that would change the dynamics of our relationship. Edward has been living up there for years, and every single room reflects of his personality. It would feel as though I were shoving my way into his space, regardless of the fact that he was inviting me to do so. I cannot imagine Mathilde and I having one of our movie nights in his living room. And H? That one-bedroom flat is certainly not big enough for three of us.

I know Edward is trying hard not to pressure me into an enormous commitment, but this is worse. I want moving in with someone I care about to be a big deal. I don't want a watered-down invitation with a 'Get out of jail free' card attached to it. The thought of moving in for a few weeks only to move back out again is unfathomable. Who does that?

I don't know how to explain my worries and concerns to Edward. The one time I tried, I made such a mash of it he thought I was trying to break up with him. Since then, I've been ducking and dodging the discussion anytime he has brought it up.

This time, I'm saved from replying by the sight of my back door and H waiting on the doorstep.

"'Urry up with the food, will ya?" H calls when he spies us coming up the walk. "'Arry said they've got cheese souffles on the menu tonight."

"They do indeed," I confirm as I dash up the back stairs and through the open door. "Has everyone made their way here?" I settle the two bags of food on the nearby breakfast table and sigh as I rub the red marks left by the plastic handles on my arms.

"Yeah, all 'ere. 'Arry's pouring drinks for Mathilde and Kate, and Bartie and Alfred are catching up on the news from the last night's university-wide Eternals meetin'." H's voice trails off as he sticks his snout into the bag, following the smells in search of the promised souffle.

I quickly scoop up the bags, saving them from the accidental destruction only a hungry wyvern can cause. Edward follows me through the kitchen into the living room and together we put all the boxed meals on the coffee table.

"I don't know why you let H run riot through your food, Nat," Edward grumbles. "He's an animal, constantly leaving a mess behind."

"He's an Eternal," I remind Edward, for all the good that it does. Edward spent too many years thinking of H as Lillian's cat. Lillian, my predecessor, didn't help since she also kept H at arm's length. H has told me more than once that I'm the first prefect to treat him as a partner, rather than as a pet. I'm sure I have my grandfather Alfred to thank for that, since he told me so many stories of the mischievous wyvern when I was a child. H was as much of a person as the characters in any of my storybooks. That he had wings and misbehaved was a bonus.

Edward's off-hand remark solidifies my decision to look elsewhere for a room to rent. H and I moving into his space upstairs could only spell disaster. Sooner or later, they are going to end up in a full-on battle.

The question now is who can I ask to accompany me on my search for a new flat? I let my gaze travel around the room, taking everyone in. Kate is first in my line of sight, but I immediately mark her off the list. She has her hands full with the fire investigation. The last thing she needs is someone turning up to ask for a favour.

Harry is next up. She'd be a perfect choice, except for one thing. Harry wants what is best for me, but I'm not certain that she and I see eye to eye on what that is. She's been thrilled to see Edward and I fall for one another, two of her favourite people here at St Margaret finding love and maybe a future together. Will she understand my desire to find a place of my own, or will she find problems with every available flat, leaving me no option but to move in upstairs? I know she means well, but something holds me back from trusting her with this task.

Finally, my eyes land on Mathilde: young, independent, no nonsense. She was on the house hunt herself last year when she moved to Oxford. I'm sure she has a good idea of which letting agents are reliable as well as what neighbourhoods will fit within my budget. She's straightforward, but also reasonable. She'd be the perfect person to help me weigh up what housing is available and find something which fits my budget and my needs.

She catches me staring at her and raises an eyebrow. I squeeze onto the sofa next to her and whisper, "Remind me to talk to you tomorrow about flat hunting. I need your help."

Mathilde grins, immediately reassuring me that she was the right person to approach. That settled, I park any remaining concerns about flat hunting, focusing instead on handing out food containers and cutlery.

When we've distributed the food and are munching away on our dinners, my grandfather steps forward. "Kate and Mathilde updated Bartie, H and I on what you spotted in the security footage. Excellent work, Nat."

"Fanks, granfaffer," I mumble, my mouth full of food, eliciting chuckles from around the room.

"I can see you're enjoying your meals," my grandfather comments with a wistful smile. He may be an Eternal, but as a ghost, unlike H, he can't eat. "While you all focus on dinner, I'll update you on my evening. Sound okay?"

We nod, happy to sit back and listen. The food is divine. None of us want to run the risk of our plates getting cold while we talk.

"Last night was the monthly leadership meeting for us Eternals, attended by the Heads of Eternals Affairs from each of the colleges. Normally Bartie would attend, but given the events of the last few days, I offered to go in his place."

Kate swallows her food and raises her hand to interrupt my grandfather. "Thank you for that, Alfred. Bartie has been a great moral support when I needed it."

"I had no doubt that he would be, Kate," he replies with a gentle smile. "At any rate, I'm glad I was there."

"What was the topic of the meeting?" I ask, in between bites.

"Our problems with the magic," my grandfather replies, his brow wrinkled with worry. "Criminals have snuck into colleges and stolen valuables, uncovered and burglarised a secret chamber, and now it seems they've set fire to the Ashmolean's archives.

We've got to identify who is behind them and put a stop to their crimes. Eternals from all the colleges here in Oxford have been working together to come up with a short list of people we believe could be our suspect."

Mathilde nearly chokes on a gulp of water. "A short list?" she says with wonder once she stops coughing long enough to get a word out. "Already?"

My grandfather beams at Mathilde, pride clear on his face. "This is what the magic does best, Mathilde. It takes a seemingly impossible problem and quickly narrows down the avenues for research."

Mathilde stares at him, eyes wide. "But how?"

"I'm glad you asked," he replies. "Thanks to Edward here, we know that anyone with the right bloodline can forge a connection with the magic..." He holds up a finger before adding, "That is, if they have access to one of the three prefect keys and use it to unlock one of the prefect desks. Just as Nat had Edward do, when she brought him to her office and convinced him to use her key to unlock her desk."

Once again, we all nod our understanding, curious to know what else my grandfather will say.

"And thanks to our discovery of Sir Christopher Wren's journal in Barnard College's secret chamber, we also have a rough idea of who the original discoverers were. We presume those men interacted with the magic enough to transform something within themselves, giving their descendants the ability to connect to the magic and carry on with the roles of the prefects."

"It's been over three hundred years since Sir Christopher stumbled across the magic of Oxford. That's eight generations of families, Alfred. How could you and the other Eternals already have a short list of potential suspects for us?" Mathilde asks.

"I agree that if you started at the top of the family tree, the list would number in the thousands," my grandfather replies. "However, we had one more piece of information at our disposal."

Mathilde elbows me, but I shrug. As hard as my brain is working, I can't imagine what other clue the Eternals had available.

"Don't hold back, Alfred," Harry admonishes my grandfather as she waves her fork telling him to get on with it.

"We know the individual had to be working at a college here at Oxford around the time that Lillian noticed things going missing, which was shortly after Kate arrived," he explains. "We flipped the genealogy chart on its head. We started by putting together a list of people who interacted with our prefects - colleagues, college fellows, researchers and the like."

Mathilde shakes her head, still unconvinced. "That has to be a large number as well, at least a few hundred people."

"Our shortlist has three names on it," my grandfather reassures her, holding up his hand to halt her next question. "To activate their connection to the magic, our mystery thief had to be here at Oxford and be near one of you. Or you, Kate and Lillian, I should say. You three held the only keys during the period in question."

Kate grimaces. "I'm not sure 'held' is the right word. Mine is sitting in my desk drawer. That's where I found it shortly after I started my role at the Ash, and that's where I left it."

My grandfather gives her a reassuring smile. "Don't worry, our logic still proves sound. Whether they needed to interact with you directly, or simply have access to wherever you store your key, it still narrows down the possibilities to a handful of people."

"Who are they?" Mathilde asks. "We must know them, or at least one of us, right?"

"I've got the list here." My grandfather fishes around in the pockets of his trousers, his expression growing troubled when he cannot find the paper in question. Fortunately for all of us, I've seen this exact situation repeat itself enough times to know how to jump in and help.

"Grandfather, your shirt pocket..."

His eyes light up in recognition, and he hastens to check. Sure enough, the folded square of paper is there, nestled between the ink pens which call the pocket home. He doesn't make a production of the event, quickly and efficiently unfolding the paper to read off the names written upon it.

His tone is grave as he pronounces our list of suspects. "After much research, the possibilities are Dr Nigel Symonds, Professor Mary Chloe Lennon, and Mr Jonathan Townsend."

"Nigel?" Edward surprises me when his voice rings out. "Nigel Symonds at St Margaret?"

My grandfather double-checks the list before nodding. "Yes, it says here he is affiliated with the college. Do you know him?"

"No..." Edward's voice trails off. "I only recognise the name from our list of fellows." He spins around to find Harry, perched on a chair behind us. "Harry, do you know him?"

"I do," she murmurs. "However, I can't imagine him as our villain, except we'll probably say the same thing about all three people on the list. He's even more bookish than you are, Edward," she says with a wink. "He's on sabbatical at the moment, working on a book, I believe."

"Does that mean he is away from Oxford?" I query. "Don't people use sabbaticals as an excuse to travel to somewhere else?"

"For most people, yes. But Nigel has always been a homebody, and his wife Emma isn't in the best health. As far as I know, they've remained here in Oxford. In fact, they're scheduled to attend our High Table dinner this Friday evening." Harry's face brightens. "I could add you and Edward to the list and arrange for you to sit near them. It might be your only opportunity to question him without raising any suspicions."

"That's brilliant, Harry," Edward replies. "I've been talking to

Nat about coming along to one, but I hadn't gotten around to making a booking."

"That's settled then," Harry says while making a note in her diary. "I'll sort it out tomorrow when I'm back in the office. Now, what about the other two people?"

"Believe it or not, I also know Mary Chloe," Edward admits, chagrinned. "She's a professor in the psychology department. Our areas overlap enough that we've co-advised a couple of students."

"Lillian knew her as well," Harry pipes up. "I'm sure of it. I remember her mentioning the name while she was working on her last major event. Is she a fellow at Teddy Hall?"

"Yes," my grandfather and Edward confirm, nearly in unison. My grandfather arches an eyebrow in Edward's direction. "Think you could arrange a visit with her? Something less formal than a meeting?"

"I could…" Edward looks up at the ceiling and I can practically hear the wheels turning in his head.

"If you know her well enough, why not invite her over for dinner? You can use me as an excuse," I offer. "Tell her I've been wanting to meet some of your colleagues. That would work."

Edward frowns, but eventually agrees. "I've never been the dinner party sort of chap, Nat. We may end up talking about work for the entire evening. Can I apologise in advance?"

"Nonsense," I say, patting him on the leg. "You'll have to change the subject sometimes if we're meant to get our questions in. It will be a learning opportunity for you."

When silence again settles on the room, Mathilde straightens up beside me, raising her hand. "I know the third person. Jonathan. He's a researcher at the Bodleian. I've seen him at staff meetings, but that's it. His area of expertise is far from my own."

"What is his area of expertise?" Kate asks.

"He oversees our legal texts. I haven't a clue how I would approach him." She shifts uncomfortably next to me.

"We'll leave him until last," I suggest. "If either Nigel or Mary Chloe is our suspect, we won't need to come up with an excuse. If they aren't, we can use the next week to figure out a way to bump into him."

Mathilde gives me a grateful smile. Clearly, she isn't as comfortable questioning suspects as I am. Although, I have gained some experience in the last six months between eliminating potential murderers here at St Margaret and chasing down leads at Barnard.

Bartie rises from his seat next to Kate, clearly deep in thought as he carries her glass over to refill it. When he finishes his task, he pauses, turning to look at my grandfather. "Alfred, you said that these people had access to a key. How can you be sure? Particularly if Nigel Symonds is on sabbatical."

My grandfather rubs the back of his neck as he replies, "We don't know for certain, but we think there is a strong chance they had the opportunity. Jonathan works at the Bod and knew Mathilde's predecessor well. As Harry mentioned, Mary Chloe interacted with Lillian during her last event. As for Nigel, he didn't go on leave until the start of this year. Lillian loved working out of the Ceremonies office here at St Margaret College, so he had plenty of opportunities to bump into her."

Bartie looks to Harry to see if she agrees. "Yes," Harry confirms. "Lillian and I were great friends, and she would work near me whenever she could. I don't have a clue where she kept her prefect key, but it isn't unreasonable to think that it might have been here at St Margaret, at least part of the time."

On that note, I push myself off the sofa and begin gathering up empty takeaway containers. "We'd better call it a night and get some rest. It sounds like Edward and I have a busy social life in our near future."

Chapter Six

Bright and early the next morning, Mathilde, Kate, and I huddle up for a quick cup of coffee before we start our workday. We're in Kate's office, steaming lattes in hand, sitting around her desk chatting, when we hear a knock at the door.

"Come in," Kate calls out. The door gives a small squeak as it swings open to reveal Francie standing on the other side of it. "Francie, my goodness. I didn't expect you here so early this morning after you spent much of yesterday at the police station."

"I didn't know where else to go," Francie half-mumbles, teetering in place as though she isn't sure whether she should come in or go away. "I didn't mean to interrupt..."

"Not at all," Kate reassures her as she strides across the room to welcome her inside. "Mathilde, Nat, and I were about done, anyway."

Mathilde and I reach over to gather our things, but Francie stops us before we can rise from our chairs.

"No, don't leave, please." She slumps into a nearby chair, letting her handbag fall to the floor. Francie looks so forlorn that Mathilde and I settle back into our chairs, pushing aside any concerns we might be intruding.

I quickly realise that Francie is wearing the same clothes as she had on the day before. Her hair is such a far cry from the silky straight of the days prior that I'd be surprised if she even ran a brush through it. One side is matted down from where she must have slept on it.

Mathilde and I turn our attention to Kate, a subtle prod for her to step in and fill the silence.

"Can I get you a cup of tea, Francie? Or a coffee? Something from the café?" Kate offers, her voice gentle.

Francie shakes her head. "My stomach is tied up in knots. I don't think I could keep anything down. But thank you... Yesterday was one of the worst days of my life. I don't understand what is happening, or why it is happening to me."

Kate opens a desk drawer and rustles around inside until she finds a packet of tissues. She passes them over to Francie, who is fighting a losing battle against the tears in her eyes. While Francie wipes her eyes, Kate asks, "What did DCI Robinson tell you? He's the one who questioned you, right?"

"Yes, it was him, along with a female officer. Neither of them told me anything. They asked question after question about my relationship with Andrei, my role here at the Ashmolean and my personal life." She sniffles again. "They took turns, going around and around in circles, asking the same questions a dozen different ways."

Mathilde sits closest to Francie. She scoots over and gives her a quick squeeze to comfort her.

Clearly anxious, Francie runs the tissue through her fingers. "After a couple of hours, I tried to convince myself I was in a TV show. Like it wasn't really happening to me, but was something I was watching from afar. I asked if I could call someone, but that only made it worse."

"Worse?" Kate asks, her expression turning fierce. "Did they mistreat you?"

"No," Francie mumbles, her face hidden behind a tissue. "They asked if I needed a lawyer. They made it seem like I was trying to hide something. They said that if I was innocent, I didn't need anyone there with me."

"Did they, now?" Kate mutters, her tone icy.

I half expect Kate to leap to her feet and march down to the police station, letting them know exactly what she thinks of their interview technique. I step in, giving Kate a moment to cool down. "I'm so sorry you had to experience that, Francie. We all are. Kate tried to convince DCI Robinson of your innocence, but he was determined to bring you in for questioning. At least it is over now..."

Mathilde gives her another friendly squeeze of reassurance, asking, "Did you get any rest last night?"

Instead of answering, Francie bursts into tears. Mathilde fumbles around with the packet of tissues, fishing out a few more and shoving them into Francie's hands.

After a few deep breaths, Francie calms down enough to answer her. "The investigators made me hand over my house keys. They had a search warrant. By the time I got home, late in the evening, my flat was filled with officers, searching through every drawer and cupboard inside. I had to get out of there, you know?"

We all nod in understanding, even though I don't think any of us can really imagine the stress Francie experienced in the last twenty-four hours.

"I phoned a friend, one I knew wouldn't ask too many questions, and asked if I could stay the night. I told her there was a water leak in my flat. I didn't think to pick up any clothes or an overnight bag. I asked an officer to leave my keys with my neighbour and I dashed out of there. I collapsed on my friend's sofa and slept there, before coming straight here this morning."

"Oh hon," Kate's voice is heavy with sympathy. "You poor thing. You need to rest. One of us can take you back to your flat.

We can help you tidy it up, fix you something to eat, whatever you need."

Francie gives a wan smile, her lower lip trembling, a sure sign that her tears lie near to the surface. "Thank you. I will take you up on that, but not yet. I'm not ready to face the sight of my flat in disarray, or to be alone in there. If it's okay, I'd prefer to stay here as long as I can, lose myself in my work so I can get my mind off everything else for a little while."

"Of course," Kate replies, her soft gaze almost motherly. "When you are ready to go home, if I'm not with you, then call my mobile. Don't worry about interrupting my schedule."

Tears well in Francie's eyes, but for the first time, I think they might be ones of relief rather than despair.

"Thank you for being so lovely, Kate," Francie replies after she wipes her face clean. "I tossed and turned all night, worrying about what you must be thinking. I had nothing to do with the fire, and I certainly wouldn't have done anything to endanger Andrei. I can't figure out why the police were so insistent... and yet here you are, trusting me without asking a single question."

Kate lays her hands flat on her desk. "Yesterday, before you left, DCI Robinson said you were captured on the security feed from the evening of the fire. I asked the Security team to send me a copy, so I could see for myself what happened that night." Kate waits until Francie meets her gaze. "Nothing I saw made me suspect you. You were clearly distraught, not furtive. Do you want to tell us what happened?"

Francie closes her eyes, colour draining from her face. Whatever happened in the Archives building is not something Francie wants to relive, but Kate was right to ask. We need to know what happened, what Francie saw and anything which might be useful in our search for the real arsonist.

Francie speaks, her eyes still squeezed shut as though she can't bear to face us as she tells us what happened. "I told you that

Andrei and I had been seeing each other for a month. In the last few days, it seemed like he was distracted, almost as though he was pulling away a bit. I thought surprising him at work with a nice dinner might help..." Her voice trails off before rising again. "I was so stupid."

"I take it he didn't appreciate the effort?" Kate asks, stating the obvious.

Francie shudders. "He was awful. Horrid, really. If I hadn't been standing in front of him, I would have sworn I was speaking to a different person. He shouted at me for interrupting him at work, calling me stupid and needy. I was shocked and barely knew what to say. He said he'd never really cared for me and I shouldn't bother him any longer."

I rock back in my chair, equally stunned by Francie's tale. "Did he offer any explanation?"

"No," Francie whispers. She clears her throat and tries again. "His face was so cruel, his words filled with anger. I stood there like a fool, taking the verbal beating, the bag of food still in my hands. He practically chased me out of there."

"That's what you threw into the bin outside? The bag of food you'd brought?" Mathilde queries.

"Yes, I spotted the bin in the courtyard. I wasn't thinking. All my hard work, all that food. I shoved it inside and went back home to cry myself to sleep."

"And then you woke up to the news of the fire and Andrei's death," Kate states, providing the end to the young woman's story.

Francie nods her head as fresh tears track down her face.

Kate offers to get Francie a glass of water, and this time Francie accepts. As Kate rises from her desk to get it, another knock sounds from the door. Francie looks up from her pile of used tissues, panic in her eyes.

"Stay here. I'll speak to whomever it is," Kate reassures her, and then she cracks open the door to slip outside of it, pulling it closed behind her.

"Try to put it all behind you," I suggest to Francie as I hold up the small bin for her to discard her used tissues. "I've dealt with more than my fair share of mysteries in the last few months. It's terrible that the police questioned you and searched your flat, but the worst is over."

"Nat's right," Mathilde adds, offering Francie a new packet of tissues. "Stay in here as long as you need. I am sure Kate won't mind. When you feel up to going home, either Kate or one of us will go with you. We won't leave you on your own until you are ready for us to do so."

Francie gives us a grateful — if tremulous — smile.

The sound of raised voices coming from the hallway captures our attention. With the door closed, we can't make out the exact words. However, it sounds like Kate is arguing with a man, her voice getting louder and colder as the discussion goes on. The jiggling door handle is our only warning of her return.

"This is ridiculous!" Kate growls in frustration as she reenters the room. "I don't care what you think you found. She didn't do it."

Francie whips her head around, her eyes growing wide as Kate marches back to her desk, with DCI Robinson and a woman officer trailing behind her.

"Francie," Kate calls, pulling Francie's gaze back in her direction. "I know you didn't set the fire in the archives. I can't put a stop to this," she explains, waving her hands at the two police officers, "but I will figure out who the real culprit is."

"I don't..." Francie stutters, her head twisting left and right as she looks between Kate and the officers, "I don't understand..."

I watch in growing horror as DCI Robinson steps towards Francie. With his hands on his hips, he towers over her, his menacing glare causing her to whimper. "Francie Zhao, you are under arrest on suspicion of setting fire to the Ashmolean archives and the causing the murder of Andrei Radu."

The other officer circles around him, reaching out a hand to pull Francie to her feet. Apparently, this is the last straw for Kate, as she leaps in between the two women, preventing the officer from handling an obviously terrified Francie.

Francie lets loose a wail of terror, shocking me out of my frozen state. For everyone's sake, we've got to calm Francie down before the police escort her from the building, as they seem determined to do. I rush over to push the door closed, buying Francie a moment of privacy.

DCI Robinson is unfazed by the hysterical young woman sitting before him. No doubt he's seen his fair share of criminals proclaiming their innocence. He reads from a small card, "Francie Zhao, you do not have to say anything. But it may harm your defence if you do not mention when questioned something which you later rely on in court. Anything you say may be given in evidence."

Francie breaks down into sobs, gripping onto the side of her chair as though that will somehow save her from being taken away.

"Stop it!" Kate shouts at the group, her voice echoing off the modern glass and steel furnishings. "No one is going anywhere until you've explained yourselves and Francie has calmed down. I will not have you drag a member of my staff kicking and screaming from this building, particularly one whom I know to be innocent of the charges you are levelling against her."

"Are you interfering with a police activity?" DCI Robinson asks, his voice furious.

"No, I am not. I am trying to avoid a very public scene in a university institution, one which will no doubt result in the university president lodging complaints against yourself and your fellow officer." Kate points to the empty conference table nearby. "Now please, have a seat and explain what is going on."

The other officer waits to see how DCI Robinson responds, only moving towards a chair after he does.

"This will not change the outcome," the Chief Inspector warns as he settles into the chair. "Nor does it change the fact that Ms Zhao is under arrest. She is welcome to speak up, but we will note everything she says as part of the case record."

I slide into the chair next to Kate as she nods her understanding. Mathilde remains by Francie's side, stroking her back with one hand while passing her tissues with the other.

When Francie's sobs quiet, DCI Robinson begins, "As you are aware, yesterday we brought Ms Zhao in for questioning regarding her presence at the site of the fire shortly before it began. We also executed a search warrant, visiting her flat to check for evidence of her involvement with either the fire or the theft." He asks Kate, "I understand you have determined some items are missing from the archives. Is that correct?"

"Yes," Kate replies, her tone clipped. "We are still working up a full list, but the fire damage complicates it. However, there are gaps in shelves and drawers which cannot be explained."

DCI Robinson motions to his assisting officer and she pulls a file from her messenger bag and passes it over. He rustles through the papers until he finds the ones he wants. "I believe we can fill in some of those gaps, Ms Underhill. Here are photos of items we found hidden within Ms Zhao's flat. We were planning to ask you to send someone to the station to examine them and make a formal identification."

Kate's eyebrows shoot up to her hairline as she accepts the stapled packet of papers. I follow her head as she turns towards Francie, her face communicating a silent question. Francie shakes her head furiously, her face white with confusion and fear.

Even though I've only recently met Francie, I cannot imagine that anyone is that good of an actress. I'd be shocked if she knew stolen items were stashed in her home. Surely if she did, she would have used yesterday evening to make a quick getaway. She wouldn't have slept on a friend's sofa and reported in to work.

I can see that Kate arrives at the same conclusion. She asks DCI Robinson, "If I may, where were the items found inside the flat?"

This time, the woman replies. "We found the smaller items tucked away behind furniture. The larger items were stashed inside of storage boxes and within Ms Zhao's suitcase."

Francie leans forward, her eyes blazing. "That's not true. I haven't taken so much as a pen from this building. This doesn't make any sense! I had nothing, nothing at all to do with the fire. Why is this happening?"

DCI Robinson stares at her. "Only you can tell us the why, Ms Zhao. Frankly, that isn't my job. My task is to discover the who and the how. The evidence is clear."

I know I should remain an observer, but his tone puts me on edge. "Evidence? What of Edward's call to you yesterday, and the evidence we noted in the security feed? Can you truly say that you've run every possibility to ground and are confident you aren't arresting an innocent woman?"

DCI Robinson finally acknowledges my presence, shifting to glower in my direction. "I am competent in my job, Ms Payne, which you would know if the heads of St Margaret and Barnard colleges hadn't stood in my way and prevented me from conducting a proper investigation. Don't think that your sheer luck in solving those crimes indicates a lack of skill on my part. I wouldn't have achieved the rank of DCI if I wasn't qualified."

I gulp but keep my back straight. "I don't mean to disparage your work, Chief Inspector, but we're talking about a young woman's life here. Won't you at least consider getting an expert to take a second look at the security footage?"

DCI Robinson shoves the papers back into the folder and slams it shut before passing it back to his partner. "If Ms Zhao wants to argue her innocence, she can do so in the courtroom. I have said all I have to say on this matter."

He pushes back from the table, signalling an end to our conversation, and then he crosses the room and pauses in front of the closed door. "Ms Underhill, if you could please send someone to the station to identify the items we recovered, it would be most appreciated. If Ms Zhao will come quietly, we can skip the handcuffs and exit through the rear entrance. That is as much as I can do."

Mathilde helps Francie to her feet, whispering words of comfort and encouragement in her ears. Francie somehow holds herself together as the two officers escort her from the room, closing the door firmly behind themselves.

Kate's jaw is clenched so tightly, I fear she is going to break her teeth. Without asking permission, I grab the speakerphone from the middle of the table and quickly tap in a familiar set of numbers.

Kate and Mathilde retake their seats as the beeps of the ringing phone fill the space.

"Hullo, Professor Thomas speaking," Edward states in response to the call from an unfamiliar number.

"It's me," I jump in. "Francie's been arrested."

"Arrested?" Edward's voice echoes across the line. "For what?"

"Arson, theft and murder, if DCI Robinson is to be believed," Kate answers. "He showed up this morning with another officer and they arrested Francie, right here in my office."

Silence fills the line as Edward parses her words. Seeing that Kate is in no mood to explain, I pull the speaker closer and recount our morning.

I hear the creak of Edward rocking back in his chair and imagine him running his hand over his face. "Why can't we ever have a straightforward problem?" he groans.

"Welcome to the world of magic," I reply. "Now you know how we've felt over the last six months. But there has to be a way to nudge DCI Robinson in the right direction."

"Like you did with me when I was investigating the murders of Chef Smythe and Ms Evans?" Edward lets his question hang. "Trevor Robinson is a good police officer. I've known him for a long time, and I have never had reason to doubt his methods or to complain about the way he's handled a case. His reputation is sterling."

I begin, "But this time —"

"I know. I know," Edward mutters, his voice echoing my frustration. "This time he has it wrong. But look at it from his perspective. This is the third unexplained death on university grounds in the last six months. For the last two, he was forcibly kept away from solving the crimes. Dr Radcliffe fought hard to keep him from questioning her students, unknowingly letting the murderer hide within their midst. Then, Master Finch-Byron blocked out the police to protect himself."

"I don't want to keep him from doing his job," Kate interjects. "In fact, I want him to do just that. He needs to keep looking for the right person. We need all the help we can get."

"I hate to say it, but I think we're on our own once again." Edward huffs out a sigh. "Trevor's promotion to DCI came through last month. That's despite the situations at St Margaret and Barnard. It is only because his reputation is well-regarded that he got promoted even though he didn't solve those murders. But he cannot afford to have another mishap here. He needs the arsonist identified and put behind bars as quickly and efficiently as possible."

Edward's words lay heavy across the room. I glimpse Mathilde and Kate out of the corner of my eye. They are both staring off into space, their minds working as quickly as my own in search of a solution. Francie cannot go to prison for a crime she didn't commit.

"All right, so that's settled," I say, putting force behind my words. "DCI Robinson isn't going to act unless we force his hand. We either need incontrovertible evidence of Francie's innocence, or we need a new culprit for him, ideally delivered straight to his doorstep."

When Mathilde and Kate look unconvinced, I lean forward and address them directly. "We can do this. We've done this before. It won't be easy, but for once, we'll have Edward's expert help from the start."

Edward adds, "Nat's right. Thanks to the Eternals, we've got a list of potential suspects and plans for interviewing them. I suggest we add more research on Francie and Andrei into our plans. If Francie didn't steal those items and hide them in her flat, there's one other person who had the same access and opportunity."

"Andrei?" Kate asks, her eyebrows raised.

"Yes, Andrei," Edward confirms, his tone grim. "I hadn't thought about it before, but our arsonist may have had someone helping them from inside the museum. Someone who could be bribed to pan and move the security cameras around so they wouldn't be captured on the feed, and then open the door to let the arsonist inside. It would explain why we're having trouble recovering the footage from the interior camera."

Kate admits, "That certainly puts a new perspective on the

security footage, Edward." Her eyes skip around the room, but it is clear we don't have any choice other than to proceed on our own. She looks in my direction and then Mathilde's, double-checking that we agree with the plan. When she is satisfied, she stands. "You three are going to have to take the lead on the investigations, at least for the next couple of days. I've got to contact Francie's family, make sure she has a lawyer and then call together my senior team so we can figure out how to head off the internal rumour mill before Francie's reputation is ripped to shreds."

Chapter Seven

By the time Friday rolls around, I am ready to curl up in a blanket on my sofa with takeaway curry and reality TV. Unfortunately, tonight is the night Harry has booked Edward and me places at St Margaret's High Table dinner. I try to drum up excitement thinking about the four-course dinner of Michelin-star-quality food, but the reality is I'll be spending most of our meal questioning the first of our potential suspects from the list the Eternals put together.

"H!" I call from my bedroom doorway. "Can you keep an ear out for Edward and let him in when he gets downstairs? I'm jumping into the shower."

H flaps out of the reception room with a jar of cheese dip in one hand and a spoon in the other. "Sure, Nat. I'll take care of 'im. Don't worry." He flies off towards the front of the flat before I can say anything else.

That sorted, I lock myself in the bathroom and set to work, washing away the worries of the day and replacing them with a fresh attitude. Who says we can't make quick work of our questioning and spend the rest of the evening enjoying a fine meal and interesting conversations? It will be nice spending an evening talking about something other than Francie's arrest and the problems with the magic. Deep in thought, I jump when a loud thud echoes through the wall, overpowering even the sound of the running shower.

"What in the world?" I mutter, twisting off the taps, suds running down my neck. "H?" I shout. "Everything okay?"

"Fine!" he replies, but his tone makes it almost sound more like a question than a confirmation.

I weigh up the idea of exiting the shower to double-check, but I'm already behind schedule and I can't afford to lose five minutes trooping around my flat, leaving a trail of wet footprints behind me.

I'm nearly done when I hear another strange sound, this one almost like the sound of glass breaking. "That can't be good," I grumble as I turn the water off once again. "H? Aiiitttcchhh!" I shout, getting louder when he fails to reply. "Did you knock something over?"

This time, Edward's deep voice responds. "I bumped into a vase. All okay, no need to get out!"

Reassured, I restart the water and rush through the final steps of my shower routine. I grab my towel off the radiator, luxuriating in its warmth, and step one foot out of the tub. My other foot is mid-air when a thundering clatter rattles the bathroom door.

After wrapping the towel around myself, I wrench open the bathroom door and go flying to see what is going on. As I dash down the hallway, my wet feet squishing and sliding across the wooden floor, I hear the crashing sound of a picture hitting the ground. Grunts and groans echo from the front of the house. My feet slip as I take the corner into the kitchen, my wet hair swinging behind me, leaving a spray mark on the wall.

As I hit the kitchen tile, the sound of breaking glass followed by a deep male roar sends my heart racing. With a last leap and a tight grip on my bath sheet, I finally enter the front room, my eyes skimming over all the signs of destruction to land on the culprits.

"Ugh! Are you two at it again?" I shout, causing H and Edward to freeze their battle to the death. H chokes back a flame while Edward's face cycles from furious red to bloodless white before settling on an embarrassed pink.

"He stole my tie," Edward grumbles.

"I said I'd 'elp 'im," H gripes back.

"You were covered in cheese dip!" Edward snipes, his tone rising.

"Seriously?" I bellow. "Why can't you two get along? Look at the mess you've made!" My voice grows shrill as I point out the damage the pair have wrought while I was in the shower.

My armchair and coffee table are both lying on their sides, accounting for the thundering clatters I heard from the bathroom. My framed print of Oxford's city centre is face down on the wooden floor, a sea of broken glass around it. I'm fairly sure that mustard-coloured stripe on my sofa is cheese dip.

"H, you have got to stop antagonising Edward," I say, pointing my finger at him. "And you, Edward! Can you please be nicer to H? I have more important things to do with my time than to constantly referee your arguments." Both man and wyvern flinch under my verbal assault, but I am well beyond any pity for them.

I hold up a hand to halt them before they can begin making excuses. "I am freezing cold, wet and now late. I am going back into my bedroom, where I am going to close the door and finish getting ready for dinner. When I come back out, I expect this room to be in perfect order and for you two to be sitting in it. Together. Getting alonnggg," I drawl out, just in case my meaning isn't clear.

After a moment of hesitation to make sure I don't have anything else to say, the two spring into action.

"Sure, Nat, of course. You go on back."

"Oi, Nat. Nothing to it. It'll be good as new, mate."

I narrow my eyes in a final death glare before spinning around and retracing my wet footprints back to my bedroom.

Twenty minutes later, I carefully twist my door handle, opening it a crack to listen before I fully step out. I hear H's gruff voice and Edward's deep bass, and then the reassuring higher pitch of Harry. The conversation sounds friendly enough, so the men must have called a *detente* and focused their attention on putting my flat back to rights.

My high heels click on the wooden floorboards, announcing my arrival. From her seat in my armchair, Harry is the first to see me, her eyes twinkling with delight as she takes in my look from head to toe. Edward twists sideways, following her gaze, and looks star-struck when his eyes hit mine. Even H is shocked into silence.

"Don't you clean up nicely!" Harry exclaims as she rises to her feet to come over and say hello. "Do I want to know why I found H lighting your sofa cushions on fire when I got here?"

"Probably not," I reply with a grimace. "Let's just say that the sofa cushions weren't the only things H needed to demolish so that the magic would step in and replace them. There are a couple of people here who should be pretty darn happy that magical restoration was even an option."

Harry doesn't take long to figure out what happened, rolling her eyes at the two men in my life. "How about we move on to a more pleasant subject?" She backs up, to take the full sight of me in. "That dress is gorgeous!"

I twirl around in the doorway, letting the silky hemline swirl against my calves. When I saw the midnight blue fabric in the shop window, its tiny silver stars sparkling in the shop lights, I knew I had to have it. The cowl neckline is just reserved enough to be appropriate for a college event, but the silky sleek lines showcase my curves. A narrow silver belt cinches my waist. One look at Edward's face confirms the dress was worth every pound I spent.

"Will I do, Edward?" I ask with a cheeky grin, jutting my hip out in a sultry pose and flipping my sleek hair over my shoulder.

"You'll be the star of the evening," he says when he finds his voice.

"Are you saying that because of the stars on my dress?" I ask.

Edward pushes up from the sofa, striding over to take my hand and press a soft kiss against my knuckles. "No, Nat," he replies, "I'm saying that because you look absolutely gorgeous."

I pull my hand back and step forward to pat him on the cheek, arching an eyebrow as I say, "That's almost lovely enough to make me forget what I saw in here earlier."

"Err, yes," he stutters out in a quintessentially British fashion. "We've sorted everything out, nothing to worry about."

Sure enough, my front room is in perfect order, with nary a glint of broken glass nor any streaks of cheese dip in sight. I usher everyone back into the room, taking my usual position on the sofa.

"Okay, Harry," I start. "What can you tell us about Nigel and Emma Symonds? Any interesting tidbits we can use as conversation starters? Or maybe a favourite topic?"

"I've got a few suggestions," Harry replies with a grin. "Bartie and I put our heads together. However, before we leap into them, I thought it might be useful for me to give you an overview of how a High Table dinner functions."

"Oh! Is that necessary?" I ask. "I assumed it was like any other formal dinner."

H flaps his wings, pulling my gaze in his direction. "It's a ceremony, Nat. At Oxford. You should know better than most 'ow people 'ere like to add a bit faff to even the simplest of events."

"Good point," I concede. "Very well, Harry. The floor is yours."

Harry settles deeper into her chair, clearly in her element. "As H implied, High Table dinners are a cornerstone of the Oxford experience, for both our fellows and our students. The students can invite friends along, although they must all dress appropriately, and they are seated at the main dining tables which run the length of the room. Our fellows and special guests sit on the raised dais at the far end of the room, literally sitting at the high tables."

"Like the Hogwarts dining hall?" I ask with a smirk, knowing how much H hates it when I compare anything at Oxford to the Harry Potter films. He snorts out a puff of flame in my direction in reply.

"Exactly! The inspiration had to come from somewhere," Harry notes. "Now, you won't go straight into the dining hall as the evening is divided into three parts: pre-dinner drinks, the dinner itself, and then after-dinner drinks. The first part takes place in the Senior Common Room and is fairly relaxed. Our fellows and their guests are invited to enjoy a glass of bubbles or fresh juice while they wait for the students to take their seats. Once the students are all inside, a steward will come to collect your group."

"I always hate that part," Edward admits with a grimace. "They parade us past the poor students who simply want to enjoy a nice dinner with friends."

"Sounds like an appropriate start to an Oxford ceremony," I quip.

Harry shakes her head at us before returning to her explanation. "You'll need to move quickly to find your place setting at high table. Fortunately, tonight's group isn't large so there is only a single high table. Everyone stands behind their chairs until Dr Radcliffe says the blessing, and only then may everyone be seated."

"The blessing is in Latin," H warns, "so don't be expectin' to understand it."

"Right," Harry confirms. "Once you're seated, it is like any other dinner. Fair warning, keep a very close eye on how much wine you drink. The wait staff are known to top up the glasses. It's not until you stand up to leave dinner that you realise how many you've had."

"I'll drink plenty of water," I reassure her. "I've got plans with Mathilde tomorrow, and I do not want to ruin them with a sore head."

"Good," Harry says with a nod of approval. "Once the dessert course is over, Dr Radcliffe will once again rise to her feet and call an end to the dinner. Everyone at the high table will exit at this point, and one of the stewards will escort you to another room for after-dinner drinks."

"After-dinner drinks are actually offered by the fellows, rather than by the college. Once inside the room, Dr Radcliffe ceases to be the host, and the most senior fellow in attendance steps into the role. You don't happen to know who that is tonight, Harry?" Edward asks, looking in her direction.

"I do," she answers with a strange smile. "Our most senior fellow tonight is Nigel Symonds."

"That's convenient," I remark.

"Particularly for you, Nat. I've placed you beside him for the after-dinner drinks portion of the evening. I thought it would give you a good excuse to pester him with questions without raising too many eyebrows. Once he hears this is your first high table experience, I'm sure he'll be happy to answer most anything you ask." Harry glances down at her wrist and then leaps to her feet.

"Look at the time! You two need to be on your way if you're to make it to pre-dinner drinks."

"The conversation topics?" I remind her as I pull on my coat. Dinner may be a short walk away, but British evenings are notorious for turning cool with little warning.

"Ah, yes," she says, digging a paper from her pocket. "Nigel is a keen rower and a fan of cricket. Bartie thought those might be useful starting points for asking about his time here at Oxford. Emma, on the other hand, loves anything to do with the royal family and is always happy to discuss her distant connection to the crown. This might be a reach, but perhaps they have aspirations beyond their reach... Ones which might suddenly seem achievable if they could use Oxford's magic."

Out in the hallway, I pull my door shut and lock it tight, giving Harry a quick squeeze before dashing off. "Thanks for always being such a dear, Harry," I whisper in her ear.

"It's my pleasure, Nat. Now hurry along and don't forget, watch out for the bottomless wine glasses."

The Senior Common Room at St Margaret is one of my favourite places in Oxford. With its robin's egg blue walls and comfortable seating, the fancy coffee machine and plate of biscuits, there is nowhere I'd rather sneak away for an hour or two with a good book in hand. They designed the room for exactly that purpose, providing a retreat for weary professors who need a break from their research.

As we step inside, I can feel the last bit of tension release from my shoulders. The room is fairly full with what looks to be about twenty people, but for once, I'm a guest and not the event organiser. A few people glance our way as we come into the room, but no one waves to me with a request or a question. Edward passes me a glass of prosecco and I begin to feel excited at the prospect of seeing an Oxford ceremony from the viewpoint of an attendee.

"Edward, Natalie, so lovely that the two of you could join us this evening," Dr Radcliffe says as she welcomes us with open arms. "Do you mind if I borrow Natalie for a moment? I was just discussing the autumn gala with two of our distinguished guests, and I'm sure they'd be delighted to meet the woman behind it."

"Not at all," Edward says after I nod my head in agreement. "I see Nigel is here this evening. I'll go find out how he is progressing with his plans to write a book while on sabbatical."

I try to keep half an eye on Edward so I can see which of the attendees is our suspect since I've never met him, but I quickly lose Edward amidst the clusters of people standing around the room. Dr Radcliffe leads me towards the back, where a man and woman are standing together.

With his grey hair, ruddy face and solid shoulders, I'd guess the man to be in his late fifties. He stands tall in his double-breasted navy suit, swirling a glass of prosecco. The woman beside him is a great deal younger, likely close to my own age. A wisp of a woman, she is draped against his side, in a demure frock offset with thousands of pounds' worth of jewellery that screams old money. Her wide eyes make her look like a deer in the headlights.

Dr Radcliffe passes me a glass of bubbly from a nearby table and then makes quick work of the introductions. "Natalie, this is Lord Denzil Gowlington and his wife, Lady Ingrid. Lord Denzil's daughter read history here at St Margaret, and we've enjoyed his support for a number of years as a result. Lord Denzil and Lady Ingrid, allow me to introduce Natalie Payne, the brilliant visionary behind last year's Autumn Gala."

"It's my pleasure," I say automatically as I extend my hand to Lord Denzil. His grip is firm, if slightly sweaty, his voice booming. Lady Ingrid's handshake feels like I'm holding a dead fish. Her voice is breathy as she says hello, and I pull my hand back as quickly as is appropriate. We fall into small talk, mostly discussing the gala and where I found such an authentic-looking group of actors and costumes to impersonate St Margaret's residents from years past.

With my back to the rest of the room, it's impossible for me to resume my search for Edward, Nigel, and his wife Emma. I can only hope that Edward is having some luck with his efforts. If not, there are still dinner and drinks ahead of us.

When the steward arrives to call our group to dinner, I make my excuses and rejoin Edward's side. "Did you have any luck?" I whisper.

Edward's frown says it all. "I asked about his book and that was all he talked about for the last ten minutes."

Hand in hand, Edward and I exit the Common Room, filing in behind the others as we walk along the hallway which leads to the dining hall. We nod our hellos at Catherine Morgan when we pass her portrait. Edward gives my hand a reassuring squeeze, which quickly turns tighter. With the dining hall doors swung open for our arrival, he barely has time to whisper in my ear before we have to walk inside. "Um, I just realised that Harry and I forgot to tell you one thing."

"What?" I whisper back, my voice pitched so he can hear it over the din of the packed room.

"The seating arrangements! We won't be sitting together. They split up all the groups, so that everyone has a chance to speak with someone new."

I struggle to make sense of his words and wonder how he and Harry could have possibly forgotten to mention that little tidbit of information. So much for my vision of a date night with Edward. Sounds like I might not see him for the rest of the evening.

There are no further opportunities to question Edward as we

arrive at the dais and make our way along the length of the table to the few empty seats. I find my name card placed at a single chair between Lord Denzil and a frail woman in her sixties. A subtle glance confirms she is Emma Symonds, Nigel's wife, so at least this part of our plan has gone right. I catch myself before I pull out the chair, remembering that Dr Radcliffe has to say the blessing before we can be seated.

Students fill the regular dining hall tables from end to end. There must be several hundred, at least, all chatting away with their friends while they wait for the appetiser course to be served. The level of volume in the room is so loud, I can barely hear the people on either side of me. Edward is at the other end of the table, one seat down from the head of the table, and I can only hope that the kindly looking older gentleman on his left is Nigel.

I turn to my right, smiling at the older woman. "Hullo, I'm Natalie Payne."

"Emma Symonds," she replies, or at least I think that is what she says. Her voice is weak, barely audible above the noise of the room.

"I'm here with my partner, Professor Edward Thomas. And you? Are you also a guest?" I ask, hoping I can ease her into a conversation. I have to practically lean against her to make out her words, as she points towards the older man seated beside Edward.

When Lord Denzil's voice booms out from my other side, I almost breathe a sigh of relief. Questioning this woman, in this room, with this many people around us, is going to be impossible unless I find a megaphone for her to use.

"I say, young lady," he states to me in between gulps of wine. "I am positively ravished. I do hope they bring the first course soon." His pronunciation is utterly posh to the point of being comical, identifying him as an Etonian man to everyone within earshot.

I make several further attempts to engage Emma in conversation, but they quickly fizzle out, either because I can't hear her responses or because Lord Denzil decides I'm his audience for the evening. The only positive is that he doesn't seem to expect me to reply to any of his remarks, as he guffaws at his own jokes and regales me with tales of his recent polo match with Charles. Prince Charles, naturally. From there, he moves on to his new Aston Martin and the challenges of finding good help for their villa in Spain. I can only nod my head in commiseration as I wonder whether I can get away with escaping to the loo.

When Lord Denzil enjoys his chocolate mousse, I catch Edward's eye, arching my eyebrow in a silent question. He half-shrugs while giving a slight shake to his head, apparently not having much better luck. More than once I wish Harry hadn't warned me about the bottomless wine glasses. I'd like to accidentally drink myself into a stupor. Anything to put an end to another one of Lord Denzil's tales.

Finally, Dr Radcliffe rises from her seat at the head of the table and issues the invitation to adjourn to another room for a glass of port before we make our way home.

"Seating arrangements for this portion of the evening?" I murmur to Edward when he meets me at the bottom of the dais.

"Shuffled again, I'm afraid," Edward says with an apologetic smile. "But on the bright side, you're unlikely to be near that obnoxious man again. I could hear his voice all the way at the other end of the table."

"Tell me about it," I grumble as I pretend to massage my ear.

The next room is more understated, with three tables laid out in a U-shape, each one holding a beautifully arranged cheese and fruit platter at its centre. Decanters of port and sweet dessert wine are dotted around, ready to be offered to the guests. Despite feeling full from the three-course meal, my mouth waters at the sight of a dish of chocolate truffles and tiny chocolate squares stamped with the college's crest.

Edward gives my hand one last squeeze before he splits off. "Good luck, Nat," he whispers as he points me towards the empty chair beside Nigel Symonds.

"You must be Edward's Natalie," Nigel says when I take my seat. I turn, ready to retort that I am no one's person but my own, but I swallow the words when I see his face. Despite a hefty build, which no doubt harkens back to his years as a rower, his expression is so full of warmth and kindness that I immediately put him in the same category as my grandfather Alfred. His bushy white eyebrows frame his soft brown eyes; he gives me a gentle smile as he offers to pour me a glass of port.

"Yes, I'm Natalie Payne. You must be Nigel Symonds. I sat next to your wife at dinner."

When I mention her, he searches the room, finding her seated near Edward. His love-filled gaze is tinged with a hint of sadness, as though he knows his years with her are running towards their end.

Nothing about this man leads me to believe he is our arsonist, but perhaps that is how he has remained hidden all this time. I harden my heart and begin my questioning.

"Edward tells me you're on sabbatical. It must seem strange not coming into St Margaret every day after all of your years here."

"Yes," he agrees with a laugh. "The first morning, I puttered around my house for hours with no idea what to do with myself. Thankfully, my Emma was there to rescue me from myself."

I accept the plate of chocolates from the woman on my right, helping myself to one before handing the plate to Nigel. "And now?" I ask once his attention is back on me. "Has so much togetherness time worn off the shine?"

His eyes get that faraway look as he loses himself to his

memories. "Oh no, Natalie. Far from it, and no one is more surprised than I am. All those years I spent with my head stuck in one book or another, always doing research. I let my job distract me from the insightful, sharp-witted, funny woman I married. She has become my greatest resource as I work on my book. Anytime I find myself at a loss for words, I turn to her. After so much time as a professor's wife, she knows my subject matter almost as well as I do."

"Yes, I can see how that might happen," I admit, thinking of myself and Edward. He may be the criminologist, but I'm quickly proving my crime-solving abilities.

Silence falls between us as we sip our port and nibble on chocolates, cheese, and fruit, each lost in our thoughts.

Nigel picks up his napkin, wiping a smear of chocolate from his fingers. "Take some advice from an old man, Natalie. If you think Edward might be the one, don't waste your best years focusing on your careers. I was a fool to take so long to realise what a gift I have in Emma. Now all I can do is to make the best of the time we have left."

His words provide the opening I need to dig deeper with my questions. "What if there were a way to stay here in Oxford for an eternity, never losing one another? Would you take the opportunity if it presented itself? Hypothetically," I add when he arches an eyebrow.

"Ah, to be young and still so filled with hope. To answer your question, should a genie appear tomorrow and grant me three wishes, I would use one to lengthen our time here together. However," he says, holding up a finger to halt me from asking my next question, "Emma would have my hide. She firmly believes we must live our best lives now and not waste time hoping for a miracle. She'd use her wishes differently — likely to provide for our children or to fund the local animal rescue, or some other community initiative."

I weigh his words, but I can't find a single hint of guilt. He is a man in love, not a man filled with desperation. Nor would he look so sad if he knew of the existence of the Eternals.

I'm suddenly sorry that I spent my dinner stuck listening to a buffoon instead of his wife. Who better to guide me through the start of a relationship with an Oxford professor than someone who has done it successfully for so many years?

I don't have to fake the interest in my voice when I finally reply. "She sounds like an amazing woman, Nigel. I hope we can arrange a more informal opportunity to get to know you both better."

Chapter Eight

"How was High Table last night?" Mathilde asks as she lets me into her flat. It's bright and early on Saturday morning, perfect weather for our mission of finding me a new flat to rent.

"Oh goodness, where to start!" I reply as I follow her into the kitchen, a bag of croissants and two coffees in hand. "The food was exceptional, but that was to be expected. I sat next to a bore of a man, Lord Denzil, and he blathered his way through three courses. If I never hear another polo story, it will be too soon."

Mathilde snickers at the grimace on my face. "And our suspect, Nigel Symonds? Were you or Edward able to question him?"

"It turns out that High Table is a terrible time to question anyone, particularly a potential suspect for a major crime," I say with a frown. "The room was so loud, I honestly couldn't hear a word Nigel's wife said, and she sat next to me at dinner. Edward didn't fare much better. Fortunately, I had a good chat with Nigel when we adjourned for after-dinner drinks."

"And?" Mathilde asks, waving her croissant in the air as she motions for me to spill the news.

"It's not him." When Mathilde looks disappointed, I add, "It was a long shot, Mathilde, and we only suspected him because of his family tree. He was absolutely lovely, and the way he talked about his wife made my heart melt. I'm glad I got a chance to meet him."

Mathilde's face softens when she sees me smile. "I'm glad the dinner was productive. Now that we've eliminated Nigel, who's next?"

"Mary Chloe Lennon, Edward's colleague," I confirm. "Edward phoned her to invite her to dinner, but she insisted we come to hers instead. She lives in a gorgeous cottage in the Cotswolds, so it was an easy yes. We're going there next week."

We turn our attention to our food, quickly finishing our breakfasts. I help Mathilde tidy up the crumbs, and then we are out the door and on our way.

"What's our plan for the day?" Mathilde asks as we hit the pavement.

"I've made appointments to see two places," I say, double-checking my planner. "The first is up in Headington and the second one is back in the city centre. Since the weather is so nice, I thought maybe we could walk to the first one and then bus back into the centre for lunch before we see the second."

"Sounds good to me! Lead the way, Nat!" Mathilde insists, standing back with a flourish to motion me onwards. We quickly fall into step side-by-side, winding our way through the warren of streets which are typical of Cowley, the neighbourhood where Mathilde lives.

When I mapped the directions, the website failed to mention that the first part of our walk would be straight uphill. Whatever plans I had to chat with Mathilde fall by the wayside as we huff and puff our way up the steep streets, climbing our way to the top of the Headington Hill. Even the cars driving upwards growl their frustration with their gunned engines as they struggle to scale the narrow streets.

A bus stop conveniently sits at the top of the hill; Mathilde and I collapse onto the empty bench, trying to catch our breath. A passing bus slows, its driver catching our eyes to see if we need a lift. Unfortunately, it's going in the wrong direction, so we wave it along and return to our feet.

"Only a ten-minute walk from here, hopefully with no more mountains to conquer along the way," I announce after a quick consultation with my mobile.

"It should be easier going from here," Mathilde reassures me. "Before we get to the first viewing, it would be good to know what exactly you're looking for in a flat."

"Honestly, I'm not too picky. All I need are a clean room and bathroom, and friendly roommates."

"Roommates?" Mathilde arches an eyebrow. "You've been living on your own for the last six months. I'm surprised you'd opt to return to shared accommodation."

I take a moment before I answer her question, once again questioning my decision. "I have so enjoyed living on my own. I really don't want to move back in with other people. However, I want to buy a house here in Oxford. Shared rentals are so much cheaper and will go a long way towards helping me save up the rest of what I need for a deposit."

"Home ownership in Oxford?" Mathilde asks, double-checking she heard me correctly. "That is expensive! I can see why you'd make the sacrifice, though. I'm also putting money away in savings, but my goal is still well off into the future."

We return to a comfortable silence as I follow the directions on the screen. "It's the next street up ahead on the left, and then we need to look for number ten."

"Nat?" Mathilde's voice is hesitant. "If you need an

inexpensive place to live, why don't you take Edward up on his offer for you to move in upstairs with him?"

"Have you ever moved in with a partner?" I ask instead of answering her question.

"No…" she trails off in confusion.

"Neither have I, Mathilde. Maybe it is silly, but I always thought moving in with someone I'm dating would be an important step forward in our relationship."

"It would be," Mathilde agrees.

"That's the problem. Edward has been treating it like an invitation to sleep over on his sofa, not a deepening of our relationship. I imagined having a discussion with my partner, talking about our feelings for one another, where we thought our relationship might go and why moving in together is right for us. Instead, I got a casual offer, the kind you'd toss out to a friend who is sofa-surfing while they look for a place of their own."

Mathilde flinches, her face screwed up in disgust. "Yeah, okay, I can definitely see why you would turn that down. I'm not the candlelight and roses kind of gal, but even I would walk away from that kind of offer."

I glance at Mathilde out of the corner of my eye. "Do you think maybe Edward isn't serious about me?"

"What?" she squawks, caught off guard. "That man is completely smitten with you. If I had to guess, I would say he is more likely clueless about what it is he has done wrong." She flips her long hair off her shoulder and then nudges me with her elbow. "Do you want me to talk to him?"

"God no! Definitely not." I blurt. "You are right, I'm sure. And maybe moving in together right now would put unnecessary pressure on our relationship. Plus, Edward and H keep butting heads. They wrecked half of my front room last night fighting over a necktie."

"You seem awfully blasé about your flat being messed up." Mathilde says with a worried look on her face.

I shrug off her concern. "The two of them sorted it out while I finished getting ready for High Table. But as long as Edward is determined to view H like a pet, they are going to keep at it."

"Nothing about that situation sounds appealing," Mathilde agrees as we make our final turn. "Hopefully, this place is better."

As we round the corner, Mathilde stops dead and asks, "Is that a shark sticking out of the top of the house?" Together, we stare at the building from across the street.

"The housemate wanted advert I saw definitely didn't mention anything about a shark," I reply when I can find my voice again.

From the information in the advert, the house seemed promising. Set one block in from Headington's high street, it has good access to shopping and public transport. There were photos of the front garden, the common areas, and the available room. I didn't think twice about the lack of a photo showing the full front of the house. Now I know why they didn't include one.

It is a typical terraced house, midway through a long row of family homes, each with a postage stamp-sized garden out front. If you removed the towering replica of a grey and white shark crashing into the rooftop from the picture, the place would be perfect.

"I've heard of this house, but I hadn't seen it before today. It's infamous, Nat," Mathilde says, her voice full of wonder. "As long as the shark's head isn't coming through your bedroom ceiling, this might actually be a pretty cool place to live."

"There are two flatmates living here already; they are looking to fill the place of one who recently moved out," I explain to Mathilde. "They're offering the master bedroom, which includes an ensuite. It's worth a look, even if it has a twenty-five-foot shark sticking out of the roof."

"Here goes nothing," I whisper as I press the bell, alerting the residents of our arrival. The wooden door looks freshly stained and the windows are spotless.

"Hiya," a twenty-something man says, looking surprised as he opens the door to welcome us inside. "You're Nat?"

"Yes, I'm Nat, short for Natalie, and this is my friend Mathilde. Thanks for agreeing to show me the room this morning."

The man stares at me, somewhat thunderstruck, but shakes himself out of it and ushers us into the house. "Andrew, *Natalie* is here," he shouts up the stairs, putting emphasis on my full name. With a sinking feeling, I suspect that they thought 'Nat' was a man.

"Were you expecting a man?" I ask gently. "The ad didn't specify that you wanted a male housemate, but if that is the case, we can go. It's fine."

"No, no," he insists, shifting his demeanour to a more friendly one. "It's my fault for making assumptions. It's cool! Our last housemate was a woman." He sticks out his hand. "Sorry, I've forgotten all my manners. I'm Bill, and the other tenant is Andrew. He'll be down shortly."

Once the introductions are over, Bill invites us to follow him deeper into the house. When I ask about the shark, he explains it was erected overnight years ago as protest art and caused quite a lot of stir in the town when it happened. The owner spent years fighting for permission to leave it. "The landlord doesn't mention it in the vacancy listing because he doesn't want a bunch of random lookie-loos asking to see the place when they have no intention of renting it."

Reassured by Bill's explanation, I set my initial concerns aside and return my attention to assessing the possibilities of living here. That's when the smell hits my nose.

It starts with a hint of gym shoes, worn too many times under less than ideal circumstances. A quick look around identifies the source, an overflowing shoe rack tucked away behind the front door. We step into the front room and the situation does not improve. What I can see of the furniture matches the photos, but most of it is buried under sweaty workout clothing draped around to air out.

"Did you forget I was supposed to come by this morning?" I ask, trying not to wrinkle up my nose.

"No. Why do you ask?" Bill replies nonchalantly.

"No reason…" Out of fear he might ask us to sit, I jump in with a request to continue the tour rather than waiting for the other housemate to present himself.

The dining room from the photos is now an indoor gym, complete with free weights, a treadmill and an exercise bike.

"Andrew and I both work long hours," Bill explains as we stand in the doorway, "and we realised it would be much easier to fit in our workouts if we installed the equipment here at home. If you move in, you'd be welcome to make use of it."

"Um, thanks," I mumble. I hadn't looked closely at Bill, being distracted by the shark and the name confusion, but now I note his muscular arms and strong shoulders. He has the kind of bulk that can only come from hours of dumbbell lifting. Fine for some, but I'm more of a quick run kind of gal. I'd prefer a dining table.

In the kitchen, a large platter of fresh fruit catches my eye, reviving my hope in the place, but then I notice the bags of protein powder and jugs of muscle-building shakes lining the shelves. Stored in their midst, H's stash of crisps and biscuits would look completely out of place. The basin is overflowing with dirty pots and pans, and protein bar wrappers surround the bin.

"There's a back garden as well, right?" I ask, pointing towards the exterior door on the far side of the kitchen. Having an outdoor space is key to H's happiness, not to mention my own. Unless they hire a cleaner, I can't imagine myself spending too much time inside.

"Oh yeah," Bill exclaims, clearly pleased to show it next. "It's amazing. We turned it into a miniature version of the Tough Mudder course."

Mathilde and I can't stop ourselves from turning to look at one another, horror painted on both of our faces. Thankfully, the other roommate makes his appearance, saving us from having to troop our way around a giant mud pit.

Andrew is even more muscled up, his hand nearly crushing mine when we shake hello. The testosterone level in the room is so high, I start to involuntarily sweat.

"Why don't we have a seat and get to know one another," Andrew suggests, swiping a t-shirt and jumper off the kitchen chairs before pointing Mathilde and I towards them.

I prepare myself to answer questions, but I might as well have not. After repeating their introductions and including their jobs, the two men pivot the conversation to tell me what they want out of a new housemate.

"Our last housemate, Lana, was awesome," explains Bill with enthusiasm. "She was always puttering around the house, tidying things up or making home-cooked meals. The front garden was her pride and joy. To be honest, we're hoping to find a female housemate, so it's cool that Nat is short for Natalie and not Nathaniel."

The more the men talk, the more obvious it is that they aren't looking for someone to rent a room. No, they are hoping to land a live-in cook and cleaner, someone to handle all the domestic tasks without complaining about the eau de locker room. Given my propensity for ordering takeaway and H's habit of leaving empty cheese wrappers around the house, I can't see myself fitting the bill.

Mathilde must reach the same conclusion, as she gives me a pointed look when I ask to see the available room. "You two go ahead. We'll be right behind you," she says, holding back so the men have no choice but to follow her instructions. She lowers her voice to a hoarse whisper. "Nat! Are you sure you want to see more? It sounds like they want a live-in cleaner, not a housemate."

I may agree with her, but I also know that finding a free room for rent in a house of professionals, and not students, is the equivalent of a needle in a haystack. I can't dismiss any option out of hand. Besides, I won't be living there forever, and the rent here is a bargain.

"This is the first place we're seeing. We have to stick it out. It might end up being the best of a bad bunch!" I whisper back and then dash ahead to catch up with the others. "The room might be gorgeous. You don't know!"

The master bedroom is on the first floor, where Bill waits for us to catch up. "I'll let you look around the room on your own." With that, Bill twists the knob to open the door and then retreats deeper into the hallway.

The room is bright, decently sized and, oh my word, the light fixture is a shark's head.

My gasp is loud enough to make it into the hallway, calling Bill back from where he stands. "It's cool, right?" he says exuberantly. "It's not the actual shark head. The owner had the fixtures made bespoke and then he installed them in each of the bedrooms."

"It's a talking point, that's for sure." I keep my back to the door, lest Bill see the trepidation on my face. I can't imagine laying down to sleep with a shark's toothy grin threatening me from above. Even H might draw the line here. I give the rest of the room and the attached bathroom a cursory look before beating a hasty retreat.

At the front door, I thank the two men again for showing me the room and promise to get back to them within a week. Outside, the clean air clears my nose and head.

"Mathilde, I know it is a bit of a walk, but would you mind too much if we headed to the centre on foot? It's all downhill..."

"Fine with me," Mathilde agrees. "I think we could both use some time to clear our heads. I really hope this isn't the best option available to you, Nat, because... Wow. I don't even know where to start." She steps back until she can see the shark's body crashing into the roof, with broken boards scattered around it. "The shark house! I just... I mean... Yeah."

On the bright side, at least I know for certain that Mathilde was the right person to bring along on my flat hunt. Anyone else would berate me for even considering taking a room in a shark-infested home where I'd be expected to be the domestic help. But Mathilde knows that reasonably priced rooms are hard to find.

Still, I can't help crossing my fingers as we make our way to the next place on my list.

Mathilde wipes her mouth with her napkin and pushes back from the table. "I think we should revisit your criteria for selecting a new flat."

Giving up on my attempts to pick up the last rice grain on my plate of sushi, I set my chopsticks down and nod my head in agreement. "Yes, I might have been hasty when I said wasn't picky. It turns out I'm not keen on giant fish, locker room smells or housecleaning." When I consider how ridiculous that last statement sounds, I have to laugh. My chuckle turns contagious when Mathilde joins in and before long, we're both making jokes about the morning.

"Remember when you asked Bill if they had forgotten you

were coming over and he had no idea what you meant?" Mathilde remarks.

"That was nothing compared to your face when you saw the light fixture in the bedroom," I chortle.

Mathilde shudders at the memory. "There is no way I could sleep with that thing above me."

"My thoughts exactly," I concur.

"All right, enough of rehashing the last place." Mathilde waves a hand to the waiter and motions for the bill. "Where are we off to next? You said something in the centre?"

I double-check my notes, refreshing my memory on the specifics. "Shark house was the least expensive place available... and now we know why. You'll be pleased to know that we're moving to the opposite end of the cost spectrum. It's a studio in a new building two streets over. The photos on the building website looked really gorgeous, and the description said there is a small park nearby. It's a little more than I had hoped to spend, but after this morning, I think I can make my money stretch if needed."

The address leads us to a brand-new high-rise behind the city's new shopping centre. On the plus side, I could walk to any of the colleges from here and there is no shortage of food options. On the downside, having to stroll past all the shop windows will wreak havoc on my resolve to save money.

The exterior is glass and steel, the afternoon sun illuminating a shimmering reflection of the Oxford skyline. Only four stories tall, the building would barely be of notice in any other metropolitan area, but due to Oxford's strict guidelines on building height, it towers above most of the surrounding area.

"Do you see the park?" I ask Mathilde, perplexed by the sea of tarmac surrounding us.

"Maybe it's on the other side?" she replies. "Come on, let's see the inside before we worry about a play area for H."

The building's reception area is lovely, if a bit aesthetically cold. A trio of potted plants placed near the security desk do little to absorb the echo of our footsteps make on the tile floor.

"Hullo," I say as I approach the security guard. "I have an appointment to view the flat for rent."

The guard flips through his papers until he locates the right note and then places a quick phone call to the sales office to let them know of my arrival. Soon after, a woman emerges, wearing a smart dress, heels and with her hair smoothed into a neat knot at the base of her neck. She clicks her way over to us, offering a welcoming handshake as she introduces herself as a member of the building sales team.

"Sales office?" I ask nervously. "The flat I'm here to see is for rent, right? I'm not looking to buy just yet."

"Don't worry," she assures me. "Our primary focus is on selling the remaining units, but we also act as onsite management for our investment owners who rent out their flats."

She leads Mathilde and me into the lift, pressing the button for the top level. With a bright smile, she gushes, "The views from the studio flat are lush. Just wait!"

The lift dings and the doors open into a narrow corridor lined with numbered doors. Thankfully, a deep carpet covers the floor, cutting down on the noise of our voices and footsteps. The sales agent stops halfway down the hall, retrieving an oversized keyring and searching until she finds the one with the correct tag. I expect her to lead us inside, but instead, she steps back and motions for us to go ahead.

"Go on in. I'll wait for you here."

With Mathilde close behind, I move into the flat. The view from the floor to ceiling glass windows is indeed gorgeous, but it in no way makes up for the fact that the flat is tiny. Miniscule. The entire flat comprises a teensy galley kitchen with an eat-in bar, a lounge area with a two-person love seat and television stand, and finally a double bed and side table tucked against the windows. Despite the minimum of furnishings, there is barely room left to move.

Mathilde shuffles around to let me pass by on my way back to the doorway. I stick my head out to find the sales agent standing in the hall. "Excuse me, are you sure this is the right flat? It doesn't look at all like the photos."

"Oh dear," she murmurs, shifting uncomfortably on her feet, "I told Steven to take new photos. He's been using the ones from our model unit instead. I thought he'd updated the listing, but based on the look on your face, I guess not."

"Err, no... It's a little smaller than I expected."

Realising she has a problem, the agent switches into full-on sales mode. "Yes, it's narrow, but look how long it is." She strides inside the flat, calling over her shoulder, "We call this our boxcar floor plan. It's very popular now, particularly with the interest in the tiny house movement and minimalism. And look at these windows!" she exclaims when she reaches the bedroom area. "They really open up the space, almost make you feel as though you are living in the clouds."

"Clouds, yes," I mumble, thinking feverishly. At least H can fly, I remind myself. "The website mentioned a nearby park. Can you see it from here? And do these windows open?"

The agent scoots to the side, making a small space for me to stand next to her at the foot of the bed, so we can both see out of the window. "If you look over to your right, across the roundabout, you can see the tops of the trees. That's the park. As to the windows, for health and safety reasons, they are sealed shut."

She plasters on a big smile, doing her best to encourage me. "Why don't you take a little more time, really envision yourself living here? I'm sure you'll fall in love with the space. I'll be out in the hall."

Having ended her sales pitch, she exits the flat, pulling the door shut as she leaves to give us a moment of privacy.

I really try to imagine living here. The kitchen appliances are shiny new, albeit small. The furniture is in pristine condition and the view is unparalleled. I almost convince myself that it is workable when Mathilde's voice interrupts my reverie.

"This isn't boxcar, it's prison block," she says while trying out the loveseat. "I don't think you and H would last a week in here. He'll be bouncing off the ceiling, and every time he sneezes, his smoke plumes will trigger the smoke alarm."

My shoulders drop in disappointment. I know she's right, even if I'm loathe to admit it. But the determined part of me refuses to admit defeat. I straighten up and give the flat a proper assessment, peering into the cupboard and bathroom, checking out the kitchen and gazing out of the window.

For her part, Mathilde leaves me to it, flipping through an interior design magazine someone left in the flat. When there is nothing left to see, we thank the agent for her time, take a copy of the rental paperwork, and I promise to get back in touch soon.

"Anything else to see today?" Mathilde asks and I shake my head no.

"That's it. I've got appointments to see two other places next Thursday. You free to come along again?" I give her a hopeful glance, pleased when she promises to see me through all the options.

As we call it a day and head our separate ways, I'm left pondering the question: Am I going to end up living in a shoebox or a shark house?

Chapter Nine

On Sunday, I scour all the local news sites and online boards looking for more adverts for rooms and flats, but to my dismay, nothing new shows up. Late March is a terrible time to house hunt. Since we're midway through the university calendar and close to the Easter holidays, few people are making moves at this time. I force myself off the sofa for a run and then reward myself with a takeaway curry and a movie for dinner.

Edward messages later in the evening, letting me know the results of his test of the college's video cameras. Sure enough, when my grandfather walked in front of him, the camera footage blurred, hiding him from view. I can't help but wonder how our suspect discovered the technique.

The return to work on Monday promises plenty of distractions. First thing on my agenda is a meeting with Mathilde, Will and Jill, where Mathilde will show us the items for the exhibition. Despite that, I had been at Barnard and had seen the contents of the secret chamber spread across the old library. I was so distracted by the murder investigation that I barely have a clue of what they found stored away inside. I'm looking forward to the tour. Surprisingly, even H asked to tag along, promising to be on his absolute best behaviour.

As agreed, we all meet in one of the Ashmolean's staging areas, currently set aside for planning the final layout of the exhibition. Tables covered with journals, books, artefacts, and paintings fill the plain, white room. A small notecard explaining what it is accompanies each item. The items are so varied; it is nearly impossible to know where to begin.

"Sorry I'm late," Mathilde calls out as she makes her way in from the hallway. "My housemate had moved my keys, then my bicycle tyre was flat, and finally I got stuck when a large tour group blocked the cycling lane on Magdalen Bridge."

"Oxford problems," Will and Jill remark in unison, making us all chuckle. Jill adds, "Housemate, bicycle, and tourist troubles... You ticked every box."

"Hopefully that means I'm good for a long while." Mathilde says with a grimace. She drops her bag on a nearby chair before inviting us to join her at the first table. "Before I show you the individual items, I thought it might be useful for me to give you an overview of our discovery, providing a frame of reference, if you will."

Looking chagrinned, Jill confesses, "That would be fab, Mathilde. It's been ages since I took a history class and I was a little worried I might not understand half of what you'll show us."

"Don't be embarrassed! If I mention someone you don't know or say something you don't understand, please speak up." Mathilde makes sure we all nod our agreement. "Great, let's begin."

I double check that H is sitting quietly before turning my attention to Mathilde.

Mathilde clears her throat and begins. "If I were to sum up the contents of this room in one phrase, it would be *the birth of modern science*. The journals and manuscripts, portraits, statues, and artefacts document the lives and work of men in the late seventeenth century — men who were passionate about exploring what they called 'natural knowledge.' These men set aside the commonly held theories at the time about why people got sick and how things work, deciding that they would take no one's word for it unless they could prove the theory themselves."

She moves around the room, pointing at different tables. "Sir Christopher Wren, Robert Hooke, Robert Boyle, even Sir Isaac Newton, utilised their insatiable curiosity to make giant leaps of advancement in the fields of math, science, architecture and philosophy, to name a few. It wasn't enough for them to make a discovery or solve a problem. They challenged one another, reviewing work, providing feedback, and creating the foundation for modern day peer review, which is fundamental to scientific advancement."

My gaze skips around the room, the display tables taking on a new light.

Mathilde crosses to a table, pointing at a contraption consisting of a metal tube, glass lens and a candleholder, and a sheaf of loose pages lying nearby. "Although the microscope was patented in 1608, it would take several decades before scientists turned their lens towards researching living creatures. This microscope was used by Robert Hooke to study the finer details of plants and insects. He sketched drawings of everything he saw, and here we have some of his draft works. He eventually published his studies in a book called *Micrographia*, which was a landmark scientific text."

She passes each of us a pair of gloves and clears off a section of the table so H can join in. Under her watchful eye, we take turns looking at the centuries-old sketches, marvelling at their detail.

As always, I'm slightly nervous about having H in such close quarters with people who don't know about the existence of Oxford's magic. However, Will and Jill seem oblivious to the oddity of having what appears to be a cat inside of a museum. At one point, I catch H putting a foot on a book, stopping Will from turning the page. Will waits patiently until H gives him the nod to go ahead, never stopping to ask himself why a cat is reading a book alongside him.

The portraits remind me of the renaissance paintings upstairs in the museums, showing men with long flowing locks or curled wigs and women with powdered hairstyles. I imagine that the daily looks were dramatically different, probably closer to how our modern scientists look in the labs here at the uni — hair pulled back, clothing somewhat of an after-thought, and full attention on whatever it is they are studying.

It takes us most of the morning to go through the room, asking questions and proposing ideas how we might bring the story to life at the grand opening.

"How about doing a time capsule theme?" Jill offers. "We could dress some of the waitstaff up like the portraits."

"It's a great idea, Jill," I say with an encouraging smile, "but too similar to what we did with St Margaret's autumn gala. What other ideas have we got?"

Mathilde steps forward. "You could decorate the rooms to match the field of study. You know, one for medicine, one for architecture, one for math, and so forth."

I ponder her idea, replying, "I like the idea of separating the fields, but it might come across as too gimmicky if we use microscopes or addition signs in the decor."

The room goes quiet as we continue to mull. I can feel the pressure to create something spectacular and memorable weighing on my shoulders. I struggle to remember what made my last two events successes. It wasn't necessarily the theme itself, as much as it was the brilliant representation of the story we needed to tell. At St Margaret, I needed to use the event to strengthen the college's connection with the magic of Oxford. I did so by reminding everyone of the college's long history. At Barnard, I took their celebration of the first female students and turned it into a recognition of the centuries of women who laid the foundation, creating the environment which would eventually welcome women as equals rather than inferiors.

"Mathilde," I speak up, breaking the silence. "What was the phrase you used to describe the discovered objects?"

"Birth of modern science," she answers. "The men you see in the portraits had a passion for study. Sir Christopher over there," she says, pointing to a portrait of a man in an enormous brown wig, "was so keen to collaborate. He introduced the idea of having a society for learning. He got royal support and founded what is now known as the Royal Society, the highest-recognised organisation for scientists in the UK. It is invitation-only and extremely well-respected. Their motto is '*Nullius in verba*' — or in modern-day language, '*Take nobody's word for it.*'"

I contemplate what Wren, Hooke and the others would choose if they were here. Would they want a swish event with cocktails and ballgowns? Despite the styling of their portraits, somehow I doubt it. It seems more likely that those men would have preferred to push up their sleeves and get to work on their experiments than to strut around like a group of wealthy dandies.

Tapping my finger against my lips, I push myself to see beyond the glitz of a typical exhibition grand opening. "Maybe we should follow in their footsteps, focusing our attention on the questions they were asking, and problems they wanted to solve, rather than on the men and their discoveries. After all, what are these journals, objects and portraits, but evidence of the work they did here? They represent trials and failures, successes and steps forward," I muse.

As I wind my way through the display tables, letting my gaze skip around, I see how this could all come together. Before I can voice my thoughts aloud, Mathilde remarks on the time and reminds me she and I have a busy afternoon planned, and we need to hurry to lunch if we want to eat.

We gather our things and I suggest we take one last look before we leave. "We've got plenty of logistical work to do this week, with ordering party furniture, selecting a caterer, and taking security requirements into account. While we cross some of these more tedious tasks off our list, we can unleash the backs of our minds to think about the creative aspects. We know the story we need to tell; let's take our time figuring out how to best do it. Agreed?"

Will and Jill don't need to reply. Their grins are answer enough. Just like me, there is nothing they relish more than an event-related challenge.

"Where are they off to?" Mathilde asks when Will and Jill dash out of the Ashmolean's main doors.

"I arranged for them to meet with a new vendor in Birmingham," I explain as I wave goodbye. "They'll grab a sandwich to eat on the train and won't be back until late this afternoon."

"Oi, missies," H calls out, flapping his way in front of us. "Do you mind iffen I take off too? I can scavenge a sausage roll from the cafe and then 'ead off to 'ang around with Xavvie? I've 'ad enough meetin's to last me for a while."

"Sure, H," Mathilde replies, "or you could get Xavvie to take you upstairs to the restaurant. They've got cheese soufflés on the menu." H gives us both a toothy grin, shooting a jet of excited flame before flying off to find his fellow Eternal.

"Perfect! Our next stop is lunch with Nancy and Agatha, two volunteers here at the museum," Mathilde announces, looking at her watch. "They are probably already down in the cafe. We'd better hurry." She strides off, assuming I'll follow behind.

"Wait up, Mathilde," I say when she takes off again. "Can I ask you a question on our way downstairs?"

"Of course," she quips.

"What happened to the journals and manuscripts which reference Oxford's magic? I didn't notice any of them amongst the items you showed us this morning."

"It turns out Finch-Byron's desire for secrecy did us a favour. Kate and I are the only living people who know what was inside the hidden chamber. With your grandfather Alfred's help, we ferried all the sensitive items over to the Bodleian Library, where the Eternals stored them someplace safe." Mathilde skips down the stairwell, descending to the lower level where the cafe is located. "The Eternals can keep the average researcher from finding them but make them available should any future prefects need the information."

"That's handy." I snag Mathilde's arm, pulling her into an alcove near the bottom of the stairs. "Before we go into the cafe, can you give me a little background information on Nancy and Agatha? Why are we meeting with them?"

"We need to know more about Francie and Andrei, right? Particularly about the early days of their relationship. You know, how they met and their interactions with one another." A mischievous look flashes across Mathilde's face. "At first, I thought we could check the security tapes, but then I realised there might be something better."

I arch my eyebrow in a silent question.

"Agatha and Nancy are the queen bees of the gossip circuit here at the Ashmolean," Mathilde says with a cheeky grin. "Kate said that those two hawk-eyed older ladies don't miss a thing. She arranged for us to meet them for lunch today. If anyone knew about Francie and Andrei's relationship, it's them."

When we enter the cafe, it isn't hard to pick out Agatha and Nancy among the busy tables. The two white-haired women have commandeered a four-top in a prime corner location, providing them an unobstructed view of every table in the place, including the order counter. Their faces might be heavily wrinkled, but their sharp eyes catch even the smallest detail.

Mathilde waves hello and points towards the counter to let them know we'll grab food and come over. They give the barest nod of acknowledgement before returning to their duties as unofficial sentries. Kate was definitely right in her description of these two.

I elbow Mathilde to get her attention and then whisper, "Those two old biddies could give Granny Grantham from Downton Abbey a run for her money." Mathilde shushes me, stifling a snicker as we step up to the counter.

Food in hand, we present ourselves to our interview subjects, standing there until they give us permission to be seated. From a distance, the women look so much alike that at first glance; I thought they were sisters. But now that I am closer, I realise that the similarity is by design rather than by relation.

They have the same white hair styled in tight curls to hide its thinness. The scarves around their necks are pinned with large broaches and are artfully draped over their jewel tone cardigans. Their jewellery is subtle but expensive; their makeup goes in the opposite direction, with bright blue eyeshadow, rosy cheeks and vibrant coral lipstick. Despite their bird-like statures, there is an aura of power around them — one that can only come from old age and vast knowledge.

"Hi, I'm..." I say but stop when the woman in the sapphire blue cardigan interrupts me.

"You're Natalie Payne, Head of Ceremonies and you are..." she shifts in Mathilde's direction, "Mathilde Seymour, from the Bodleian. Yes, we know."

The emerald-green-cardigan woman picks up the thread. "I'm Agatha and this is Nancy. We've seen you two walking around the museum recently. Kate mentioned you wanted to speak with us. We considered this request and decided it would only be right to assist wherever we can."

I doubt that is the case, but I paste a smile on my face.

She continues, "You all seem to know each other well. How did you meet?"

Putting more pressure on Mathilde and I to respond, Nancy adds, "You three couldn't be more different, yet you seem thick as thieves. It makes a person wonder."

I wait for Mathilde to reply since she arranged the meeting, but she gently kicks me under the table, jolting me into action. Good thing I'm quick on my feet.

"No secret there," I say with an innocent smile. "Mathilde and I started around the same time and made friends at a new-employee welcome event. We got to know Kate when she joined us at Barnard College earlier this term. Mathilde worked with Kate to catalogue the contents of the secret chamber. I happened to be there organising a big event."

Agatha and Nancy exchange glances, apparently deciding my answer passes muster. Nancy gives me a regal nod. "What do you need from myself and Agatha? We're only volunteers here; I'm not sure we'll know anything of value."

I know a test when I hear one. If we get this wrong, we won't find out anything. I lean across the table, looking straight at Nancy and Agatha. "You may be volunteers, but according to Kate, nothing happens here without you knowing about it. You can go wherever you want in the museum, talk to everyone, and see all. If you can't help us, no one can."

The two older women settle back into their chairs, clearly

pleased with my flattering description. I slide my foot over to tap Mathilde's ankle, passing the baton back her way.

Mathilde takes a fortifying sip of her water and jumps in. "I'm sure you know the police have arrested Francie, accusing her of setting fire to the archives."

Nancy frowns. "That DCI Robinson could give Idris Elba a run for his money, but that doesn't excuse him from hauling off our Francie. There is no way the girl did what he claims." She punctuates her statement with a loud harrumph.

"Exactly our thoughts," Mathilde echoes, leaning forward conspiratorially. "DCI Robinson thinks Francie was stealing from the museum. You two had plenty of opportunities to observe Francie on her own, and her interactions with Andrei. What do you think?"

This time Agatha harrumphs in displeasure. "I never understood how those two ended up together. Sure, Francie was moon-eyed over Andrei when she first started working here, but all the young gals are like that. He was a handsome bloke, and he sure knew it. If I were fifty years younger, I'd have taken him out for a spin." She wiggles her shoulders suggestively, causing Mathilde and I to blush.

Nancy rolls her eyes, accustomed to her friend's antics, and then sips her tea, looking thoughtful. "Francie's initial infatuation with Andrei didn't last long. She's dedicated to her job, and she takes her position as Kate's assistant seriously. You two should have seen her while Kate was off at Barnard, sorting out that secret chamber they uncovered. Francie worked herself to the bone trying to keep on top of everything."

Agatha nods. "She was stressed, and it showed. She'd look nice enough when she came into work in the morning, but by the end of the day, she'd sweated through her make-up and her hair was frazzled. I don't think she sat down, always running around, trying to keep on top of everything. That said, she seems to love her job. Would you agree, Nancy?"

Nancy makes a tsking sound. "She works too hard, if you ask me. I was glad when Kate returned to the museum, taking the weight off Francie's shoulders. Young woman like that needs to have a personal life. Sew some wild oats like we did. Right, Agatha?"

"Mmmhmm," Agatha concurs, her eyes focusing off in the distance. "We could tell you some stories about Oxford in the 1970s. Marching with the women's liberation movement... lovefests in the University Park..." She trails off, lost in her memories.

I start to ask Agatha to tell us more, but Mathilde gives me the evil eye, reminding me to stay focused on our task at hand.

Mathilde leans in, her expression serious. "How did Francie and Andrei get together? Do you think she approached him? You said she was interested beforehand. Do you think she finally got around to acting on her feelings?"

Agatha purses her lips. "I don't know for sure, but if I were a betting woman, I'd put my money on him having asked her out."

Nancy bobs her white head up and down in agreement. "Which is strange, if you know either of them. Francie is pretty enough, but she is a far cry from the other women I've spotted snogging with Andrei outside in the smoking shelter. From day one, I thought he had to be up to something, but Francie was so starry-eyed. Who was I to say anything? She's old enough to make her own mistakes."

Agatha reaches over to pat Nancy's hand. "That's the truth. I was alone at the information desk with Francie several times in the last few weeks. I tried to start a conversation, but Francie immediately began gushing about how great Andrei was, and how lucky she was, and how she could hardly believe it. I saw little point in bursting her bubble. I thought it would work itself out in the end."

"Always does," Nancy agrees with a wry frown. "If I'm honest, Andrei disappointed me. He played a good game, but a zebra can't change its stripes. He was a love 'em and leave 'em type, always half an eye out looking for the next attractive woman to come along."

"Francie never struck me as the type to have a casual affair," Agatha explains. "She's too single-minded and too dedicated to her work to let a man be a distraction. Andrei was the opposite. It was bound to end. We were waiting to swoop in and offer her a shoulder to cry upon when the relationship either blew up or fizzled out. However, neither Nancy nor I could have envisioned this outcome."

I offer to refresh their cups of tea, giving us all a moment to ponder their words. It is really sounding like Andrei was up to something, but why did he drag Francie into the middle of it?

Chapter Ten

We leave the two older women sipping their teas in the cafe, promising to meet again for a slice of cake and a happier chat. I have no doubts that the two of them have plenty of interesting stories to tell.

Mathilde jogs up the stairs, leading me past the visitor information desk and out through the front doors. When she pauses at the corner to wait for the pedestrian light to change, I ask where we are going.

"Andrei split his shifts across the Ashmolean and the Pitt Rivers Museum," she explains over the beeping sound of the crossing sign. "We've got as far as we can with our investigation at the Ash, so I thought it was time we checked out his other workplace."

She speeds her way across two different lanes of traffic and turns left in front of St John's College, heading away from the city shopping district. The cobblestone pavement is slick with rain, forcing us to slow down as we walk towards the Lamb & Flag pub. Mathilde makes a sharp turn into the alley beside it.

I look around with interest, realising I've never taken this shortcut before. The surrounding buildings are all part of the university, either providing housing for students at St John's College or offices for the various departments. It is one of the few parts of town that actually feels like a university campus.

"How many Eternals are there at the Pitt Rivers?" I ask, curious to know more.

"There are several Eternal creatures living in the Natural History Museum, but not the Pitt Rivers. Like the Ashmolean, the Pitt Rivers only has one. In fact, Xavvie is going to meet us there and introduce us to him," she adds. "He doesn't go there very often, because he prefers to stay close to Kate, but in this case, he thought they could compare notes and provide a more rounded view of Andrei."

"Sounds perfect!" I am genuinely enthusiastic. "The Pitt Rivers is connected to the Museum of Natural History. Is that right? I've been meaning to visit them both."

"Yes, that's correct," Mathilde confirms as we reach the end of the alley. Across the street, just beyond a lush green lawn, sit the museums in question. The stately building, with its yellow-orange stone and neo-gothic windows, somehow strikes a balance between awe-inspiring and welcoming. The giant concrete dinosaur footprints running across the grassy lawn might have something to do with it.

Mathilde nudges me when the pedestrian crossing light changes, jolting me out of my enthralled state. "Wait until you see the inside, Nat. It is even more incredible than the exterior."

The rain picks up, chasing us inside the stone entrance. The sounds of children giggling and parents calling them to wait echo in the small space. We quickly weave our way through the crowd of visitors, many of them very young, and dash up the stairs into the museum proper. Despite the cloudy day, the glass roof floods the room with daylight. Flowery ironworks and colossal columns divide the sprawling open space into three arcades filled with displays.

My eyes scan the array of signs, but I can't see anything that indicates where the entrance to the Pitt Rivers might be. "Where do we get into the Pitt Rivers?"

"It's easy," Mathilde gives me a cheeky grin. "We walk past the dinosaurs and then make a left at Charles Darwin, and we'll see the doorway in front of us. I'll go on ahead and let Xavvie know we're here. You can take a minute to have a look around."

Mathilde confidently strides off ahead, walking along the central corridor, seemingly oblivious to the towering dinosaur skeletons posed mid-step.

The nearby displays shed light on Oxford's Palaeolithic history, showcasing dinosaur bones that had been found in the nearby quarries and hills. Knowing I don't have much time, I skim over the text, focusing more of my attention on the animals on display. H told me that the Oxford Dodo is an Eternal, but I have no idea what other creatures within the museum can come to life.

I'm pondering the likelihood that the dinosaurs themselves might be Eternals when something catches my eye. "Wait a minute, is that one breathing fire?" I mumble, trying to keep my voice down. I back up a step and lean sideways, spotting a glimpse of a familiar leathery grey wing.

"Did I scare ya, Nat?" H shouts from his perch inside of the mouth of a Megalosaurus.

I roll my eyes but can't stop a smile from blossoming on my face. "I see Xavvie didn't come on his own. I should have known you wouldn't miss an opportunity to turn another one of Oxford's famed museums into your personal playground."

H gives me a toothy smirk before sending another jet of flames shooting from the skeletal head. Even knowing it is only H, the scene is still somewhat terrifying. I really hope the dinosaurs aren't one of the museum's Eternal creatures.

Lost in thought, I feel something tugging on my trousers and look down to see a small child, no more than three years old if I had to guess, standing beside me. Her black hair is pulled up in piggy tails and she's wearing a bright pink princess costume. I give her a bright smile, remembering my childhood spent wearing dressing up clothing year-round.

Her brown eyes are wide open, staring unblinkingly up at the dinosaur. She pulls her thumb out of her mouth and uses it to motion upwards.

"Kitty. Meowwwww. Nice kitty!" she cries out in a tiny voice. She waves her little hands in front of her, encouraging H to jump into her arms. "Here, kitty kitty!"

Uh oh, it looks like the magic is less effective at distracting children than it is on adults. I need to get H out of here before we end up with an audience of ankle-biters. Not that H would mind, but Mathilde will be annoyed if she has to pull us out of a crowd of toddlers. "Hurry, H. You've been spotted."

H shifts nervously when he spots the little girl and realises it's him she's calling. He barely stifles a sneeze before he launches himself out of the dinosaur's jaw and swoops to land at my feet. He pauses long enough to let the girl stroke his back, and then we skedaddle.

I hurry to keep H within eyesight, following him to a doorway marked with a sign announcing it as the entry to the Pitt Rivers Museum.

I'm dumbstruck by the sight in front of me. Where the natural history section was large, airy, and open, the Pitt Rivers is the exact opposite. There are none of the traditional museum displays, but the floor is littered with dozens and dozens of curio cabinets, holding thousands of objects.

An older gentleman — dressed in a loose khaki jacket, blue

jumper, an impressive cravat, and even more impressive mutton chops — steps out of the shadows at the bottom of a wide staircase, waving a hand in our direction.

"Hullo up there," he calls from his post. "Hurry along, Xavvie and Mathilde have gone ahead of us."

I pull my gaze from the maze of wooden display cabinets so I can pay attention to the narrow steps and reach the bottom safely.

"Henry Fox, my dear," says the man, clicking his heels together and standing board straight.

"Natalie Payne," I reply, holding out a hand in greeting. "Why do I get the sense you left a military title out of your introduction?"

"I earned my fame in the Crimean War, rising to the rank of Lieutenant General before I retired. After a hundred years as an Oxford Eternal, one hardly needs to demand pomp and circumstance at every introduction." His stern features soften, and he bends over to give H a warm pat on the head. "Let's move out of here before we wake up the shrunken heads. Follow me. We've marked one of the break rooms as out of order, so we won't be disturbed."

"Shrunken heads?" I whisper to H. "Are there really shrunken heads on display here? Actual heads, not paper mâchè or something?"

"Yeah, Nat," he whispers as a tremble runs down his back. "They're a bit much even for me, and that's sayin' somethin'."

I shove that thought firmly out of my mind. Shrunken heads might sound fascinating, but shrunken heads who can make noises? No way. Not today.

Henry keeps to the perimeter of the room, leading me past a glass case filled with wooden carvings and tribal costumes, and then out of the museum into a modern stairwell. "The break room is upstairs," he explains as he jogs up a flight and turns to the right. Two doorways later, I find Mathilde and Xavvie relaxing inside a cosy nook.

"So that's what took you so long..." Mathilde gives me a knowing grin when she spots H at my side. "I see you picked up a stray on your way through the museum."

"Oi, missie!" H gripes good-naturedly, sending a puff of smoke wafting towards her face.

I join her on the leather sofa, falling into its deep cushions and sighing with relief. Between spending all morning on my feet and then the brisk walk here, my feet were crying for a rest.

Henry lays claim to the armchair, and Xavvie rolls closer in his wheelchair, closing off our circle. H susses out the situation and finally decides Xavvie's lap looks like his most comfortable spot. He leaps up, turns around and flops onto his side, a small stream of smoke curling from his nostrils as he closes his eyes to grab a catnap.

"Xavvie explained what happened at the Ashmolean. I'm sorry to hear about all the troubles there. He said you want to know more about Andrei. I'll help as best as I can." Henry scratches the full length of his sideburn, which starts by his ears and stretches along the side of his jaw. "Where to start..."

Xavvie looks skyward as he gathers his thoughts. "I'm assuming you also noticed a change in his behaviour, Henry. Around two months ago, I would say. Perhaps we should start there."

"Yes, that's as good a place as any," agrees Henry. "Andrei reminded me of the men in my troops. He arrived here two years ago, proud to be commissioned as part of the museum's security team. It isn't a demanding job, however, keeping watch over millions and millions of pounds' worth of objects lends a certain cachet to the role. As the months passed by, I could see the monotony wearing on him."

Xavvie interrupts to explain, "I overheard him talking to another guard, complaining about his shifts at the Pitt Rivers. He said he spent more time searching for lost children than anything else. I suspect he preferred his shifts at the Ash because it attracts a different demographic of visitors. More single women in their twenties and fewer children. He was a bit of a rake, you know."

"What happened two months ago to drive this change of behaviour you mentioned?" I ask.

"One manager within the security team retired and Andrei was keen to take his place. He'd have done well in a role with more responsibility," Henry clarifies, "but the Head of Security eliminated the position. There was nothing personal about the decision, but Andrei sure took it that way. I'd often hear him grumbling to himself as he made his late-night rounds of the museum."

"Why didn't he quit if he was so unhappy?" Mathilde queries, her curiosity genuine.

"I thought he might, at first," Henry says, pulling a pipe from his jacket pocket and beginning preparations for a smoke. "Then, one day, it was again as though someone had switched a light off. He stopped searching the job ads. He became... more furtive? That's the best way to describe it. I'd come across him in the storage area, taking overly long with his rounds. His phone stopped ringing with calls from women. He developed a great interest in the items on display."

"*Oui,*" Xavvie chimes in. "I saw something similar at the Ashmolean."

I look back and forth between the two men. "And neither of you thought to mention this to Kate?"

Both men look abashed. Xavvie replies, "I thought several times of mentioning it, but you all had your hands full with the discoveries at Barnard. I never saw Andrei doing anything wrong, and it didn't seem right to burden Kate with uncertainties and vague suspicions."

"I blame myself," Henry confesses in between puffs on his pipe. "Xavvie and I thought we'd catch onto Andrei's game, or otherwise find it was nothing. But we couldn't spend all our time trailing behind him. We have our own responsibilities to help our researchers and inspire our visitors. Not to mention the number of objects in both museums which seem to have a magic of their own. Whatever happened, it slipped right underneath our noses."

Mathilde and I exchange glances, both of us unsure what to do with this new information. We need to know more about Andrei, and there is only one person left who might shed some light. Francie. Good thing Kate and I are going to visit her this week.

Chapter Eleven

F or the first time in ages, I'm ready to go somewhere before
Edward. It's been a while since I've seen him. He was away
all weekend at a work event. On Monday, I spent all day with
Mathilde getting a tour of the secret chamber contents and then
interviewing people for more insights into Francie and Andrei.
Today was Edward's busy day, with a lecture class to deliver and an
afternoon of tutorial sessions.

I've been looking forward to this evening, hoping we can use
our drive into the Cotswolds to compare notes on what we've
uncovered so far.

"Knock knock," I call out as I open his flat door and step
inside. "Shall we head out? I've got Harry's car parked outside."

"Nearly." Edward's reply is faint, coming from deeper inside of
his flat. I follow the sound of his grumbles to find him holding a
tie in each hand, taking turns to trial them in front of the mirror.
"I think the red tie goes best, but will it come off as too
aggressive when we question Mary Chloe?" He swaps them again,
huffing in frustration.

Sensing the need for an intervention, I step into the room and
take both ties from his hands. "Stop thinking about this as an

interview with a suspect and try to approach it as dinner with a friend." I hold up a more casual polo shirt and wait as he unbuttons his starched white shirt and rehangs it inside the armoire.

"I'm supposed to be a professional, Nat. Why is it so hard for me to decide on a tie?" Edward gives me a hangdog look. "Also, I can't bring myself to believe Mary Chloe could be the evil mastermind behind all the thefts and the fire in the archives. She's a colleague, for goodness' sake! I've worked with her for years, shared students with her, sat across the table at lunches and dinners."

I make a quick decision that we can afford to be a few minutes late. There is no way we can leave with Edward so discombobulated. I'll spend the entire dinner trying to cover up for his awkwardness. "Come, sit down here on the bed for a minute. A couple of good exhales to calm yourself." I coach Edward through a quick relaxation exercise until he stops twitching.

"Thanks, Nat. I don't know what got into me. Or rather, I do, but I don't want to admit it. I've been staring at the date in my diary all day, planning out conversation starters and follow-up questions, and hating every minute of it."

"If it makes you feel any better," I offer, "I spent a day thinking Harry might have been the one to kill Chef Smythe. I was in complete misery, both at the thought of it and with the pressure of needing to confront her."

"Harry?" he repeats, his voice full of disbelief. "Harry and Chef Smythe were like oil and water, but murder? It wouldn't even have crossed my mind."

"I couldn't imagine it, but I had to ask the questions and rule her out based on evidence and not my gut feeling. Neither of us suspected the real killer, so it goes to show how easy it is to make a mistake."

Edward rises from his seat on the edge of the bed, tucks his shirt in and rolls his shoulders back. "Alright, let's do this."

I can still feel the tension coming from him, but given we're already late, I decide it will have to do.

"I'll drive. I know the way," Edward offers, holding out his hand for the keys to Harry's car. I drop them in and follow him down the stairs and outside into the carpark in front of our building. We make quick work of starting the car and are soon on our way.

The stop-and-go traffic requires Edward's full attention, so I use the first part of the drive to catch up on my emails. Typing long replies on my phone is not my favourite way to communicate, but it is a necessity given how little time I spend behind a desk. Once we clear through the last major roundabout, I tuck my phone back into my purse and start a conversation.

"How was your conference this past weekend? Bump into any old friends or hear any interesting speakers?" I leave my real question unvoiced. What I want to know is whether he told anyone about us.

Edward relaxes as he recounts his trip to Southampton. Although the speakers were good, the bland catered dinners left a lot to be desired. I get a secret thrill of pleasure when he wraps up saying that several of his colleagues expressed an interest in meeting me and encouraged him to bring me along to their next event.

"How about you, Nat? I was so caught up getting packed for my trip, I forgot to ask what you had planned for the weekend."

Do I want to tell Edward I went flat hunting, particularly at when he is already stressed?

"I hung out with Mathilde, had a really pleasant walk around the city," I answer, but in my head, I'm thinking *please let him drop it, please let him drop it.*

"Did you see anything interesting? Any new areas? Your

parents are coming up soon. We need to come up with a plan of where to take them."

I grasp onto his second comment like a lifeline. "Yes, we do. My dad grew up here, but I bet he hasn't done a lot of the touristy things. Isn't that always the way? Everyone thinks they'll get around to visiting their own hometown's treasures, but anytime a holiday comes up, they go away."

Edward chuckles, agreeing with my assessment. "Okay, so tourist favourites are on the yes list. Did anything catch your eye?"

Sweaty roommates, dirty clothes and shoebox-sized flats? Can't mention any of that. I grasp at straws. "The shark house? Have you ever seen it? It's up in Headington. Crazy, really!"

I launch into a detailed description of the grey shark and the artfully broken roof tiles. Edward seems really interested in what I'm saying, so I keep going. "And yet it's right there, in the middle of a row of houses on an otherwise quiet street. And the crazy thing is that inside the house, the bedroom light fixtures are designed to look like a shark's mouth."

"What?" he says, taking his eyes from the road to look over at me. "I had heard about some of the other facts you mentioned, but I've never heard anyone talk about the inside of the house. I thought it was privately owned."

Oh no.

"Were they having an open house, Nat? Is that how you saw the inside?"

"Um, not exactly an open house," I mumble, spinning my wheels as I desperately search for a way out of this conversation.

I can see the exact moment when Edward catches on to my real activities. His jaw clenches and I can hear his teeth grind.

"You were flat hunting, weren't you? You actually looked at a room inside the shark house?"

"I didn't know it was the shark house until I got there," I say in my defence. Not that it helps. "I didn't even know there was a shark house at all."

"I see," he replies, his tone hinting at his unhappiness. "Where else did you and Mathilde happen to walk on Saturday?"

"The centre?" My voice wobbles, making it sound more like a question than an answer. "Near the Westgate. There's a new high rise there..."

"A high rise? And a shark house?" His voice grows louder with disbelief. "You would rather go off on your own and live in a house with a giant fibreglass predator crashing through the ceiling than move in with me?" His jaw ticks as he struggles to contain his sadness. "I don't understand, Nat. I thought things were going well between us."

I rush to reassure him. "They are going well, Edward. Really, magical problems and fires aside, I've never been happier."

His shoulders drop but he musters what he really wants to say. "Then forget about rushing to find a new place to live. Move upstairs with me."

And there it is, another half-hearted invitation leaving open the option that it might only be temporary. My guilt over covering up my weekend activities evaporates. He may not like it, but me moving in and back out again soon afterwards won't do anything good for our relationship. I don't want to play house. But how to make him understand?

"It's not just me, Edward. I've got H to think about as well. Last week, you two were at each other's throats. Your flat upstairs isn't big enough for the three of us."

Edward huffs a frustrated grunt, his sadness turning to frustration. "It's not my fault. H looks for opportunities to needle me. He plays the innocent when you come into the room, but it's all him, I swear!"

"Gah! It's not all him, Edward. You are as much at fault. Every time you treat him like a pet, he retaliates. He doesn't want you to see him as an animal to be shoved out into the garden with a bowl of kibbles. H is an Eternal, with four hundred years of experience viewing our world. If you would treat him more like an equal, all of this nonsense would stop."

Edward swings the car into a narrow drive and comes to an abrupt stop. His cheeks are pink with anger. Whatever work I did to calm him before we left was a waste of time. Our little conversation in the car has ruined the mood. And now we've got to go inside his colleague's home and figure out whether she is a criminal in hiding.

I unbuckle my seatbelt and lean over, resting my head on his shoulder. "I don't want to argue with you, Edward. Really, I don't. I know this evening is stressful enough as it is. Let's put this conversation on hold and try to make the best of tonight. I'll take the lead on questions. You can relax."

He lets out a ragged sigh before sliding his hand into mine and tilting his head to tuck me against him. We sit nestled together in silence for a moment. Finally, but yet still too soon, he lifts his head and squeezes my hand. "Come on, we'd better get inside, or she'll wonder why we're sitting out here."

The woman who opens the door has an artful white streak running through her deep black hair and she is wearing a caftan. Those two things, plus the broad smile on her face, are all I need to know to confirm I'm going to like her. She is clearly a woman comfortable and confident in herself, and not one to bend to conform to the expectations of an Oxford professor, particularly a female one.

"You must be Nat," she drawls in a broad tone, with a hint of up-country in her accent. "I'm Mary Chloe. Please come in." She envelopes my hand in both of hers, patting it gently. There is no

way to describe her other than to say she exudes warmth. I can
see why Edward would be fond of her.

Her home is the same. Brightly coloured rugs cover the
wooden floors and the walls are crammed with framed
photographs and original prints. While I wait for Edward to
finish unlacing his shoes, I step further in to take a closer look.
"Are these yours? I mean," I correct myself, "are you the artist?"

"That depends on whether you like them," Mary Chloe replies
with a grin.

I don't have to fake my enthusiasm. "They're wonderful," I
gush. "The vibrant colours and your brushwork. These should be
on display somewhere."

She waves off my compliments and leads us to a sitting room,
offering us a glass of wine. "I'm delighted you got in touch,
Edward. I'd heard through the grapevine that you were seeing
someone, but I couldn't believe it unless I saw it with my own
eyes."

"Erm, yes," Edward squirms on the sofa, wiping a hand across
the back of his neck. He looks so much like a little boy caught out
that I can't help but feel a moment of tenderness. "I suppose I
was waiting all these years for Nat to come along."

Mary Chloe peers at him over the rim of her wineglass,
weighing his words. "Well said, Edward. Now sip your wine and
tell us how you met."

As we take turns interrupting one another, correcting details,
or adding in the other's point of view, I realise this is the first
time we've had to tell someone our origin story. Everyone else I
know has been there since the start. They know exactly when my
feelings towards Edward turned from annoyance to frustration to
a hint of something more. They were witness to my struggle to
see how I could mesh saving the magic of Oxford with a love life.

Now, reliving the memories of our early days, I'm reminded of
how far Edward and I have come. We had time to learn about one

another, seeing how we behave at work and with friends. We may not have been dating for long by most standards, but we didn't start off with a blind meeting in a pub. We're adults; who's to say that we can't fall for one another this quickly? If only I could know for sure what Edward means when he says he wants me to move in.

Edward and Mary Chloe laugh, pulling my mind back to the present. "Do you really have a devil voice?" she asks. Immediately, I know Edward must have been telling her about our first trip out to the Cotswolds to question a potential suspect. We had a flat tyre on our way back, and Edward's weak attempts to help resulted in my work papers flying out of the car and across a nearby field.

"Oh yes," I say, my eyes narrow. "I can have a firm hand when the situation calls for it. I don't use it often, but it has never failed me. You should have seen Edward leap into action as soon as the words left my mouth."

Mary Chloe's laughter booms again as she tries to mesh posh professorial Edward with the vision of a man frantically gathering papers from a muddy field. "Our Edward needed someone to come along and set his world on fire. He's so strong-minded and determined, he had to find someone who isn't afraid to give it right back to him."

"My parents would say the same thing about me," I admit as I give his arm a quick squeeze. "Must be a match made in heaven, then."

"Or by magic," Mary Chloe murmurs. "Oh, we'd better move this into the dining room or dinner is likely to overcook in the warming oven. Have a seat; I'll bring in the food."

Mary Chloe's comment unbalances me, shaking my conviction that she couldn't be our suspect. "Magic?" I mouth to Edward from across the table when she leaves the room. He shrugs, but I can see he is as worried as I am. Why did she have to use that word specifically?

We work quickly to wipe the concern from our faces when Mary Chloe comes into the room bearing a tray of food. She refuses our offers to help, putting Edward in charge of opening a fresh bottle of wine and filling our glasses. He pours full glasses for me and Mary Chloe, raising and lowering his eyebrows to subtly encourage me to drink with her. Hopefully, the alcohol will loosen her lips.

"This looks amazing, Mary Chloe. I can't believe you made all of this." I pass my plate over to Edward and ask him to serve a slice of the lasagne. I balance it out with sautéed green beans and heirloom tomatoes in a balsamic vinaigrette. My mouth waters at the sight of it, but I force myself to wait until everyone has helped themselves.

With the first bite of lasagne, flavours explode in my mouth. I half convince myself that a woman who cooks this well cannot be a criminal. How could the same person build a meal so steeped in love, turn around, and burn something down? I'm ready to write-off this whole evening as a wild goose chase if it means I can have seconds. But Edward catches my eye, wiggling his eyebrows in a way that can only mean *get on with it*.

I swallow my bite and look longingly at my plate, but needs must. "Mary Chloe, I've just realised we've spent the whole evening thus far talking about us. I'd love to know more about you."

"About me?" she asks, her fork in mid-air. "I'm practically an open book. No secrets here."

Undeterred, I make a second attempt. "Your accent isn't local. Where are you from originally, and what brought you to Oxford?"

"I'm originally from a small village near York. My parents love to tell about me as a child, how quiet I was, the perfect observer. Somehow, that childhood fascination in human interaction translated into a degree in psychology at Newcastle. I came to Oxford as a post-doctoral researcher and have been here ever since."

I take my time chewing, thinking up my next angle. "I'm surprised you ended up at Oxford, rather than somewhere closer to home, like Manchester or Liverpool. Or even York itself; its university is well-regarded."

Mary Chloe settles into her chair, sipping her wine. "Oxford is, well, Oxford. When they ring, you answer. How could any academic say no to an opportunity to come here? If I'm honest..." She takes another sip. "Oxford always fascinated me. This may sound silly, but it was almost as though there was something calling me here."

"Haha," I chuckle nervously. "Nothing strange about that. Its reputation is second to none, worldwide. I suppose that's how we all wound up here."

"Ah, yes!" Mary Chloe's face lights up. "I nearly forgot that you also work at the uni. Head of Ceremonies, if I've heard correctly."

"Yes, I joined the team six months ago. I've organised events at two of the colleges, but not your college yet. Teddy Hall, right?" I pause for her to answer. "Maybe you knew my predecessor, Lillian?"

"Yes, of course. I knew her well. She was fantastic at her job; she must have left huge shoes behind for you to fill."

Edward pipes up before I can think of how to respond. "I know I'm hardly impartial, but Nat is quickly gaining a reputation for organising events that defy the imagination."

I feel a blush stealing up my neck. I grab my wine glass and hide behind it, praying my colour will return to normal before the other two notice. Who knew Edward would be so quick to sing my praises?

"That's high praise indeed, Edward," Mary Chloe remarks, seeming as stunned as I am. "I wasn't sure you even noticed the events, other than your obligation to attend them from time to time. Nat's must be something if they managed to catch your attention."

She turns towards me. "I'll have to petition Teddy Hall's governing body to put in a request for your assistance. I'm sure we must have something on the college calendar soon which would warrant your involvement."

"I'd like that," I say without an ounce of falsehood. "Each college has its own story to tell. I love that my job gives me the chance to hear all of them, and to find ways to share them with our visitors, fellows and students."

Mary Chloe's eyes narrow as she reappraises me. She must see something she likes, as she gives me an almost regal nod of approval.

On and on the conversation goes, like a game of cat and mouse, even when we move from the dining room back to the lounge. I throw out new topics, testing her interest in the museum, in antiques, in Harry Potter. I am nearly to the point of asking whether she believes in ghosts when Edward taps me on the wrist.

"It's getting late, Mary Chloe, and I don't want to overstay our welcome after you've been such a lovely host." Edward rises from the loveseat where we're tucked close together, pulling me up beside him. I may not be sure whether Mary Chloe knows about Oxford's magic, but apparently Edward has reached a conclusion of his own.

We say our goodnights, thanking her again for the dinner and promising to return the favour sometime soon. Mary Chloe surprises me with a hug, whispering in my ear before she lets me go and shoos us out the door and into the night.

❖

"What did Mary Chloe say to you?" Edward asks when we're seated in the car. I can tell the suspense is killing him.

"Are you sure you want to know?" I reply, mostly to make him squirm. He gives me an annoyed glance, silently demanding I tell all. "She told me to take good care of you, Edward. That's all. She genuinely cares about you, almost as though you were her kid brother."

"Really?" Edward asks, flummoxed.

"I think all three of us had an ulterior motive for getting together tonight. You know why we were there. For her part, Mary Chloe was clearly keen to take my measure, see how I size up against her idea of the type of person you should be dating."

"Huh," he replies eloquently. Poor men, sometimes they haven't got a clue what we women are up to.

"From her last words, I think it's safe to say I passed her test. However, I am no clearer on whether she could be our suspect. She never said anything which would outright implicate her, but then, she wouldn't do that. She's not stupid." I slump in my seat, frustrated. "Don't get me wrong, I had a lovely evening. That's why I wish I could say without a shadow of a doubt that she didn't do it. Any of it. No burglaries. No fires. No cavorting with evil Eternals."

Edward takes one hand off the wheel, leaning over to pat me on the thigh. "She didn't do it, Nat. She's innocent."

"But how can you telllll?" I whine, throwing my hands in the air.

"Did you recognise any of the artwork?"

"No." I slump further into my seat.

"Did you see any antiques, or *objet d'arte* or get even the slightest hint of an Eternal being around?"

"No, no, and no again. And I definitely would have noticed that third one. I caught my grandfather spying on me, remember? But so what? She could have hidden the evidence."

Edward swipes a hand across his brow, nearly growling in annoyance. "There's no motive, Nat! Mary Chloe is still here in Oxford. She comes into her office every day. Even if she knew about the existence of the magic — and I am not saying that she does," Edward clarifies, "why would she need to steal it, or for that matter, set a building on fire?"

I push up in my seat, ready to defend my uncertainty. "For her house? It's well beyond the boundaries."

"Her house is an oasis, Nat. It is where Mary Chloe goes to get away from everything else, including work. She's unmarried, no children. She works late and I bet she rarely ever carries work home with her."

Edward lets his words hang in the air, giving me time to reprocess everything I saw and heard. It doesn't take me long to reach the same conclusion. All those potential clues could just as easily be innocent word choices. If I hadn't placed our whole evening under a virtual microscope, would her use of the word 'magic' even have caught my attention? Probably not.

A wave of exhaustion crashes over me. It is probably all the wine I drank, but I can't help feeling like this never-ending search for our suspect is the primary cause of my weariness. Despite having access to all of Oxford's resources, magical and not, somehow this person is staying one step ahead of us.

My voice is heavy as I ask, "Do you think we'll ever catch the person behind the problems with the magic?"

"I do," Edward replies, almost offhandedly. He takes a moment to realise I meant my question. "Don't lose heart, Nat. They are getting more brazen, moving from simple theft to uncovering secret chambers and setting fires. Either we'll figure it out or they will eventually make a mistake. We will catch them."

I lean my head back against the headrest and close my eyes. I let myself drift off, dozing until a bump jostles me awake. We crest a hill and I can see the lights of Oxford bright upon the horizon.

"Are you awake?" Edward asks, his voice barely louder than a whisper.

"Yes."

He takes a deep breath. "I'm sorry for getting upset earlier... when you were telling me about your flat hunt."

"It's okay," I reply, not really wanting to revisit the topic.

"It's not okay, Nat. I was a jerk. I am sorry." Edward gives me a quick glance, letting me see the serious expression on his face. "You need to do whatever you feel is best. If that's finding a flat of your own, I understand. I don't want you to have to hide things from me. That won't do either of us any favours."

I stare forward, unsure what to say in response to his words. I don't know what I want, so how can I possibly know if I'm doing the right thing? If he showed up with flowers and a house key, asking me to take the next step in our relationship, I know I wouldn't be searching the rental adverts.

We sit in silence as we travel through the series of roundabouts which lead back into town. I'm still at a loss for words when Edward speaks up again.

"I don't have any doubts about my feelings for you, but I know it is early in our relationship. We don't have to rush into anything." He gives me a quick smile, wrapping his hand around mine. "There's no hurry. Neither of us is going anywhere. We've got all the time we need."

I mumble a response, barely able to get the words past the lump in my throat. Edward smiles again, taking my quietness as a sign of my exhaustion, rather than me being upset. Back home, he gives me a kiss at my flat door and wishes me a good night of rest before heading upstairs to his own place.

Inside, I zombie walk my way to my bedroom and flop down onto my bed. I can't help wondering whether our last conversation has left me feeling better or worse. Having Edward's understanding and support was all I ever wanted. But what did he mean by not rushing into anything? I fall asleep worrying he's having second thoughts about having offered for me to move in with him.

Chapter Twelve

An awkward silence weighs down the atmosphere in the car as Kate and I make our way towards the prison where Francie has been remanded. Both of us have tried to start a conversation, Kate telling me about her recent date night with Bartie, and me updating her on our dinner with Mary Chloe the night before. But no matter how hard we try, we end up lapsing back into silence within a few minutes.

The clipped voice of the sat nav narrator breaks the quiet. "In five hundred metres, make a left turn and you will arrive at your destination." The road signs concur, alerting drivers to the prison at the next exit.

Out of the front window, I watch as we wind down a narrow drive, passing signs reminding us to lock our vehicle doors and not to leave any valuables inside it. Unnerved, I snap the clasp on my bracelet open and closed again and again.

Kate carefully navigates into a free space in the car park and turns the ignition off. "Well, we're here. Can you pass me that bag from behind you?"

I unfasten my seatbelt and reach behind my seat, waving my

hand until I feel the rough cloth of the shopping tote. "What's in here?"

"Some more clothes for Francie. She asked me to pick up some items from her flat and bring them to her," Kate replies as she takes the bag from my hands.

I snap my head up in surprise. "She doesn't have to wear a jumpsuit?"

"No, she has more freedom while she is on remand and waiting for the trial. Thank goodness. Being stuck here is bad enough. I can't believe the courts refused her bail."

I remember when Kate got the call from Francie's lawyer, letting her know the bad news. The courts determined her a flight risk because she's a foreign national with considerable resources. When combined with the serious nature of the accusation, they had enough to hold her. Kate was livid, but there was nothing any of us could do to change the outcome. She immediately submitted a request for a visit. Today was the first available opening.

The prison is privately managed; the website promising to provide a comfortable environment for family and friends to maintain contact with loved ones housed inside. Yet, I'm not surprised when the reality turns out to be industrially bland interiors, with white walls lined with motivational posters. The visitor area turns out to be a canteen, dotted with tables where inmates can meet with their guests.

I shake my head no when Kate offers to get us a cup of coffee from the nearby machine. My stomach is already roiling with nerves. The addition of bitter caffeine would not do me any favours. Instead, I let my gaze wander, being careful not to meet anyone else's eyes. The prison is home to women and youth. Aside from me and Kate, the visitors fall into three categories: grandparents with grandkids here to visit mum, grim-faced adults likely here to check on their teen, or partners to see wives.

A burly guard steps into the room and requests we stay in our seats while the inmates seat themselves. A stream of people follow behind him, some in the shapeless prison jumpsuits and others in casual clothes. I look through the faces, searching for Francie, but can't see her anywhere in the group.

Kate sucks in air, letting it out in a soft moan as a woman separates from the rest of the group and moves our way. I nearly don't recognise her. Francie is a far, far cry from the well-dressed young woman who met Mathilde and me on our first day at the Ashmolean.

Kate pulls her into a hug, jumping apart when a guard chastises them for touching. Contrite, we sit at the table, Kate and I on one side, and Francie on the other.

Francie's dark hair is pulled into a low ponytail, the top shiny with grease. Her face is the colour of a sheet of paper. The only exceptions are the deep, dark bags under her eyes. They almost look like bruises. Her lips are stretched flat and bloodless. She is a shadow of her former self already, despite only having been arrested a week ago.

"Oh, hun," Kate murmurs, barely able to get the words out before Francie breaks down into sobs. Pulling a packet of tissues from my handbag, I pass one each to Francie and Kate and keep one for myself. Despite our promises to one another to keep a sunny outlook, I doubt Kate and I will make it through the meeting without at least a tear or two.

I make myself busy getting us glasses of water while Kate asks Francie how she is coping. She probes carefully, making sure Francie isn't being bullied or mistreated.

"Those of us on remand are kept separate from the general population," Francie explains after she blows her nose in the tissue. "There is a small library, and the television is always on. If I could find the energy or attention span needed to enjoy either of those, it wouldn't be quite so bad."

Francie launches into questions about work and various projects, clearly wanting to change the subject. Kate and I follow along, providing updates and anecdotes. I tell them both about my lunch with Agatha and Nancy, coaxing a small smile out of Francie. Half an hour speeds by with inane chatter.

"Fifteen minutes left," the guard announces loudly enough to be heard over the conversations, prodding me to move our chat along to a more useful topic.

"Francie, has your lawyer given you any updates on the investigation?" I ask. "DCI Robinson and the local department have gone very quiet."

Francie frowns, causing deep lines around her mouth. "There is no investigation, at least as far as my lawyer can tell. Once they arrested me, they stopped looking for other evidence. I guess, between the security footage and the stolen items hidden in my flat, they feel they have enough to convict me."

"Can we talk about that?" I ask gently. "How do you think the items ended up in hidden in your cupboard and tucked behind furniture?"

When she takes too long to answer, I prod, "Do you think it could have been Andrei who hid them there?"

Her reaction is immediate. She shakes her head and says no several times. "He'd been staying over a lot in the last two weeks, but I cannot believe he is the one behind this. Someone must be setting me up. Maybe they're setting both of us up."

"Both of you?" Kate reaches across the table and places her hands on top of Francie's. Her tone is soft as she says, "You don't think Andrei is behind this? He had access to the museum's storage, was inside your flat, and was there the night of the arson."

"My lawyer keeps insisting on the same thing, but I just can't bring myself to believe it, Kate," she replies, pulling her hands back to wrap them around herself. "I dated Andrei for a month, spending evenings and nights with him. Until the day of the fire, I thought things were going perfectly. We never fought. We seemed to like the same television shows and movies. He couldn't have been faking his interest in me for so long. If he had an ulterior motive, I would have known... right?"

Her question hangs over us, none of us sure how to respond.

I let Francie sip her water and then follow up. "The other morning, in Kate's office, you mentioned Andrei had been pulling away in the few days leading up to the fire. What did you mean by that? Could it be a clue?"

Francie shifts in her plastic chair, clearly uncomfortable with the conversation. I'd back off, but we can't afford to ignore a possibility just because Francie doesn't like it. No one wants to believe their significant other faked their interest, but we need to consider the option, anyway.

She closes her eyes as she casts her memory back. "He was distracted, busy. His phone would ring, and he would leave the room before answering."

Kate hesitates before asking, "Did you think he was seeing someone else?"

"What?" Francie opens her eyes wide. "No. Well, maybe a little at first. But I crept close and eavesdropped on one of his calls. He was talking about meetings and timelines. I thought maybe he was applying for another job. I know he really wanted that promotion at the museum."

I parse her words, looking for a clue. There is still something we're missing. "What about now, Francie? You've had a week of sitting here. I'm sure you must have relived that day of the fire dozens of times by now. We saw the video; we know how upset you were when you left the archives. Why do you think he was so cruel to you?"

Her face flushes and tears well in her eyes. "I can't bring

myself to believe Andrei set me up, or that he was behind the fire. If he was, why would he have ended up dead?"

I shrug, no closer to understanding than she is.

"I'm locked in jail for a crime I did not commit. For my sanity, I need to believe Andrei is innocent as well. Maybe it's naïve of me, but the only conclusion I can reach is that Andrei was trying to get me out of the archives building to keep me safe."

I pass Francie another tissue as she cries softly, her face buried in her hands. The guard announces another time warning, suggesting we wrap up our conversations.

"Francie," I keep my tone gentle, "did you ever go to Andrei's house? Maybe you saw something there that meant little at the time?" I'm grasping at straws, but I have to make the effort. We need more clues.

She shakes her head. "No. He lived in a basement flat. It wasn't very nice, so he preferred to stay at mine. Sorry."

As we stand to leave, Kate and I reassure her we're doing everything we can to get to the bottom of the mystery. When the guard clears his throat, Kate passes her the bag of clothing and we take our leave.

On our return journey, I switch the radio on and turn the volume just loud enough to save Kate and me from feeling like we have to chat. Staring out the window, I replay Francie's words in my head, trying to place them within the bigger picture of things we know. Eventually, I dial the music volume down and share my thoughts.

"Here's what I think. It has to be one of two things. Option one is that Andrei was in on the plan from the start, and he let the arsonist into the archives. In this case, it isn't a stretch to think he may have planted the stolen items in Francie's flat as a frame job. Option two is Andrei was as much a victim as Francie is. Maybe our arsonist made a mistake and thought Francie's flat was Andrei's. The arsonist could have hidden the stolen items there, with a plan to make Andrei take the fall. Francie did say he was staying with her a lot." I make a fist and shake it in the air. "Ugh, both seem equally possible. Where have you landed, Kate?"

Kate drums her fingers on the wheel. "More or less in the same place as you. I still firmly believe Francie is innocent, but I've got a giant question mark over Andrei. Unfortunately, when it comes to him, I don't think we can put much stock in Francie's opinion. She's too biased, blinded by her emotions rather than logic. As she said herself, she can't bear to think he might have been using her from the start."

Our conversation lapses again as we each return to our thoughts. Only when we pull off the ring road and merge into the traffic heading towards the city centre does Kate speak again. "Where do you want me to drop you, Nat? Your flat? The Ash?"

"Andrei's flat," I mumble, half serious.

Kate gives a wry laugh in response. "Yes, I wish. His death was so recent that I bet it is sitting there untouched. But how would we get in and make sure no one catches us?"

I think back, remembering how someone once helped me open a locked door. One of Barnard College's Eternals had unlocked a door to let Edward into the master's lodge. If the trick worked once, there's no reason it won't work again.

"Take me to St Margaret. H and my grandfather were planning to spend the day with Bartie. I'm sure they'd help. One can unlock the door, and another can act as a look-out."

"Are you serious?" Kate asks, one eyebrow raised.

"Absolutely! I mean, yes, it is slightly ridiculous to think about the two of us as cat burglars, but I can't see any other way to learn more about Andrei. Maybe there was another reason he kept Francie out of his flat. Maybe the evidence is just sitting there, waiting for someone to stumble across it. Come on, Kate. Are you in?"

She shakes her head, high spots of colour popping out on her cheeks. "I can hardly send you off on your own. I guess so." She turns into my drive but leaves the car idling. "Should we get Edward to come along?"

I take a second to consider her question but quickly arrive at a hard no. "If things go horribly wrong and someone finds us inside Andrei's flat, I think we could talk our way out of trouble. We could say that Andrei had carried some important files home, and we found the door open, etcetera. It would sound weird, but I think most people would give the two of us the benefit of the doubt. If Edward is with us... a man who knows the law well..."

"Yes, quite. I see your point."

I open my door and exit the car, putting an end to further discussion. I slow my steps as I listen for Kate following behind. Only when her footsteps crunch on the gravel do I hurry over to the side gate to St Margaret's gardens.

Bartie, H and my grandfather are easy to find. All three of them were practicing meditation in the gazebo of the Fellows Garden. As I get close enough to see inside, I realise that two of the three are actually napping, which makes much more sense. I rap on the glass, startling my grandfather and H awake and pulling a smile from Bartie.

Kate and I quickly explain our plan, amazed when the three agree to come along with nary a word of naysaying. I tell myself that they've agreed because our plan to search Andrei's flat is good, and not because they know we're likely to take off on our own if they refuse to join us.

Back inside my flat, Kate uses my laptop to log into her files at the Ashmolean, searching up Andrei's address. "He lived in Marston, near the hospital. It will be much faster if we drive."

Kate and I resume our places in the front, with Bartie, H and my grandfather crammed into the backseat of Kate's little Mini. I have to stifle a laugh when H attempts to use a jet of fire to claim more space, forgetting for a moment that the other two are Eternals as well. Sensing the looming trouble in the back, Kate distracts us with a request to assign roles and agree a firm plan. After typing the address into my phone, we use street view to get the lay of the land.

"Missies," H announces after conferring with the men in the back, "ya 'aven't anything to worry about. Bartie, Alfie and I 'ave it all under control. We'll make sure the way is clear for you."

"Bartie can stay out front and keep an eye out," suggests my grandfather. "I'll pop inside, make sure the place is empty, and then unlock the door. The stairs to the basement unit are on the side of the building, so you shouldn't be visible from the street as you descend unless someone is keeping a close watch."

We debate where to leave the car, but eventually decide to park it in the first space we see. After all, if we're planning to claim we have a legitimate reason for being inside Andrei's flat, there's no point in parking far away.

Andrei's building is a concrete block of flats built on a side road in a residential area. I can hear passing sirens fade in and out, a steady reminder of the large hospital which sits a few streets up the hill. The building is set close to the pavement and is painted an unobtrusive ivory-colour. After all the time I've spent looking at rental adverts, I estimate that the flats inside are likely not inexpensive, despite the lack of frills in the building itself. This neighbourhood is a prime choice for the many doctors, nurses and other staff at the hospital.

Kate and I linger near the car, pretending to be in a deep conversation while we wait for H to return with news on my grandfather's recon mission. When H gives us the okay, we speedily make our way to the stairwell, descending out of sight.

I am not sure what I was expecting, but Andrei's flat is as

impersonal as the exterior of his building. The front room consists of a small kitchen and a seating area. The air smells stuffy, typical of a house which has been closed up for an extended period.

"There's hardly anything in the refrigerator or the cupboards," my grandfather calls when he sees us walk into the room. "Backs up Francie's claim that he stayed over at her place."

A small hallway leads to a shower room with a toilet and further along a bedroom. There are no photos or art on the walls. No knick-knacks or keepsakes on any shelves or tables. The bedding and the sofa are shades of blue.

"Did he move in recently?" I ask Kate.

"I don't think so. I didn't see any record of a previous address on his employment record and he'd been working at the Ash for a while."

"I'm not seeing much of anything here," I grumble when even the bins are empty. "Shall we divide the two rooms and have a quick rummage in his drawers?"

Kate scrunches her nose up in distaste but nods her agreement, anyway. "In for a penny, in for a pound."

Ten minutes later, we're still empty-handed. All we've found is a listing of the television channels, a half-empty pack of cigarettes and three lighters. Hardly the smoking gun of evidence we hoped to uncover.

We regroup at the flat door, all of us looking morose. I put my hand on the doorknob, but before I can turn it, H dashes off towards the back of the flat.

"H?" I shout, "Where are you going? We looked back there. Let's go."

"Wait a minute," he shouts back, his words garbled. The sounds of a door opening and metal hangers sliding across the rail give us some clue what H is doing, but no explanation. "Aha!" he shouts again. "I knew somethin' was weird about this place."

Perplexed, Kate, my grandfather and I track along the hall until we find H in the bedroom, hovering above an open suitcase.

"I remembered that the police found stolen goods in Francie's suitcase. I spotted this 'ere piece of luggage in the cupboard, but thought little of it. But when we didn't find anything else, I came back to check."

"What's inside, H?" I ask, trying to see around the bed. "More stolen goods from the Ashmolean?"

"No, missie. There's clothes. Lots of 'em."

"Clothes? You called us back here to see clothes in a suitcase?" I give H a hard look.

"Yes," he says, punctuating his response with a puff of smoke. "What 'ave you got in your suitcases at 'ome, Nat?"

"Err, nothing."

"That's right. Who keeps a suitcase packed full and stuffed in the back of their cupboard? Not a normal person, I tell you." H tilts his head up, daring me to contradict him.

"That's a really good point, H." I shift my attention to Kate. "Want to have a quick look? You're the only one here who can tell us whether the clothes are ones Andrei normally wears."

Kneeling beside the open case, Kate shifts the top layer of clothing, doing her best to peer underneath without dishevelling everything inside. "I recognise the shirts. The trousers all look the same to me, but what's here seems to be in good condition."

My grandfather offers, "Could it be a suitcase he was planning to take to Francie's house? Maybe a new set of clothing?"

Kate closes the case and puts it back where H found it. "If Francie lived far away, I might buy it. But a fully packed suitcase? And no personal items anywhere in the flat? If he was planning to take it to her place, why was it stuffed in the back of his cupboard? This is strange enough to set off alarm bells for me."

I nod to show my agreement with Kate. "This seems more a

go bag, like you see on television or in the movies. The kind people prepare when they're planning to run off in a hurry."

Kate strides across the bedroom and motions us back to the front door. "Great, one more piece of utterly confusing information about Andrei. Let's get out of here before we get caught. Hopefully Edward can make some sense of all of this, because I certainly cannot."

Chapter Thirteen

I tap my bank card to pay for our coffees right as Mathilde turns up in the coffee shop. "Just in time," I say, passing her a latte.

"Thanks, Nat. I definitely need the extra jolt this morning. I stayed up late binge-watching old Inspector Lewis episodes, and I forgot to turn my alarm off this morning." Mathilde adds a heaping spoonful of sugar, blowing on the top of her drink before taking a gulp. "I woke up early and couldn't get back to sleep."

"Classic bank holiday error," I say with a laugh. "At least it's Easter, so we've got four days off in a row. You'll have plenty of time to catch up on your sleep."

We fall into step on the pavement, weaving our way around the other people who are out enjoying the lovely spring day. As we walk, I update Mathilde on the trip to the prison and subsequent search of Andrei's flat.

"Andrei had a fully packed suitcase hidden in his cupboard?" Mathilde narrows her eyes, weighing up what that might mean. "It's odd, that's for sure. What did Edward think about it?"

"He is as perplexed as the rest of us," I reply, looking worried. "It would be so much easier if we'd found a note stuffed in a drawer or a convenient copy of his phone or bank records sitting around. Our only hope now is the security footage from inside the archives building. The fire damaged it, but Edward hopes one of the local tech experts can recover it."

"I'm surprised the footage wasn't synced up with the cloud somewhere," Mathilde replies.

"The automated back-up system runs at midnight. We've got perfect copies of all the previous days, but not after midnight of the day before the fire. Kate is having all the local hard drives relocated to fire resistant cabinets, but that doesn't help us with this case." Frustrated, I kick a pebble into a nearby garden.

"Aw, chin up, Nat." Mathilde gives me a friendly bump with her elbow. "We're doing everything we can to help free Francie and to identify the real culprit. There's nothing we can do over the long weekend; everything is closed. I suggest we try to relax a little, catch our breath after a crazy busy week."

"Good point, Mathilde. Shall we turn our focus to the two flats we're seeing today? I really hope one of them works out because there is nothing else out there right now."

"There's always Edward's flat..." Mathilde reminds me, raising and lowering her eyebrows suggestively.

"Don't you start," I chastise her. "These two look much better on paper than the last set we saw. The first is a long-time local resident who rents out the extra room in her converted attic." I double-check my phone before adding, "It's on the next street."

We shortly turn onto a quiet, tree-lined street in North Oxford, not too far from my flat at St Margaret. The houses are a mix of single-family homes and semi-detached houses, all of them standing several stories tall with nice-sized gardens out front.

"There is an entrance to Port Meadow not too far from here," I explain to Mathilde. "I could walk to work through the meadow and avoid the noise of passing cars and buses."

"H would love that," she concurs, looking positive about the possibility.

We find the correct house number painted onto the kerb at the end of the drive and pause a moment to take in the view. No sharks crashing into the roof, so at least that worry is out of the way. The garden is well-tended, with green grass and blossoming daffodils. The house stands alone, one of the smaller ones on the street, but that isn't necessarily a bad thing. I stare up at the dormer window on the top floor, which must be the bedroom currently available to let, and try to imagine the view.

"Looks promising," Mathilde offers up, sounding hopeful. "Shall we ring the bell?"

I nod and together we follow the short path to the front door. The old metal doorbell sends ringing tones pealing through the house, loud enough for us to hear them. They are quickly followed by the sound of footsteps and the click of the lock tumbling over. The door swings open, revealing a middle-aged woman standing inside, half hidden in the shadow.

"Hallooo," she says, breathily. "Are you Natalie Payne?"

"Yes, that's me." I step forward, holding out a hand. When she fails to take it, I let it drop back to my side.

"Anddd you arrrree?" she asks, slightly huffed, as she shifts her view to Mathilde.

"This is my friend, Mathilde. She's keeping me company today." When the woman frowns, I add, "I hope that's okay?"

"Yesss," she answers, pursing her lips, "however I'll need her to wait in the front reception room while we speak. Come in."

I step inside, blinking as my eyes adjust to the dim inner lighting. The woman walks further in, holding out an arm to indicate the front room where Mathilde should wait. Now that I'm inside, I can see her better. She's wearing a tie-dyed shirt and a long flowery peasant skirt, Birkenstocks poking out from underneath. Her wavy dark hair flows over her shoulders, nearly down to her elbows, parted in the middle of her forehead in the classic hippie style. Dozens of bracelets clink on her wrists as she motions us forward.

The hallway and front stairwell look normal enough, but something about this woman's mannerisms is making me uncomfortable. Nonetheless, I continue deeper into the house, passing by framed record covers and macramé wall hangings. I try to imagine myself living here, but the first thing that comes to mind is a vision of H using the knotted rope art as a jungle gym, swinging his way around the house.

The front reception room is comfortable enough, with a love seat, wicker chair and giant beanbag dotted around the space. The shelves are packed with books, in some places two levels deep. The paperback spines are creased from frequent readings. There is no gym equipment, no sweaty workout clothing, and there is already more space than was in the boxcar flat.

Mathilde raises an eyebrow as she moves into the room and takes a seat on the small sofa. She mouths, "Will you be okay?" giving me a meaningful look before she settles in. I paste on a happy face and give her a confident nod, even though it is certainly weird that the woman will only speak to me on my own.

"Follow me, Natalie," she says in a singsong voice, leading me to the kitchen at the back of the house, dark with the curtains closed shut. She tells me to sit at the small breakfast table and lights a dozen candles placed along the countertop. Finally, she pulls out the chair across from me, sitting down. She lights a stick of incense and places it in the holder on the table.

A narrow band of smoke trails up from the centre of the table, scenting the room with an intense woody smell, with hints of spice coming through. I blink rapidly, trying to stop my eyes from watering, and scratch an itch on my arm. The woman stares intently, assessing me from head to toe, leaning sideways when the table blocks her view.

"I am Jane, keeper of this abode. Welcome, Natalie." She folds her hands into the prayer sign and nods in greeting. "Tell me about yourself."

"Um, yes, sure," I stutter while scratching my other arm and then my leg. "As you know, I'm Natalie Payne. I work at the uni, only recently moving up to Oxford from London."

"Are you a researcher?" Jane asks, wafting a hand over the incense smoke to distribute it around the room.

"Uh, no. I'm a member of staff. I lead the Ceremonies team." I shift to scratch my cheek and use the opportunity to catch a tear threatening to well up in my burning eyes.

"Ceremonies? Oh lovely," she answers, her tone heavy with some unknown meaning. She leans back in her chair, unaffected by the candle smoke and incense which seems to trigger every allergy I have. Tilting her head, she assesses me again.

I wish she'd hurry, or at least open the back door and allow some fresh air into the place. I don't dare ask any questions of my own. It is all I can do to keep up my attempts to subtly scratch all the places that itch. My arms, legs, neck, and face are not on board with her over the top efforts to create an atmosphere in this otherwise normal-looking kitchen.

Eventually, my need for air overtakes everything else. "Is there a garden out back?" I push up from my chair, intent on opening the door.

She holds out a hand, stopping me in place. "Yes, but that is my private space. It is not included in the common area. It must be kept in perfect order, otherwise I risk using the wrong ingredients in my spell work."

"Spell work?" I gulp.

Jane sidesteps my question. "All in good time, my dear. Now, before I take you up to the room, I need to know more about your background."

I talk fast, the itching sensation now beginning to burn. I have got to get out of this room. "I'm from London, born and raised. My father, however, grew up in Oxford. My grandfather worked for the uni. I guess that is what brought me here. That's it, rather bland." I force a weak smile onto my face.

She stares at me, picking up her lighter and running the flame along the stick of incense. The smoke doubles and then trebles. I cough, but she ignores me. Finally, seconds before I'm ready to bolt from the room, she abandons the lighter and incense stick and holds out her hands, waving her fingers in an invitation for me to set my own on top. Years of lessons in grace and manners overtake my screaming doubts. I set my hands on hers, trying desperately not to shriek when she slips her hands out and puts them on top of mine, trapping me in place.

"Let's talk about your blood, Natalie. Blood is important for my work." She demands, her voice raising in volume. I panic, my eyes flying open, my mouth in a perfect 'O' shape. The sound of heavy footsteps pound along the hallway, jerking me out of my frozen state.

"Nat? Nat?" Mathilde's voice intrudes. "Sorry to interrupt," she calls from the kitchen doorway, her eyes flying open at the scene in front of her. "Bartie sent a text. He needs us to come right away. Some kind of emergency. I hate to pull you from here, but we should go."

Jane's hands tighten on mine, and for a moment, I fear she won't let go. Her gaze darts between me and Mathilde, measuring her chances of keeping me there. I can't even imagine for what reason. I jerk my hands back when I feel her grip loosening, jumping to my feet and grabbing my handbag from the floor.

"Oh dear. Bartie, did you say? He wouldn't text unless it was something truly urgent." I shove Mathilde from behind, encouraging her to walk faster as we all but dash to the front door.

I hear Jane's chair scraping against the floor as Mathilde's hand hits the doorknob. Mathilde doesn't stop, twisting the knob and letting in a whoosh of fresh air in her eagerness to get outside.

I pause in the open doorway, spinning around to call out behind me, "I'm so sorry to run out, Jane. Thanks for showing me the place. I'll be in touch." Then I pull the door closed behind me and quick foot it to the pavement.

Mathilde is waiting in front of the next house, bursting to release a stream of commentary. I hush her, wanting to get as far away from that disturbing woman as I can before we say anything.

When I deem us a safe distance away, I slow my steps and give Mathilde a look. "Bartie texted, huh?"

"Oh yes," she replies, her upper lip twitching as she struggles to keep her face serious. "He wanted you to pick up some sage and mandrake from Jane's witchy garden."

I roll my eyes, not yet prepared to laugh at the situation, although Mathilde has clearly found the humour in it. Her fake text from Bartie, of all people, was the icing on the cake. "Yes, yes. Laugh it up. That was terrible and I'm fairly certain I'm allergic to that house. Even if I weren't, I'd rather live in the shark house than with a wannabe vampire witch, and given our connection to the magic, that's saying something."

I check my watch, surprised to see that half an hour has passed. Apparently, the candle lighting and incense-burning coupled with the intense, assessing gazes, took up more time than I realised. Thankfully, the itchiness dies down once we are outside, but my eyes are still watering. I'm in no condition to view another flat right now, particularly one which is my last hope of finding a somewhat normal place to live.

I dab my eyes with a tissue, setting Mathilde laughing again. "Lunch?" I propose, and I stride off without waiting for a response.

❖

We settle on having an early lunch at a nearby sandwich cafe, returning to our discussion of Andrei and Francie, trying to guess why Andrei was so insistent on making her leave on the evening of the fire. Maybe it is all the episodes of the crime drama Mathilde watched the night before, but she is insistent that Andrei had to have been up to no good. For my part, I'm happy enough to discuss anything other than my housing situation, so I keep the conversation going by arguing the alternate viewpoints.

The cafe door has a string of bells attached to it, which Mathilde sets to ringing when she pulls it open. Although the place is half-empty, she makes a beeline for a nearby table. "I'll stay here and reserve the table while you go order."

"Okay, but there aren't many people here, Mathilde. You can come look at the menu. I don't think anyone is going to steal the space away in the next two minutes."

Mathilde already has her phone out of her pocket and is typing away. She waves me on, requesting a jacket potato with cheese and beans and a sparkling water. I hop into the queue, taking my time to consider the sandwich display while I await my turn. It takes longer than I expect, thanks to Mathilde's jacket potato, and several minutes have gone past by the time I make it back to the table with the tray of food.

Mathilde quickly puts her phone away, giving me a gracious smile as she helps me divide the plates and drinks between us.

"What was that about?" I ask as I open a pack of cheese and onion crisps.

"What was what about?" she replies, blinking innocently.

"Um, you, your phone and your production about needing to protect the table. Were you texting someone? Maybe telling Kate about our latest flat visit."

Mathilde blushes, the flush on her neck and cheeks robbing

her of any chance of a defence. "I didn't text anyone. I was looking at something on the internet."

Sounds reasonable, except for the crimson colour of her cheeks. "What were you looking up?"

She avoids my question, taking a bite of her food and chewing slowly. I narrow my gaze, letting her know she isn't getting away with it. Finally, she swallows, sets her fork down and looks me in the eye.

"Nat, are you sure you really want to move out of St Margaret?"

"What?" I ask, dumbfounded. "Of course I don't want to move out! Who wants to move out of rent-free housing? But it isn't as though I have a choice here. Someone else is due to move in at the end of the month."

She takes another bite of potato and chews it slowly.

"What were you looking at, Mathilde? Where is this coming from?"

"Don't get mad, but on the walk over here, I couldn't help but wonder if maybe you were sabotaging your own flat hunt. You say that there are only four places available, and the three we've seen so far have been something out of an absurd romcom. The shark house, a shoebox, and then a room in a witch's coven? It seems too crazy to be true."

My sandwich bite turns to sawdust in my mouth. "Were you looking at the letting agent adverts? Were you checking up on me?"

Mathilde throws her hands out. "I know it seems bad, but I thought that if you were doing all of this on purpose, so you'd have an excuse to end up living with Edward... Maybe I would be a better friend if I helped you come to that conclusion sooner and saved us more horror stories."

I level my gaze at her. "Well, what did you find? See anything golden which I may have skipped? Something new that popped up this morning?"

She casts her gaze down to the table, pushing her food around her plate. "No, nothing new. You were right, there's hardly anything available. It's crazy! When I was flat hunting, there were a dozen places in my budget, and several were strong contenders in the end. Sorry for doubting you."

She looks so downcast that I feel the last of my indignation fizzle out. "It's okay. I'd probably become suspicious if I were in your shoes. I can honestly say I have never encountered anything like this. I'm beginning to think the universe is working against me."

We go back to our lunches, eating in silence. Still feeling guilty, Mathilde treats us to a cuppa and a slice of flapjack when we finish our meals.

"Are you sure, really sure, you don't want to move into Edward's flat? Because it may be your only option, Nat."

I pass Mathilde a napkin, motioning to my lips to alert her to the crumbs stuck to her mouth. As she tidies up, I pick up my napkin and begin tearing it into ever-smaller shreds. "Am I being silly, wanting roses and candlelight and a serious discussion about deepening our relationship? Should I call it a day on this fruitless search and move in upstairs?"

Mathilde stills, really considering the situation. I hold my breath, not sure what response I'm hoping to hear.

"No, Nat. I don't think you are being silly." She smiles when I exhale in a rush. "You love a good ceremony. Well more than the average person. That's clear in many ways, and your relationship with Edward is no exception."

"What do you mean?" I ask, genuinely perplexed by her words.

"The man lives upstairs from you. You were working in the same college for three months, bumping into one another in hallways, dining hall and common rooms. And yet nothing happened until he asked you, formally, to go out on a date. Anyone else would have got together months earlier!"

"Yes, that's true. I never thought about it…" my voice trails off.

"Of course you didn't! It isn't a conscious decision. It is who you are."

"Maybe I'm putting too much emphasis on this," I admit, thinking back to all those nights before we started dating, when I sat downstairs from Edward and wondered what he was doing. "I could be different this time. More relaxed, stop worrying so much."

Mathilde reaches her hand across the table, rescuing what little is left of my napkin from my hand. "I don't think your living situation should require you to change your personality. We've got one place left to see. Let's check it out, and then we can plan from there."

I look down at the pile of white napkin-paper confetti scattered atop my dessert plate. "Thanks, Mathilde. You're a good friend."

As we pass in front of the entrance to one of Oxford's posh independent schools, Mathilde asks for the third time, "Nat, are you *sure* we're going the right way?"

I roll my eyes and point at the screen of my phone. "The directions are super clear, and you've already made me remap it just in case I mistyped the address. It is definitely back in this neighbourhood."

"I've got a bad feeling about this place already," Mathilde grumbles as she begrudgingly restarts walking.

You'd think from the way Mathilde is going on that we are

standing in a run-down part of town, with drug dealers stationed on every corner. But we're in one of Oxford's wealthiest enclaves. Every house is a mini mansion with a Tesla or Range Rover parked out front. I admit, it is hard to believe that a block of flats could be situated on one of these gorgeous, tree-lined streets, but that's what my maps app says.

"Why don't you try the street view mode?" Mathilde suggests.

I come to an abrupt halt, spinning around to face her. "Look, this is the last shared flat available within my budget. If it turns out to be some sort of tenement building or, even worse, a bulldozed pile of rubble, I don't want to know about it until we get there. Now, have some faith, okay?"

Mathilde straightens up and reshapes her frown into a neutral smile. "You're right, Nat. Sorry. It's just that the last three places have been so bad... finding a flat in this neighbourhood, so close to the centre, seems unbelievable."

"Maybe I'm due for some good luck," I reply. "We make the next right and it will be at the end of the cul-de-sac."

We pass by a sign for the neighbourhood tennis courts and spot an entry to a hidden park before we finally turn onto the street in question. Somehow, it is even more idyllic than we could have imagined, with an enormous old oak tree growing in the centre of the cul-de-sac, casting a dappled shade across the pavement. Behind it is a small block of flats. Mathilde and I pause on the pavement, hardly able to believe our eyes.

From the perfectly manicured lawn to the wrought iron window boxes blooming with a riot of coloured bulbs, the building looks straight out of a storybook. Large wooden shutters frame every window, painted to match the light blue trim around the front door. It takes no effort for me to imagine myself lying on a picnic blanket in the front garden, H swinging from limb to limb in the giant oak tree.

I shove my phone into my handbag, march purposely to the

front door, and ring the bell for the correct unit. A tinny voice invites me to come upstairs, followed by the buzzing sound of the automated lock opening.

A pair of young women, appearing to be in their twenties, wait nervously at the top of the stairs. Mathilde and I quickly introduce ourselves and follow them inside the top-floor flat.

If I thought the exterior of the building was gorgeous, it is nothing compared to the lush, welcoming interior of the flat. The furnishings look like something from a magazine. There's a comfortable seating area, a wall covered with built-in bookshelves, and a cushioned window seat that looks perfect for an afternoon of reading. The eat-in kitchen features a white wooden table with four colourful wooden chairs. The same colours are echoed in the art on the wall and the flowers in the window planters.

"I'm Paula," says the blonde woman, her hair cut into a stylish bob and her clothing straight out of a Top Shop advert. She points over to the other woman, a curly brunette with a friendly smile, and adds, "and this is Lily. We're the other flatmates, but I guess you figured that out already."

They invite us to take a seat in the front room and we chat away, almost as though we are old friends who haven't seen each other for a while. Both women are in their mid-twenties, working in office jobs in Summertown. They each have boyfriends but make a point of staying in at least one night a week for a girls' night of chatting and television.

After my previous experiences, I ask lots of questions, certain there must be something wrong with this flat. It seems too good to be true. But no matter how I try, I cannot find anything to dislike. The flat is spacious, airy, and full of natural light. The view of the leafy oak branches almost makes me feel as though I'm living in a forest instead of near the centre of town.

Once we've established that we like the same television shows, all enjoy a good takeout and that the monthly rent includes a weekly housecleaner, I'm ready to grab my suitcase and move straight in. There's still one thing left to double-check.

"I have a cat. Would that cause a problem?"

"Oh no, not at all," Paula gushes with enthusiasm. "We've been saying for a while now that we want to get a little pet for the house, but we couldn't decide which one of us would be the official owner. This would solve the problem perfectly!"

"He can be a little, um, rambunctious," I add, and Mathilde nods her agreement.

"He sounds super cute and fun!" Lily chirps. "I spotted the most adorable cat toy at the shops the other day. I bet your cat would love it!"

Mathilde and I exchange glances, both of us hardly able to believe my luck. After one horrid option after another, this place is like a dream come true.

"Shall we show you the rest of the flat?" Paula proposes, rising to her feet. We fall into step behind her. "There are three bedrooms and two full bathrooms. One bath is on this floor and the other is upstairs."

"Two full bathrooms? That is a luxury in an Oxford flat," Mathilde states, looking even more impressed.

"The available room is the last in the hallway," Paula explains, pausing when her mobile rings in her hand. She gives the screen a quick look and suggests, "You two go on ahead while I answer this call."

She disappears into one of the other bedrooms, her voice muffled as she pulls the door closed behind her.

Mathilde waves me forward, impatient to complete this final check of the house. If the room is half as nice as the rest of the place, I'll sign the rental agreement before I leave. The door opens with a small creak, revealing not a bedroom, but an oasis. There is a sleigh bed with a carved wooden frame, built-in cupboards and two oversized windows framed with sheer white drapes. The top half of the walls are painted a pale green, while the bottom half is white wainscoting. There is a small bedside table and even a desk tucked in between the two windows, perfect for my late-night email checking sessions. Above the desk is a trio of shelves decorated with small plants, a framed print, and plenty of space for me to add my own items.

"You have to take this place, Nat!" Mathilde insists in a hoarse whisper. "This is a once in a lifetime find. If you don't take it, I will."

"No way," I say, giving her a firm look. "This flat is mine. You've already got a place."

We split up inside the room, one of us checking out the side table and desk drawers, the other peeking inside the cupboard to assess the storage space. We regroup on opposite sides of the large bed, each of us pushing down on the mattress to check the firmness. The sound of Paula's voice coming from the hallway stops us from stretching out across the bed.

"Um, Nat?" Paula's expression is unreadable as she steps into the bedroom. "I'm so sorry... this is awkward..." she trails off, wringing her hands.

I knew this place was too good to be true. I skirt around the edge of the bed, making my way back towards the door. "Is something wrong? Was it the call you answered? Do you need us to go?"

"That was the letting agency," Paula explains, twisting her ring around and around her finger, her unease clear. "We've had several viewings this week, as you can imagine. One of the other potential tenants came into the agency this morning and dropped off her rental contract and the deposit."

"That stinks," I murmur, my mind in overdrive. "Maybe all isn't lost. I'm happy to do the same, right now, in fact. If the other woman's background check turns up something or if she has second thoughts, I could be first in line."

When Paula continues with her nervous gestures, I realise that there isn't much reason for hope. "I don't think you've got much of a chance, Nat. I'm really sorry because you seem so lovely. The letting agent said the woman is renting another of their properties, so they don't need to do the standard background checks. They have cleared her to move in over the long weekend."

I don't dare look at Mathilde as my heart drops into the pit of my stomach. Not only was this flat my last hope, it was also utterly perfect. We quickly say our goodbyes, thanking the two women for giving us the tour. It's hardly their fault that things didn't work out.

Outside, I force myself to turn my back on the building and retrace my steps up to the main road. My shoulders droop in defeat. I barely notice when Mathilde stops walking and have to back up several steps to see what is wrong.

"Don't despair yet, Nat, I've got an idea," she says, her tone hopeful. "There is one more resource we can check to see if there is any other available housing hiding away in Oxford."

"What's that?" I ask, "Because trust me, I've looked at every website."

"The Eternals," she responds with a gleam in her eyes. "If anyone can make the impossible happen, it will be one of our magical Eternals."

Chapter Fourteen

Unsurprisingly, no new letting adverts crop up over the holiday weekend, leaving me even more despondent about my housing situation. Maybe that is why moving house is on the top of my mind on Tuesday morning, as Edward and I take an early morning walk around the nearby neighbourhood of Jericho.

"Edward, have you ever thought about moving out of your flat at St Margaret?" As the words leave my mouth, I wonder why I've never asked them before.

"Move out of my flat?" He repeats, thinking through the question. "It's been a long time since I contemplated the idea, but I certainly did not move in thinking I'd live there forever."

"How come you've lived there for so long?" I look over at him, curious to hear his answer.

"St Margaret has several flats available for Fellows like me to use. They typically go to professors who move over before the rest of their family joins them, or to younger, single people like I was when I started at Oxford," he explains. "The original lease agreement was for six months. When renewal time rolled around, I was busy preparing for my first lecture class. I renewed the lease, confident I'd use the next six months to find more appropriate long-term housing."

"But something always came up?" I add, knowing Edward well.

"Yes, exactly," he replies with a grin. "I have a bad habit of getting caught up in my work. Until I met you, I didn't have any excuse to step away. Having a flat so near my office seemed like a good thing rather than a feeble excuse to avoid all opportunities to socialise with others."

Wrapping my arms around his waist, I pull him to a stop. "And now? You've got nothing but distractions in your life. Should I worry you will one day resent me for the chaos I've caused in your otherwise organised life?"

Edward's reply is to press a soft kiss on my lips, pulling me close against him. The sound of a passing car reminds us we're standing in the middle of the pavement — perhaps not the best location for a private moment together.

"Back to business," I say, twisting out of the embrace. "How are you feeling about our assignment this morning?"

"Questioning Jonathan Townsend, our last suspect?" Edward confirms. "The good news is that I'm feeling less stressed than I was when we went to dinner at Mary Chloe's house."

"That's positive," I reply with a smile. "What's the bad news?"

"I have no idea how we are going to strike up a conversation with a perfect stranger in a busy coffee shop. How will we even know it is him? And why couldn't Mathilde do this?"

"Jonathan Townsend is hardly a stranger, even if we haven't yet met him. Shall we revisit the brief we got from my grandfather and Mathilde yesterday?" I ask, half-jokingly.

Edward scrunches his brow, looking concerned. "Yes, please. I get so awkward when I'm put into these situations where I have to feign friendliness in order to size someone up. I'm accustomed to marching in and pulling whomever I need into a meeting room for a formal conversation."

"I know you are," I agree, patting him on the arm. He looks so bashful and worried, a far cry from his normal confident bearing as an Oxford professor. I have to stop myself from reaching up to ruffle his hair.

I wait until we pass an older woman walking on the pavement before I launch into my briefing. "We've ruled out Nigel Symonds and Mary Chloe, therefore it has to be Jonathan Townsend. Bodleian researcher by day, master criminal by night. You shouldn't have any trouble asking him some direct questions."

"That's a good point," Edward responds, picking up his pace. "I need to worry less about potentially offending a university colleague and focus more on finally putting a stop to all the mayhem he has been causing. Thefts, fires and murder."

I cast a quick look in Edward's direction, making sure he isn't putting me on with false positivity. The determined set to his jaw is reassuring.

I add, "We couldn't send Mathilde to question him because she is his coworker. The last thing we need is for him to think she is spying on him. It's better if it is the two of us. If we're wrong, no harm done. If we're right, we can disappear from his sight, working behind the scenes to find all the evidence we need to take this to the police detectives."

The reminder of the next steps we may need to take pulls some of the pep from Edward's step. "Are we sure there is no better time or place to confront him than when he stops to pick up his morning coffee? Maybe I could bump into him at the Bod. Mathilde said he worked in the law book section."

"No," I say in a firm tone. "I don't want you to question him on your own, and there is no reason we could offer for why the two of us are doing legal research in the Bodleian. My grandfather said Jonathan is a creature of habit. He stops at the coffee shop every morning on his way to work, buys a latte and a muffin, eats them and then goes straight to the library. This is our best chance. Stop dragging your feet, Edward."

We make a left onto the main street, bringing the coffee cup shaped sign into view. I squeeze Edward's hand, reminding him we are in this together. "My grandfather is already inside, monitoring Jonathan. We'll go straight to the counter to place our orders. I'll take an extra long time mulling over the breakfast pastries to buy us time for my grandfather to give us an update."

"That all sounds reasonable. Once we know which person he is, how are we going to approach him? Do we wander over, pretend to know him...?" Edward's tone grows nervous again.

"Don't worry, I will come up with something. I always do. In fact, do you remember how quick I was to come up with a distraction when we interviewed Mr Johnston at his farm? We drove out there together, thinking he might have been our murderer when Chef Smythe was killed."

Edward raises an amused eyebrow. "Do you mean the time you said you thought you saw a rooster laying an egg in the middle of the carpark?"

"Hey, it worked, didn't it?" I reply, pretending to be offended.

Edward wraps an arm around my shoulder and pulls me in close against his side. "That it did. You saved me from being battered by an angry man. It just might be the first moment I saw you as something other than an irritation."

I pinch his side, making him laugh. "Aren't you the charmer, Edward? Now let's go in and put this matter to rest."

With that, I skip up the small set of stairs and push open the coffee shop door.

The coffee shop is long and narrow, with four tables upfront and the order counter placed at the back. Given the early morning hour, I'm surprised to see how busy the place is. All the tables are taken, mostly by small clusters of people. A lone man sits at one of the larger tables closest to the order counter, and it doesn't take much deduction to figure out he must be our man.

My grandfather stands near the back, leaning against the wall and practically salivating over the baked goods filling the display. My grandfather beams with pleasure when he sees me navigating my way through the tables and chairs, and I give him a subtle wave of hello.

"Do you want to order first? I can't decide what I want." I motion Edward forward while I turn my attention to the display of fresh pastries. Knowing the other customers can't see him, my grandfather sidles over, giving me a quick pat on the back to say hello before he launches into his update.

"As you can guess, Jonathan is the man sitting at the table behind us. He only arrived a few minutes before you, so you don't need to stress that he will run out before you get your food and drinks. In fact," my grandfather leans sideways and get a better view of our suspect, "he is reading the news on his mobile. Definitely not in any rush. I'll stay close just in case you need anything else."

I give him a thumbs up and then raise my gaze from the glass case up to the barista standing behind it. "Sorry, there are just so many delicious-looking options, you know? Can I have a pain au chocolat and a latte, please?"

While the barista prepares our food and drinks, I spin around, putting my back to the counter. Edward looks nervous. I give him a meaningful look, hoping to calm him down. He replies with a sheepish grin before bending over to whisper in my ear. "Have you figured out how to approach him yet?"

A quick scan confirms that all the tables are still occupied, and no one looks to be on the verge of leaving.

"Yep, it will be slightly uncomfortable to start, but just go along with me, okay?"

Thankfully, the barista serves up our tray before Edward can ask any more questions. Once Edward has the tray in hand, I take a fortifying breath and dive in.

In a loud voice, I comment, "Oh dear! There aren't any free tables." I take a few steps forward, pretending to look around before giving a small huff of frustration. On my way back to Edward, I pause beside Jonathan's table, wavering as though I'm unsure about my next action. "I'm sorry to interrupt you," I say, standing over Jonathan. "My partner and I were hoping to sit down and enjoy our breakfast... there aren't any free tables... would you mind terribly if we shared a corner of yours?"

Jonathan raises his head from his phone, surprised to see a strange woman looking at him. I can tell that he wants to refuse my request, but he quickly arrives at the same conclusion I reached. All the other tables are occupied by groups of people. He is the only single person, and he has claimed a table for four. "Er, sure. Okay," he replies, begrudgingly.

"Thank you so much," I gush. Inside, I'm disappointed that Jonathan shows no signs of being naturally chatty. I put my mind into gear, searching for a conversation starter appropriate for a complete stranger.

Edward places our tray upon the table, and we settle into the chairs. I make a big production out of my first sip of coffee, sighing and commenting on how badly I needed the caffeine. Edward is visibly uncomfortable as he stirs his coffee again and again, rattling the spoon against the side of the mug. I lay a hand on his thigh, giving him a silent reminder to settle down.

As our conversation falls into a natural lull while we eat our pastries, I let my gaze skip around. Starting with the set of framed photos hung on the wall, over to the counter, and I finally end up focused on Jonathan himself. I don't hide my assessment of him, staring openly at his balding head, sallow face and cable-knit jumper. Even if I didn't know what he did for a living, I could nail it within a guess or two. All he needs is a pair of thick glasses and the caricature of nerdy librarian would be complete.

Eventually, Jonathan feels the heat of my gaze and raises his head up to meet my eyes.

"You look so familiar," I state, pretending to be curious. "Have we met before?"

Jonathan flushes slightly while shaking his head. "No. I don't believe so." He quickly returns his attention to his phone, no doubt hoping I'll stop there.

"No, I'm sure of it. I've definitely seen you somewhere." I tap my finger against my face, seemingly deep in thought. "Do you work around here?"

"No," he replies, without looking up.

I cast Edward a quick glance, but he is no help. "Maybe Blackwell's? Do you work at the bookshop on Broad Street? I was there a lot last term."

Jonathan, determined to avoid a conversation, doesn't respond.

I ponder longer before sitting up straight, as though the answer has struck me then and there. "I know! The Bodleian, right? I have a friend who works there. I'm sure I've seen you there."

Jonathan's head snaps up, looking like a deer in the headlights. He hesitantly replies, "Yes, I do work at the Bodleian..."

And with those words, I am in. Now to keep him chatting until we can figure out whether he is indeed our suspect.

"That is so funny!" I say brightly. "Such a small world. Edward and I also work for the uni. Have you been in Oxford long?"

Jonathan shifts uncomfortably, realising he is trapped at the table. His mug is half-full, and he has barely picked at his muffin. I'm sure he's regretting saying yes to my request, but it is clear I am not going to give him any out. Unless he wants to abandon his breakfast, he is stuck answering my questions.

His shoulders slump as he flips his phone over and lays it face-down on the table. "I've been here twenty years now."

"Wow, twenty years!" I exclaim. "It's not even been a year for me yet, although Edward has been here longer. You must have started straight after graduating. Did you study at Oxford as well?"

Jonathan glances at Edward, looking for help, but finds none. Edward is sitting, his expression carefully arranged to look blandly friendly.

"I, err, read history at Jesus College."

Slowly but surely, I pull more information from him, starting from his responsibilities at the library and onto how he ended up in Oxford. His single-line responses are far from forthcoming, but he is no match for my sheer determination.

However, no matter how hard I try, I can't find any suggestion that he is unhappy with his life or his work. If anything, I'd bet money that he is already living his dream. His only ambitions appear to be to stay at the Bodleian until he is old enough to retire. He is so committed to the university; he has a good chance of coming back as an Eternal. Not that I can tell him that.

After a while, Edward loosens up enough to join in, but he doesn't have any better success. Eventually, the two end up in a deep discussion of a new legal text, heatedly arguing for and against the author's assertions. Jonathan's whole demeanour shifts, his face lighting up and his eyes shining, as he talks confidently about a topic on which he is clearly an expert.

I end up being the one looking at my phone, bored stiff by their technical discussion. Even my grandfather grows weary, waving goodbye before he disappears off to wherever he is planning to spend the day. When the phone screen ticks past

8:30am, I give a silent thanks and use it as an excuse to interrupt the two men.

"Edward darling, don't you have a tutorial at nine this morning?" I say loud enough to cause the men to pause their conversation.

"What?" Edward replies, looking confused. I wiggle my eyebrows twice and give him a very pointed look, reminding him of why we're here. "Oh yes, of course. The tutorial. We had better run, or I'll be late."

I shuffle off to carry our tray and empty dishes to the barista while Edward and Jonathan exchange phone numbers, promising to send one another a new book to discuss. Edward is so pleased with his newfound friend; he is still talking about him when we get outside and start making our way back to St Margaret.

I give him a few minutes to get it all out of his system before I cough loudly, bringing his excitement to a halt. "So our suspect — our last suspect — doesn't appear to be the guilty party."

"Huh?" Edward responds, confused by the sudden change in the conversation. "Oh yes, I almost forgot why we were talking to him. Nice chap, very well-read, I must say."

I roll my eyes and try not to laugh. It's times like these that I remember Edward is foremost a professor. There are few things in life he likes better than a good intellectual discussion.

"If none of our potential suspects are guilty, where does that leave us?" I wonder aloud.

Edward's grin disappears, and the worry lines reform around his mouth. "I'm not sure, Nat, and that makes me very uneasy. I have a tutorial session this morning. Shall we regroup with the others around lunchtime? There must be something we're missing in all of this."

I give him a solemn nod of agreement. "Come over to the Ash. We can order food in. Hopefully, we can come up with a new angle or new insights. If not, we're in big trouble."

"We are in more than big trouble, Nat. Whoever is responsible for all this chaos won't stop if we don't catch them."

I shiver at the thought of what else might happen. "All I can think about is Francie being accused of a crime she didn't even fathom committing, and how distraught she must be. We are out of leads and have no solid clues. We need to meet with Kate, Mathilde and the Eternals to work out a new strategy."

Chapter Fifteen

I had planned to meet Mathilde straight after Edward's and my failed coffee shop interrogation, but thanks to Edward's extensive conversation about legal texts, I'm running late. By the time we get back to St Margaret and I track down H hiding away in the gardens with his girlfriend Princess Fluffy, I barely have time to shoot off a quick text to let Mathilde know we are on our way.

At the Ash, H and I go straight upstairs to our meeting room turned office space in the upper level. Mathilde, Will and Jill have circled around the table, looking at what appears to be a floor plan of the museum.

I rush into the room in a flurry of activity — setting my bag down, pulling out a chair for H and digging out a pen and paper. Mathilde waits until Will and Jill return their attention to the floor plan before giving me a questioning look. All I can manage is a quick shake of my head, unable to say anything more due to the pair sitting beside her. Apparently, it is enough, because she frowns and then grows thoughtful.

I throw her a lifeline, saying, "Before I forget, Mathilde and I are meeting Kate and Edward for lunch. I think Kate has some news about Francie." I face Will and Jill. "Is that going to be a problem for you two?"

"Oh no, not at all," Jill confirms, brushing aside my concern. "We can eat a sandwich in the lounge with some of the other museum staff. They are really friendly."

After a short catch-up about our activities over the long weekend, we finally get down to business.

I study the floor plan, making note of the large room set aside for the new displays. "Mathilde, how far along are you and the museum team with the plans for the layout of the exhibition itself?"

"We've determined which items to display in groups based on time periods and subject matter. Now we're looking at the display case options, but that is as far as we've got. We didn't want to get too far into the plans until we knew what you had in mind." Mathilde checks my reaction. "Is that okay, or were you hoping we'd be further along?"

A relieved smile spreads across my face. "That is perfect! I was worried my plans might conflict, so this is great. I know my primary focus is on the grand opening event, but I think you might want to consider carrying some of my ideas into the exhibition itself."

With that settled, I pull a binder from my handbag, opening it up to reveal a series of sketches. "Here is what I'm thinking..."

Mathilde, Will and Jill look on with wonder as I explain my vision, taking turns to flip through my designs, read my notes and ask lots of questions. The plan is ambitious, requiring set design and displays spread throughout the atrium on the ground floor of the museum.

Will is quick to volunteer to oversee the design of the main entrance. "I've always wanted to do an Alice Through the Looking Glass type of theme. This might be as close as I get. Do you think Barnard College will let me visit the old library to take a closer look at the secret chamber?"

"I've already cleared it with their interim Master," I reply, pleased to see how excited he is. "Don't make the entrance too large. After the event, I thought we could move it to the doorway of the room where the exhibition will be on display."

Will pauses thoughtfully, and then stands up and moves to the whiteboard. "We could use curtains on either side. Something like this maybe..." he explains as he quickly sketches out a design, earning nods of agreement from all of us.

That settled, I switch my attention to Mathilde. "Would you mind acting as our liaison with the relevant university departments? We'll need biology, chemistry and architecture at a minimum, but I'm sure you know better than I do which ones should be involved."

"I'd be happy to do it," she answers with a grin. "I've got contacts in most of the departments and where I don't, I'm sure our team of researchers at the Bodleian can point me in the right direction."

"I guess that leaves me with logistics," Jill mumbles, looking somewhat dejected.

"Oh no, Jill," I interject. "I've got a special task only you can do."

Jill gives me a quizzical look.

"I've noticed your habit of sketching in your notebook, mainly because your illustrations are so incredible." I stop to rifle through my own notepad, searching for the right page. "Since we'll need to spread the displays throughout the open space, I was thinking we should have a bespoke illustration which will explain how they all fit together."

"Cool!" Mathilde and Will exclaim in unison.

I rest my gaze on Jill. "I'd like you to take the lead on the art design. You may want to consult some experts in the various subjects to get an idea of what illustration would best represent their area, but I will leave the final design up to you."

"Seriously?" Jill asks, her voice tinged with disbelief.

"Seriously. I'll take the lead on the logistics. The good news is that we don't have to worry about organising a dinner." I reach across the table and pull the floor plan back into the centre so we can all see it. Pointing at the map, I demonstrate how the event will work. "Our guests can enter here and work their way around the displays in the atrium. Then we can route them through the Greek World galleries to get them over to the Greek and Roman sculpture hall where we'll host the drinks and dessert reception."

With the high-level plans agreed, we dive into the details, all of us opening our laptops and start working on spreadsheets and task lists. H curls up in a ball, snoring softly, sending tiny wisps of smoke curling into the air. He looks so calm and innocent, I can't stop myself from leaning over to stroke his scaly head.

The silence of the room is broken only by the sound of fingers tapping on keyboards. I lose all track of time, as often happens when I am hard at work. When my mobile buzzes with Edward's text, letting me know he is on his way over to meet us for lunch, I'm amazed to see that three hours have passed.

Stretching in my chair, I glance up to see Mathilde chewing on her lower lips, looking somewhat worried. "What's up, Mathilde? You look concerned."

"It's just hit me how much work we've got to do to prepare for the big event. It's four weeks away. Do you think we have enough time to get all of this done?"

I respond but stop, turning instead to see what Will and Jill think. If they're harbouring concerns about the complexity of the plans, now is the time to get them out on the table. "Will, Jill, what do you two think?"

They don't respond straight away, taking a moment to consider the question, exchanging glances in an unspoken conversation. Will finally speaks up, "The art design and construction certainly add a level of complexity, but not necessarily more than we had at St Margaret or at Barnard. I think we can do it."

"I agree," Jill adds, still brimming with excitement over her own assignment.

"There you have it, Mathilde." I give H a nudge to wake him up. "We can regroup here in an hour, if that works. I'd like to get a timeline on paper before we go home this evening."

Mathilde leaps into action, helping me to tidy up the stray papers so we can get to Kate's office for an update on our search for the arsonist.

Bartie, Xavvie, my grandfather and Kate are already gathered in Kate's office, awaiting our arrival. A trio of salads, along with a basket of crusty bread, sit in the middle of her conference table. H's face falls in comical disbelief as he eyes the lunch options, not finding the greens and veg at all appetising. My grandfather heads off his complaint by twitching a napkin off one plate to unveil a four-cheese pizza, hidden away amidst the healthier options.

Mathilde drops into a nearby chair with a sigh of relief. "For a minute there, I thought H was going to stage a revolt over our lunch menu."

I stop to give my grandfather a quick hug, making up for the limited greeting I could do in the confines of the busy coffee shop. H flies over to the table, grabbing the pizza in his talons before gliding to a landing in his favourite location.

Xavvie laughs as H settles into his lap. "I do envy the Eternal creatures like H. It hardly seems fair that they can enjoy food while the rest of us are doomed to salivate over it."

H uses a claw to cut a string of melted cheese and chews

furiously before replying, "You 'ad your chance to eat all you wanted when you were alive, Xavvie. After three 'undred years as a stone gargoyle at the Bod, I think we deserve a pizza now and then."

No one can argue with that.

Kate closes her laptop and rises from her desk to join the rest of us at the table. The Eternals remain standing, or sitting in Xavvie's case, allowing the rest of us to take the seats and help ourselves to the food.

"Nat, eat while you can," Kate suggests, passing me a paper plate. "We'll wait until Edward arrives before we launch into our questions, although I'm desperate to know how it went."

"We might as well all eat," I respond, despondent. "Our update isn't going to be particularly filled with good news."

Edward arrives as I polish off my last bite of salad. I offer to kick off the discussion while he catches up with us.

"As agreed, Edward and I interviewed all of our potential suspects identified by the Eternals. First up was Nigel Symonds, professor at St Margaret. Next was Mary Chloe Lennon, a colleague of Edward's. Our last interview was this morning, with Jonathan Townsend, whom Mathilde knows since he works at the Bodleian. Have we missed anyone?" I ask, looking to the Eternals in the room for confirmation.

My grandfather unfolds a piece of paper from his pocket, giving it a quick skim. "Other than you three prefects and Edward, Nigel, Mary Chloe and Jonathan are the only other people here in Oxford who fit the requirements for our suspect."

"Much like ourselves, all of our suspects mentioned feeling called to come to Oxford. Their admiration and respect for the institution was clear." I cast my mind back to our conversations, searching for anything else which stood out. "Despite going into every conversation thinking I was interviewing a potential suspect, I quickly warmed to all of them, finding commonalities and chatting so long that either Edward or I lost track of time."

Kate frowns. "For all we know, that could be part of how the magic of Oxford works. Those of us with the strongest connection to the magic can't help but have an affinity for one another. It could explain why we all became such fast friends."

"If that's the case, where does that leave our investigation?" Mathilde asks, posing the question that is on all our minds.

Leaning forward in my chair, I scan the room, looking to see who might step forward with a response. I notice that Kate, Mathilde, and Edward are doing similarly, all four of us turning to our Eternals for guidance on solving a problem which is bigger than all of us.

Xavvie and H seem stumped. I notice them exchanging glances and shrugging their shoulders, neither of them any further along than we are.

Bartie is staring off into space, deep in thought, clearly pondering the question. Finally, my grandfather leaves his post against the far wall, crossing to the middle of the room where we can all see him clearly.

"Maybe it will help if we talk this out," he suggests. "Let's start at the beginning of the magic. Wren and Wilkins stumbled upon its existence. They told their small cohort of like-minded intellectuals and together, they put in place a system to keep the magic hidden to protect it from nefarious actors who would use it for malevolent schemes."

"Yes," Mathilde says with a gleam in her eyes. "Afterwards, those same men continued to collaborate for the rest of their lives. In fact, collaboration and peer review were central to their interactions with one another. It would make sense that their passion for working collectively could have influenced the human interaction with the magic of Oxford."

"It could also be one trait we all inherited, along with the ability to see the magic." I sit back in my chair, my mind spinning. "If that's the case, then it is unlikely that any descendant of the original group of discoverers would turn against Oxford or try to steal the magic for their own gain. It runs counterintuitive to our core beliefs."

The room grows quiet as we work through the ramifications of this new information. Edward catches my attention when he stops mid-sip of coffee to raise his gaze to the ceiling. His lips move in silence, as though he is working through an idea but isn't quite ready to share it with everyone else.

I call out his name to get his attention. "What are you thinking over there? You look like you might have something to add."

"This might be nonsense..." He pauses, already second-guessing himself.

"Go on," my grandfather encourages him.

"What if we've been looking in the wrong direction this entire time?" He waits to see if anyone immediately jumps in and carries on when we don't. "The originals interacted with the magic with the best of intentions, and they passed this legacy down to all of us as descendants. To create the havoc we've experienced over the past year — thefts, murder, arson — you'd need someone who feels the exact opposite of what we do. They would need to resent Oxford and all that it stands for, to where they are willing to inflict pain and suffering on those of us living, working, and studying here."

"If our good intentions date back to the originals, where would our suspect's negative feelings find their roots? An unknown original?" I shrug, adding, "I guess it's possible. We are still missing pages from Wren's journals."

"Wait a minute," Bartie pipes up from the back of the room. "We're looking for a pair of individuals, correct? We've long thought that there must be a rogue Eternal sitting at the helm, and a living person doing the dirty work. What if the pair are directly related to one another?"

Mathilde chimes in, "That's right, I'd almost forgotten that. It would make perfect sense for there to be a direct connection, but I'm not sure that makes it any easier on us. Why would one of Wren's presumably close friends turn against him?"

"They wouldn't," I say, as the truth dawns on me. "But I'd be willing to bet that people as large as life and as influential as Wren, Wilkins and their group must have had enemies. Or maybe competitors is the better word. What if one of their intellectual competitors somehow found out about the existence of the magic? Would they tell someone?"

"No, I don't imagine they would," my grandfather posits. "They could hardly lay claim to the original discovery, therefore any announcements would only add to the glory of Wren, Wilkins and the others."

"That's where we need to restart our search," I announce, sounding convinced. "Can the Eternals search the university's historical records to see if there is anyone from that era who fits the bill? And if so, can you see whether they might conveniently have a direct descendant who is connected to the university?"

Bartie looks to his fellow Eternals, checking that they are all in agreement. When he sees all their heads nod in unison, including H, his face tightens in grim determination. "I'll call a meeting of the Heads of Eternal Affairs from the various colleges straight away. If such a person exists, I am sure we can find them."

With that, he disappears from the room, leaving the rest of us feeling a lot more hopeful than when we first came in.

Chapter Sixteen

I check my mobile for the third time since lunch, but it still shows no missed calls and no messages. I had hoped the Eternals could work their magic and identify a new suspect for us overnight. However, given it has been over twenty-four hours since we met over lunch, it isn't looking promising.

To keep my mind occupied, I arranged meetings with the logistics suppliers we'll need for the exhibition's grand opening — security, audio-visual, caterers and even a strings trio. I've run from one office to another all morning long, stopping only to pick up H and grab a quick bite at home. Now I'm in the depths of a warehouse measuring the heights of various platforms and daises. To think Edward was wondering why I keep a tape measure in my handbag.

"H, would you mind holding this end in place?" I wave my free hand to get his attention. H dives off the top of a nearby metal shelf and lands by my side.

"Sure thing, Nat!" He waits for me to move my hand and then he shoots a jet of flames onto metal end of the tape measure, melting it into place.

"That wasn't exactly what I had in mind, but I guess it will do as long as I work quickly." I back up six steps, align the tape to the opposite end and make a note of the nearest number. When I hear the telltale sound of the tape winding itself back up, I drop the tape measure and jump backwards before I get smacked with it.

"Maybe next time you could hold the end in place instead." I grumble as I bend over, searching for where my handy tool ended up. Right as my hand lands on its plastic case, I hear a wonderful sound. My mobile is ringing.

I scurry to my feet, tucking my hair behind my ear before answering. "Hullo?"

"Nat, it's Kate. Where are you?"

"I'm at a party supply warehouse in Botley. What's up?"

"How quickly can you get back to the Ashmolean?" she asks in a rush. "Edward's expert came through. He retrieved the interior footage from the archives building."

"That's amazing!" I snap my fingers to keep H from wandering off. "H is with me. We'll cycle straight over. Should be there in twenty minutes, max."

"That's perfect!" Kate exclaims. "I've got to track Mathilde down and Edward is already on his way over. Come straight to my office when you get here."

Message delivered, Kate ends the call, leaving H and me to gather my measuring tape and notes so we can be on our way.

Normally, H spends our cycle rides flipping in and out of the basket, but after Kate's call, he agrees that time is of the essence. "Do you think we'll see who really set the fire, Nat?"

"I hope so, H. Poor Francie has been locked away for two weeks now. If the video proves who was really inside the archives, it should be enough to set her free." I carefully weave my way around the traffic leading into the city centre.

As soon as it flows again, H flies out of the basket and lands on the back of my bicycle. Inspired by his wheelchair staircase adventures with Xavvie, he grips his talons into the metal frame and sets his wings to flapping. With the added momentum, we make it to the Ashmolean in record time. While locking up my bicycle, I can't help but marvel at how the magic makes the rest of the world overlook a cat riding behind me.

I make sure to greet Agatha and Nancy, who are on duty at the information desk when we walk inside. I wind my way through the maze of galleries until I reach the hallway where Kate's office is located.

Kate is sitting behind her desk when I come into the room. She looks up with surprise. "Wow, you made it here sooner than I expected, Nat."

"I had a little help," I confess, holding the door open so H can follow me inside.

"You two have a seat," she says, motioning towards the conference table. "Edward and Mathilde should be here any second. Edward is bringing the file over on a USB drive."

"He knows us too well. If he'd emailed the file, there is no way we would have waited for him to get here." I get to work pulling chairs from the table and turning them around while Kate presses the button to lower the video screen. By the time we finish situating all the chairs and getting cups of tea, Edward and Mathilde arrive.

"Hurry and pass me the drive, Edward," Kate commands as soon as he comes in the door.

"Hello to you, too, Kate," he replies with a laugh, passing her the object in question. He gives me a quick hello as he takes the seat next to mine, Mathilde settling at my other side.

It takes Kate only a moment to load the drive and open the folder.

"Here we go," Kate says and clicks on the file. When the video player pops up on the screen, we fall silent and she presses play. "Andrei would have come on shift at four in the afternoon, and then would have been moving around as he checked all the buildings. I'll skip ahead until we spot him."

The camera is positioned near the ceiling in one corner of the room, providing a bird's-eye view of the storage area. For Mathilde, Edward, H, and I, it is the first time we're seeing the inside of the archives building. We lean in collectively, studying the layout.

The room stretches wide, with a generous walkway running along the side of it, allowing a clear path to enter and exit. The rest of the room is divided into storage aisles using metal shelving units. Kate explains that the door we see is the one on the back of the building, which opens into the courtyard.

"Is this the only camera inside the building?" Edward asks, frowning.

"Unfortunately, yes. The cameras were only there to keep a record of entries and exits into the building. There are exterior cameras at both the front and back entrances, as we saw in the earlier video. This one is positioned to show anyone walking into the storage space. And before you ask, I've requested that more cameras be installed to remedy this issue." That said, Kate returns to her seat and restarts the video.

Finally, we catch our first glimpse of Andrei. He steps into the bottom of the frame, entering the storage area from the front of the building. He strides confidently in and out of the aisles of shelves, presumably checking that all is well. When he finishes his checks, he returns to the front and disappears from view. Moments later, he returns with two large plastic jugs of the type typically used to carry flammable liquids. He carries them into an aisle, out of sight.

"That answers whether Andrei was involved," Kate grouses. "He must have repositioned the front exterior camera before he came to check this building. I remember it moving around and then it froze at a weird angle."

A few minutes later, Andrei reappears, talking on his mobile. He ends the call and makes his way back to the door. Due to the camera angle, we can see Andrei opening the back door and standing there deliberately blocking the camera from allowing us a clear view of whomever is in the doorway.

"Maybe this is when Francie showed up," Mathilde suggests.

However, when Andrei steps back, it isn't Francie we see. Instead, there is a figure dressed in a dark-coloured hoodie and black trousers. When the person steps inside, they hunch over and hold a backpack in front of their face, taking care to avoid being caught on video.

"I knew someone else was in there!" I exclaim. Before I can say anything further, something even more strange happens. "Wait. Did something fly in behind them?"

Kate pauses the video so we can all move closer to the screen. Sure enough, a black crow is now perched on top of one of the metal shelving units, its beady eyes looking straight into the camera. As I return to my seat, I notice H has his head cocked sideways and appears to be deep in thought.

I tug on his tail to get his attention. "Recognise something?"

"That's no bird. That's some kind of Eternal," he growls. He motions to Kate to keep the video moving, shaking his head no when she asks if it is someone he recognises.

The dark figure is careful to remain deep within the aisles, out of the sight of the camera. The crow, however, stays in view. It flies from one shelf to another, using its beak to pull open boxes. Andrei's activities are also visible. Wherever the crow lands, Andrei follows behind, ladder in hand. He climbs up and picks boxes up and then passes them to the other person standing below.

"They're stealing my collection!" Kate gasps, realising what the pair are doing. "They are pawing through my storage boxes and helping themselves to whatever they want."

Mostly, Andrei stays in sight, perched at the top of the ladder so he can follow the crow's flight and know where to move to next. When he jerks around, nearly falling off the ladder as he turns to stare at the door, we can guess what happened.

"This must be when Francie arrives," Mathilde murmurs next to me.

Andrei waves at the figure, presumably telling the person to hide, and then descends the ladder and rushes to the main walkway. He barely makes it there in time to stop Francie from coming further inside.

Andrei freezes in place for a second, clearly unsure how to handle her unexpected arrival. With bags of food in her hands, there is no doubt she has every intention of staying for a while. They discuss back and forth for a minute, her smiling and Andrei shaking his head. He raises a hand, pointing at her angrily, his shoulders huffed up as he looms over her. Francie recoils as though she's been struck and then bursts into tears.

Andrei's efforts to remove her from the building become desperate. He turns her around and marches her back to the door. He pulls it open and practically shoves her out of it. When the door slams shut, he runs a hand through his hair, clearly stressed.

"And now is when it is going to get really interesting," Kate says, her voice grim.

Sure enough, Andrei, still heated from his argument with Francie, calls out to his partner in crime. He gestures wildly for the dark figure to finish up whatever they are doing.

Together, they make quick work of their flurried search of the back rows, leaving open boxes half-hanging off the shelves. The crow takes flight, circling above them. Finally, Andrei and the hooded figure exit the aisle closest to the door, each carrying a large shopping bag.

Andrei returns to the aisles while the hooded figure stays at the door, with his back turned to the camera. He bends over to double-check the contents of the bags. The crow swoops down, landing on the floor beside him.

"Them two are up to somethin'," H splutters, nearly singeing me with a wayward flame.

Andrei reappears from the aisle with the jugs from earlier in hand. He pours the liquid along the floor of the main aisle and up towards the front part of the building. Then he scatters bins full of discarded paper on top.

"Andrei made certain the fire department would struggle to get into the building." Edward rubs his chin, considering the implications. "But if he poured the accelerant, how did he end up stuck inside?"

The next few minutes of video provide the answer. The crow flies back up towards the ceiling, cawing to catch Andrei's attention. The hooded figure, still kneeling near the door, shrugs and then motions for Andrei to follow the bird.

Andrei grabs the ladder and makes one more trip to the top of the shelves, this time in the furthest back corner. The crow waits until Andrei is trying to tug the storage box from the shelf. It launches itself from a nearby shelf, darting straight at Andrei, wings flapping furiously. Andrei throws his arms up to ward off the attacking bird, and in doing so, he loses his balance. The last we see of him is his face, a rictus of horror as he falls backwards, his arms waving in a desperate attempt to save himself.

Its job done, the crow circles the room, gliding down to land beside the arsonist. The arsonist nods at the bird, confirming there are no loose ends, and then pulls a box from his pocket, strikes a match, and tosses it into the room.

The last thing we see is the smoke rising as the pair leave the building.

Mathilde leans over and whispers, "How on earth are we going to explain the crow to DCI Robinson?"

"Let the magic sort it out," H suggests from his perch on the table behind me. His voice drops to a mutter. "A bird, of all things. I can't wait to get my 'ands on it."

I shift sideways when H punctuates his mutter with a huff of black smoke. "One step at a time, H. First, let's get Francie freed, and then we can figure out how to stop the real arsonist from committing another crime."

Edward adopts a determined look as he pulls his mobile from his jacket pocket and searches through his contacts for DCI Robinson's name. "Hullo, Trevor. Edward Thomas here. I have an update on the interior footage from the Ashmolean archives. One of our computer science students has retrieved it. Could you come to the Ashmolean and pick up the drive? Now? Excellent, we'll be in Kate's office."

He disconnects the call and then scans the room, looking each one of us in the eye. "He was close by, so we shouldn't have long to wait. How do you want to handle the discussion with DCI Robinson?"

Mathilde and I each turn towards Kate. After all, she is the director of the museum. We may be equal partners, but this is her domain. She doesn't respond straightaway, her eyes shifting left and right as she mentally plays through all the options. When she settles on one, she pushes back her chair and rises to her feet.

"First and foremost, we do not want DCI Robinson to walk into this room and feel like he is stepping into a firing line." She motions for Mathilde and me to stand. "You two, could you move to the far side of the conference table?"

Mathilde and I nod, shifting the chairs back into place before assuming our assigned positions. I push my chair back enough to make space for H to sit on my lap.

"Edward, would you sit in the chair closest to the door? We'll leave the seat at the head of the table free for DCI Robinson. I'll stay at my desk so I can run the video."

We shift uncomfortably in the silence as we wait for a knock to sound at the door announcing his arrival. We're too nervous to even attempt a conversation. The video should exonerate Francie completely, but I can't help worry that DCI Robinson will claim it is inadmissible or find some other reason to continue to hold her.

When the knock sounds, all four of us jump in our seats and H shoots a jet of flame out of his nostrils, singeing the edge of the table. Mathilde and I brush the ash away as Edward goes to open the door and lets the Chief Inspector in.

The two men exchange hearty handshakes and then DCI Robinson beelines for Kate's desk, saying hello to her. It's only when he turns around that he realises Mathilde and I are here as well. We grin sheepishly, murmuring our hellos without getting up.

"I've cued the video up on my screen," Kate says. "If you wouldn't mind having a seat, we can watch it straight away. I'm sure you'll find it as interesting as we did."

DCI Robinson takes the proffered chair, but glowers at Edward as he does so. "You should have delivered the video footage straight to the police department, Edward. Regardless of what it shows, it is evidence in a criminal case. Hardly fodder for a group movie night."

"I asked him to bring it here," Kate interjects. "I have as much vested interest in uncovering the truth of what happened that night. If you must blame someone, it should be me."

"We all want the same thing," Edward reaffirms, his tone cool but still friendly.

DCI Robinson's expression softens, barely, but enough that Kate takes it as approval to press the play button on the video.

"Andrei makes his first appearance on the video further ahead," Kate explains, as she drags the cursor forward. "I'll skip to then and slow down as we go through the hour leading up to the fire."

I'm grateful Kate had us move to the far side of the table, as we're now perfectly positioned to keep an eye on DCI Robinson's reactions without him noticing. Although he tries hard to keep his face stoic, the dark-clothed visitor and the crow provoke a clear response of surprise. His brow furrows as he narrows his eyes, concentrating on the action playing on the screen.

DCI Robinson's head shifts, a sure sign he is following the bird's flight around the room, leaving me reassured that he can see it. I expect him to comment on the crow's actions, but once again the magic of Oxford steps in and smooths over the strangeness. By the time there is nothing left to see but smoke, his mouth is pulled downward in a grim frown.

We wait for his pronouncement, but all he says is, "That was unexpected."

I glance at Edward, expecting him to speak up, but he sits quietly, leaving DCI Robinson space to think about what this new information will mean for his case.

Kate shows much less patience. "Francie is innocent. You have to free her."

The Chief Inspector turns in his chair, arching an eyebrow. "The footage suggests that Francie was not a conspirator in the fire, but there is still the matter of the stolen goods hidden in her flat. This isn't sufficient to rule her out of having been involved."

"What?" Kate exclaims, the word exploding out of her mouth before she can stop herself. She takes a second to calm down before she says anything else. "I have said all along that I thought Francie was as much of a victim here. This video perfectly aligns with everything she's told us about the night in question. As for the stolen items, it could have just as easily been Andrei. He had access to the museum collection and her flat. He could have stashed the items there, planning to frame her for the crime."

DCI Robinson stares at Kate, unfazed by her emotional plea. His tone is stern when he answers her. "Ms Underhill, I understand your position here. However, I cannot free an accused suspect from jail on one piece of partial evidence." He holds up a hand, stopping her from replying. "I said before that I would investigate all possibilities supported by evidence. Until now, there was nothing to suggest Mr Radu was involved. The video changes this. But you have to step back while we do our job."

Edward gives Kate a nearly imperceptible nod, silently conveying that this is the best outcome she can hope to achieve right now.

Kate takes another deep breath, loosening her shoulders. "Very well, Chief Inspector. I trust you will work as quickly as possible to sort out this matter."

As DCI Robinson stands to leave, Edward speaks up. "Would you agree, Trevor, that the video is evidence enough that Francie is not responsible for Andrei's death?"

"Yes," he answers, wondering where Edward is going with the question.

"In that case, could the Magistrate's court revisit the question of bail?"

DCI Robinson's eyes flash, giving me hope that Edward's suggestion might be viable. It's all I can do to hold firm in my chair as the Chief Inspector considers Edward's request. He leaves us hanging, holding out a hand to Kate so she can pass him the USB drive.

He puts the drive in his pocket, gathering himself up to leave. Only then does he stop and look at us all.

"I'll do my best," he answers and then takes his leave, saying nothing else.

Chapter Seventeen

I don't see Kate again until the next day, when we all regroup at my flat for an update from the Eternals. I catch sight of her walking into our carpark and can't help but notice how much lighter her steps are. She's barely in the door before Mathilde and I jump in with our question.

"Any news on Francie?" we ask, practically in unison.

"She's home," Kate replies with a much-relieved sigh. "DCI Robinson came through and was able to arrange bail. Her mother and her lawyer picked her up early this morning."

Finally, a piece of good news. I give Kate a quick hug in celebration. "I'm sure the investigation will eventually exonerate her. The important thing is that she isn't locked away any longer. Is she going to take some time off?"

"Yes," Kate replies as she shrugs off her jacket, hanging it on the nearby coat rack. "It was tricky to arrange, but I worked out a month of leave for her. I want to make sure she can get any help she needs. This entire experience has been incredibly traumatic for her."

Harry is the next to arrive, carrying a platter of sandwiches and crisps over from St Margaret's dining hall. "Sorry I'm late. Did I miss anything?"

We reassure her we're still waiting on Edward, Bartie and my grandfather to join us. I wish they'd hurry. I've been sitting on the proverbial pins and needles, waiting for our lunch meeting to roll around.

Although the sandwich array looks lush, not a one of us helps ourselves. We're too nervous to eat. If the Eternals' new suspect ends up being another dud, we're fresh out of ideas of where to look next. After seeing the footage of the night of the fire, we're even more frantic to stop our arsonist. Stealing our magic and causing chaos is one thing, deliberately trapping a man inside of a burning building is another.

Finally, we hear male voices arriving through my garden door. I quickly plate up a cheese sandwich for H. We may not be hungry now, but I'm hoping the news will be good enough to reactivate our appetites.

Unsurprisingly, H leads the pack, flying over our heads to land on the back of the sofa and laying claim to his waiting plate. Edward follows behind, deep in conversation with Bartie, and my grandfather is the last one to enter the room. My grandfather assumes his normal position leaning against my mantle. Bartie sits on the arm of the lounger next to Kate, and Edward helps himself to the food. Only when he moves to sit beside me does he realise he is the only one other than H holding a plate.

"Er, sorry. Was I not supposed to help myself?" He shifts awkwardly, clearly unsure whether he should eat it or put it back.

"No, not at all, luv," Harry answers, leaning forward from her seat behind the sofa to pat him on the shoulder. "I can't speak for the others, but my stomach is churning too much to think about food." Kate, Mathilde, and I nod in agreement.

"If the rest of you aren't going to eat, perhaps I should just go straight into my update," my grandfather suggests, motioning to Edward to dig in. "I have good news. The Eternals have identified a new suspect, one which seems much more likely than anyone on our previous list. In fact, we're almost certain we've found our man."

"That's great," I gush, feeling immediately relieved. "Who is it?"

My grandfather pulls a piece of paper from his shirt pocket, taking ages to unfold it and smooth it out. "Before we get into our modern-day arsonist, I think it best if I back up and start from his Eternal connection to Oxford."

"Seriously?" I whine as my shoulders tighten up from the tension in the room. Instead of replying, my grandfather tilts his head and gives me that look of disappointment which I hated receiving as a child. Suitably chastised, I sit back in my chair and force my shoulders to drop from my ears.

He adopts his teacher pose, giving his notes a quick glance before launching into his explanation. "When we last met in Kate's office, we all agreed that our search needed to start much earlier in time. We Eternals took on the task of identifying a contemporary of Wren, Wilkins, and the other members of the Philosophical Society. We started with Sir Christopher Wren, but eventually widened our research."

"I take it you found someone, Alfred?" Harry asks my grandfather.

"We did, Harry. As you all should recall, John Wilkins founded the Oxford Philosophical Club, of which Sir Christopher Wren was a member, and recruited several of the greatest intellectual minds of the time to join."

Mathilde pipes up from beside me. "Did they have a rogue in their group?"

"No, but that is where we started our search. They were a tight-knit group, likely because their ideas were often considered to be radical. They needed to depend on one another's support. Instead, we shifted our search to look for feuds."

"Feuds?" Mathilde sits up straighter, her eyebrows raised. "Of course! Why didn't we think of this sooner?"

This time, Bartie is the one to answer. "Once you discovered the journal in the secret chamber at Barnard College, we were all focused on Sir Christopher Wren. Although I'm sure he had his enemies, none of them were well-known enough to be anything other than a blip in history. We had to widen our search, expanding to look at the other early members of the Royal Society. That was when we found our likely culprit."

After clearing his throat, my grandfather finally reveals the identity of the historical figure whom he believes is behind our troubles. "This man was vocal in his hatred of Oxford and Cambridge, accusing the universities of holding a monopoly over the educational opportunities in England. He attacked them in writing, speeches, and articles, and drew the ire of Wilkins and later other members of the Royal Society. Despite being a brilliant philosopher, he remained an intellectual outcast in England, primarily because he was an arrogant arse. His feuds with Wilkins and the others are legendary, almost as well known as his name."

"Who is he, Alfred? Don't hold us here in suspense!" Harry chastises.

My grandfather blushes before replying, "His name is Thomas Hobbes."

Mathilde looks shocked. "The famous philosopher? Author of The Leviathan? That Hobbes?"

"The very one," my grandfather confirms.

"But he studied at Oxford. I'm sure of it!" Mathilde protests.

"He did, and that is how he came to be invited to visit, late in his life, providing him with the opportunity to spy on his enemies and to discover the existence of the magic. By this point, he was bitter, labelled a heretic by the government and his reputation left in tatters. He must have viewed the magic as proof positive of Oxford's unfair advantage, but he knew no one would believe him. He was nearly burnt at the stake a few years earlier. There was no way he could step forward claiming that magic existed." My grandfather folds the paper up and returns it to his pocket.

Mathilde is distracted, her mind working furiously to measure her knowledge of Hobbes against this newfound information. Kate, however, looks much less bothered to discover one of England's well-known philosophers might be behind our current problems.

"So, Hobbes came up to spy on his enemies, looking for a way to redeem himself. Instead, he uncovers their biggest secret — Oxford's magic. From what you said, I cannot imagine he would walk away from such a discovery. He likely studied and experimented with the magic right until his death, looking for a way to use it to his advantage. In doing so, he became an original as well." Kate looks to Bartie to confirm her assessment and then carries on. "Fine, I'm willing to accept this could be true. Why not? If that is the case, who is his modern-day descendant?"

"It is interesting that you should be the one to ask that question, Kate," my grandfather says, looking cheerless. "You are the only prefect who has met him. We suspect our arsonist is none other than Oswald Beadle."

"Oswald Beadle? That rat of a man?" Kate shrieks, fury colouring her cheeks.

I look to Mathilde for a clue, but she seems as confused as I am. Both of us turn to my grandfather for an explanation. All he offers is, "Xavvie had a similar response."

"Well," Harry huffs from her seat behind us. "If Kate and

Xavvie's reactions are any indication, it looks like we may finally be on the right track. Kate, who is he?"

It takes Kate a moment to swallow her initial anger. "Oswald Beadle was the Associate Director of the Ashmolean. He left the museum's employment shortly after I arrived, when I had him ejected from the premises."

"Wait a minute. Is this the person who attacked you during your first week on the job?" I ask incredulously.

Bartie puts a hand on Kate's shoulder. "You were attacked at work? How am I just now hearing about this?"

"Perhaps you could back up and take us through from the beginning, Kate," my grandfather suggests, quieting the rest of us.

Kate closes her eyes for a second, composing herself, and then launches into her tale. "At that time, I didn't know why I applied for the Directorship at the Ash. I was working at the V&A Museum in London. All of us in the art community heard about the opening, but we also knew there was a strong internal candidate."

"Beadle?" Bartie interjects.

"Yes," Kate confirms. "As I said earlier, he was the Associate Director, and had been for some time. Everyone I knew presumed he was a shoo-in for the Director's job, but something made me brush off my CV and apply for the position, anyway."

"The magic," I whisper to Mathilde, making her smile.

"As soon as I set foot in the Ashmolean, I knew it was where I was meant to be. I pulled out all the stops when it came to the interview, determined to show the hiring panel I was the person for the job. Even though the interview went well, very well, I was still in shock when the university phoned and offered me the role." She pauses, lost in thought. "I accepted immediately and started a month later."

Edward asks gently, "When did you realise Beadle was going to be a problem?"

"The moment I set foot in the building," Kate answers with a wry frown. "From the first time Beadle laid eyes on me, it was obvious he hated me. And I don't use that word lightly. He resented being passed over for a promotion he felt he deserved. He never came out and said it, but I think me being a female made it even worse. We only worked together for a week, but he would make cutting remarks in meetings, bury away briefing notes and basically do everything he could to make me look incompetent."

"That sounds awful," I commiserate. "How did you end up in a physical fight with him? Did he attack you?"

Kate shakes her head. "One of our largest donors had come in for a meeting. We were on the main floor of the museum, showing her a recent acquisition we'd made — a bust of a roman senator. Oswald had come along to the meeting under the guise of making the introductions. But he stuck around, tossing out sly remarks and interrupting me at every opportunity. It got to where I could see our donor was uncomfortable. I pulled him aside and asked him to return to his office, making my dissatisfaction clear."

"I bet 'e didn't like that at all," H says, in between bites of his fourth sandwich.

"He did not. I will never forget the look on his face." Kate winces. "He stared at me, eyes wide with shock that I would dare ask him to leave. He argued with me, refusing to accept that he had crossed a line. He grew heated, his tone getting louder. I finally told him that if he didn't take himself away immediately, his position at the museum could be at risk."

"And then he hit you?" Bartie growls, his anger clear.

"That worm?" Kate laughs. "Hitting me would insinuate he was interested in a fair fight. He backed up a step, his hands folded into angry fists, breathing heavily. Then he rushed me, shoving me as hard as he could, sending me falling into an ancient Egyptian coffin!"

We all stare at Kate, incredulous.

"Agatha and Nancy came rushing over, helping me out of the coffin while the security guards tackled Oswald."

Mathilde and I exchange glances, neither of us surprised to hear that the sprightly old birds were involved in stopping the altercation.

"It's no wonder you had to fire him," Harry says in a reassuring voice. "A person like that is not fit to work at Oxford... or anywhere."

Kate grimaces. "I agree, but I couldn't bring myself to ruin his career. I tried to put myself in his shoes, imagine how it must have felt to miss out on the opportunity of a lifetime. It took him a while, but he eventually found a new position as the director of the Torture Museum in London."

"A torture museum," Bartie guffaws. "Are you joking?"

"No, although I wish I was," Kate mumbles. Her expression shifts to one of horror as a realisation hits her. "What kind of Eternals are going to emerge from a torture museum?"

Shivers run up my spine. "For certain a crow and who knows what else, all coming our way from the darkest depths of London's brutal history."

Kate shifts uncomfortably in her chair. "I think I know when he discovered the existence of Oxford's magic. The Security office didn't get around to disabling Oswald's badge until the next day. I remember when the team told me. They mentioned Oswald had entered the museum after hours the evening before. We checked, but since nothing appeared to be missing, we let it slide. I figured he came back to pick up his things. But maybe he picked up something more."

My grandfather's face is grave. "Unfettered access to the museum for one night, plus an axe to grind? Was your key in your office, Kate?"

"It was, until a couple of weeks ago, Alfred," Kate admits. "I

LYNN MORRISON

can easily imagine Oswald breaking into my office and rummaging in my drawers. I was so new in the role, I doubt I would have even noticed if my things were disturbed. He could have picked up my key and used it to open my desk, without any idea that he was also unlocking his connection to the magic."

After a moment, Mathilde speaks up, her voice wavering. "What do we do now? Do we interview him like we did with our other suspects?"

This time, no one volunteers. Thankfully, my grandfather offers an alternative approach. "All the evidence shows that our suspect is stretching Oxford's magical borders to extend to London. Hobbes must be the Eternal guiding him. We were thinking of something more subtle. A visit to his torture museum, where one or two of you could have a look around and see if you can find proof that Oxford's magical border ends there."

Mathilde leans forward. "Do you know where his museum is located?"

"Yes," my grandfather replies. "Remember that fish and chip shop flyer you found in Barnard's secret chamber? Beadle's museum is located two blocks away from it."

I grab Edward's hand and give it a quick squeeze to catch his attention. When he looks over, I wiggle my eyebrows in a silent question. I can tell that he wants to say no, but much like me, he quickly recognises that there is no one better for the job.

"We'll go... Nat and I," Edward mumbles, clearly half-hoping someone will say no. Instead, Kate and Mathilde nod their agreement, complimenting us on our thorough investigative skills and reaffirming we're the best pair for the job.

Edward wipes his palm across his face and shrugs. "Looks like we're going to London, Nat."

"We're all three goin' to London," H clarifies. "Iffen you think I'm sendin' you and Nat off to London on your own, you're dead wrong."

Edward looks horrified at the mere thought of it. "Absolutely not!"

As I eye the pair, glaring at one another, both of them as stubborn as mules, I come to a different conclusion.

"That's a great idea, H. It will give you and Edward the perfect opportunity to bond with one another." With that said, I steal the last crisp off Edward's plate and pop it into my mouth.

Chapter Eighteen

I step out of my flat the next morning and am surprised to see my grandfather waiting in the building entryway.

"Good morning, my darling girl," he says with a smile.

"Morning, Grandfather. I wasn't expecting to see you here. Is something wrong?"

"Not at all," he reassures me. "I thought I'd join you and H on your weekend walk to get a coffee. I haven't seen much of you recently, outside of our group meetings. I wanted to check on my favourite granddaughter and see how she is getting on."

"I'm your only granddaughter, but the sentiment is appreciated nonetheless." I finish locking my door and then slide my arm through his as we head out. With my grandfather on my left and H on my right, I can't help but feel that all is good in my world.

Out on the pavement, the cars and buses whiz past us on their way towards the city centre. When we reach a zebra crossing, my grandfather pulls us to a stop. "Do you mind if we walk through Jericho? I know it's a bit longer, but there's no traffic in the neighbourhood."

I cast an eye at H, sure he will be the first to complain about having to walk extra steps, but for once he seems content to enjoy a leisurely stroll. I nod my agreement and moments later, we leave the busy road behind us.

"Mathilde tells me you're having trouble finding a new place to live."

"That's putting it lightly," I mutter. "I've got two weeks left and I'm at a complete dead end. The only places left on such short notice are well beyond my budget or outside of the ring road. I dread the thought of having to buy a car or depend upon the bus."

My grandfather pats my arm in sympathy. "Have you thought about something more permanent?"

"Of course I have," I reply. "It's not like I have any intention of moving elsewhere. What job opportunity could top spending time with you, H and our other Eternals?"

"No job in the world could be better, Nat," H agrees.

"I'd love to buy a house, something I could make entirely my own. I've been saving money while I've been living rent-free at St Margaret. However, given the sky-high cost of Oxford's real estate, I still need another six months to save up a deposit." I blow my hair out of my face, my frustration evident.

"I didn't have a much easier time house-hunting when I first came to Oxford," my grandfather admits. "I was a young man, single, with a steady income. Like yourself, I covered the ground from one end of Oxford to the other, looking at flats and small terraced houses. I was determined to find something near the pub where my mates and I met up. After several months of hunting, I finally settled on a little house, mid-terrace in St Clements. I made an offer and was just about to sign the contract when I met your grandmother."

I arch an eyebrow. "I take it grandmum didn't approve?"

My question makes my grandfather chuckle. "She never even knew about the place. I took one look at her and I fell head over heels. Finding a place with proximity to the local pub no longer topped my wish list. I stayed in my rented lodgings and put all my efforts into convincing her I was the man she was meant to marry. The day after she said yes, I took her to the estate agent's office and let her take the lead on picking out our new home."

His story warms my heart, likely as he intended. "Where did you end up living? Was it the house I visited when I was a toddler? The pretty one in the countryside?"

My grandfather pulls me to a stop and turns, pointing to the house in front of us. "It was this one. This is where your grandmother and I started our life together."

Before us stands an end-of-terrace Edwardian home, with a small garden and drive tucked behind a waist-high iron fence. The bowed front windows immediately remind me of my current flat at St Margaret, which isn't a surprise given that we're only a few streets away. The house is run down, but the bones of it are still there.

I spin around, taking in the surrounding houses that line the quiet street. I imagine a younger version of my dad riding his bicycle up and down the street. With my grandmum's green thumb, the garden was likely a riot of colourful flowers. It looks like an idyllic place to raise a family, a spacious home within a stone's throw of all that Oxford has to offer.

My grandfather recalls my attention to the present time. "The house has four bedrooms, a garage for a car and a garden shed in the back. We thought we'd have more children, but when none came after your father, we turned one bedroom into a study. We had a good life here."

"Why did you move out of it?"

"Once your father left, the house seemed awfully large for two people. Your grandmother decided she wanted to be closer to nature. We bought a little cottage with a big garden. She would potter around all day with her flowers and herbs and I'd bus into the city for work." He stops talking when his voice grows thick, pausing to clear his throat.

I pat his arm, giving him a moment. "It's a lovely home, grandfather. Thanks for showing it to me." I slide my arm back through his, ready to restart our trek to the cafe, but he doesn't budge.

"It's your home, Natalie."

I stumble to a halt, glancing at H to see if he heard the same words I did. "What?"

"This home is your inheritance. It's yours if you want it."

I try and fail to make his words compute. "I don't understand."

"Your grandmother and I never sold this house. We had money saved away, enough to pay for the cottage. We held onto the house, letting it out to young professionals like yourself and providing ourselves with an early retirement income. When your grandmother died, your father helped me sell the cottage so I could move into London to be closer to you."

"But you never sold this house?" I ask again, still unable to believe what he is saying.

"Your father thought it was a good investment. The upkeep was minimal and the rents more than covered any costs."

"But surely Dad must have sold the house at some point. Otherwise, why wouldn't he have mentioned it to me?"

"That's my fault," my grandfather confesses, sounding abashed. "I could see the spark in you, all the making of a future prefect. Before I died, I added an instruction to my Will. I left this house to you but instructed your father not to tell you about it until certain conditions were met."

My eyebrows rise to my hairline. "What conditions?"

"If you turned thirty and were not living in Oxford, he was to pass the deed to you, and let you decide what to do with it."

"And if I moved to Oxford before then?"

"In that case, your father was to give notice to the tenants and then wait one year for you to ask about it. If you didn't ask about the house within a year, he was free after that to tell you about it and leave all other decisions to you."

"But that's mad!" I exclaim. "How on earth did you convince a lawyer to write that into a Will?"

"It was my Will, Nat. You can write any instructions you want, as long as you can get a doctor to confirm you are in your right mind."

I shake my head, boggling at the complexity. "But why the subterfuge? Why not tell me straight away that I have a house sitting here in Oxford, waiting for me?"

My grandfather rests his hands on my shoulders, forcing me to give him my full attention. "I didn't want you to feel pressured to stay here. I wanted you to have a year, free and clear, to discover Oxford's magic and fall in love with the place. I felt you should meet the Eternals and decide for yourself if this is where you want to settle. I left word with an Eternal at the Bodleian to tell you the whole story before the year was up. I didn't know I'd come back as an Eternal myself."

I stare hard, still filled with questions. "What if a prefect role hadn't opened up by the time I reached thirty? How did you know I'd be here before then?"

"Lillian became a prefect before you were born. I could do the math for myself. By the time you were thirty, she would have retired, opening a place for you. If the magic didn't call you to take her place, you wouldn't have any other reason to come to Oxford. You'd be free to sell the house, take the money and buy something wherever you wanted."

I open my mouth, but find I have nothing left to ask. His plan was crazy, but knowing the ins and outs of how Oxford's magic works, I can see how it might make sense. After closing my mouth, I pivot, once again facing the house. The house that I apparently own.

"I own a house in Oxford. An empty house?"

My grandfather's eyes light up when he sees a smile stretch across my face. "It needs a lot of work after so long as a rental. However, there is nothing standing in your way from turning this into the home you dream of owning."

For the rest of the walk to the coffee shop, I pepper my grandfather for details of the house. There is a fireplace in the front room and a window seat in the largest bedroom. After so many years spent living with a flatmate, I cannot imagine how it will feel to have a whole house to myself.

My grandfather gives me instructions on how to bring up the discussion with my dad. Thank goodness Edward, H and I have already planned to go to London tomorrow. I can hardly bring up the conversation by phone and there is no way I could wait.

Eventually my grandfather begs my leave, explaining he has work to do with the Eternals. The last thing he says before he goes is, "Make sure you ask your father about his cousin Harold." And on that curious note, he disappears.

As is our custom, I pop into the coffee shop and collect drinks and breakfast for myself and H. Together, we wander over to a nearby park, laying claim to one of the wooden benches. When we finish eating and H passes me his trash, it dawns on me he is being awfully quiet.

"Something on your mind, H?"

He looks so small, sitting there with his wings tucked into his back and his feet dangling over the edge. "Thinking about your new 'ouse, Nat."

"It's so great, isn't it, H. I can't wait to go tour the inside," I gush, my enthusiasm bubbling out.

"Yeah, you're goin' to love it. It's perfect for you. You'll 'ave a great life there, everythin' you ever wanted."

My mind immediately wanders off, already making plans for the rooms. "I was thinking I could turn one bedroom into a study, like my grandparents did. It would make working from home so much easier. And the furniture! I'll have to buy so many things. I wonder if there is a nice furniture shop in Oxford... Harry will know."

I babble on, finally stopping when I notice the trails of smoke leaking from H's nostrils, something which only happens when he's downtrodden.

"Sounds really great, Nat. I'm lookin' forward to seein' it all when I come over to visit you."

My brow creases in confusion. "Visit me? Where are you going?"

"Dunno," he mumbles, huffing another puff of black smoke. "Guess I can stay in the gardens at St Margaret. Bartie will look after me."

I roll his words over in my mind, trying to make sense of them. "Wait a minute."

H ignores my comment, too busy staring dejectedly at his feet.

I wave a hand in front of his face. "H, look at me. You know you're coming along with me, right? I would never leave you behind. Never ever!"

He looks up at me, his eyes brimming with hope. "Really, Nat? But I thought... Your grandda and Lillian both left me behind when they moved into a family 'ome."

"Oh H!" I cry, sliding over to snuggle him next to me. "This whole time, you've been thinking I was moving out without you? Did you not notice I was only looking at places that allowed pets?"

"You were?" His head pops up in surprise.

"If my grandfather hadn't shown up today with his incredible news, you and I were likely going to be the newest residents of the Headington Shark House."

"Blech!" H says, pulling a face. "The only fish I like are the ones I get to eat."

I give H's scaly head a good scratch. "Ever since I was a little girl listening to my grandfather's stories, I've been dreaming of having a wyvern for a best friend. Now I'm finally here, living a life which is richer than any I could have ever imagined." I slide my hand under his snout, forcing him to look me in the eye. "You and I are family, H. Where I go, you go. My family home could never be complete if you weren't living in it."

H grins, but it quickly fades, replaced by a worried expression. "What about Edward?"

I lean back against the bench, pondering the question. "Yes, Edward... this news certainly changes the dynamics of our discussions about living arrangements."

H tugs on my sleeve. "I can be nicer to 'im. Make more of an effort. I know 'e is important to you."

"He is, but so are you. If he's equally willing to make things right with you, then maybe he can join us, too."

Our beautiful Saturday morning disappears behind a dark cloud and a steady downpour. H and I, however, don't mind the weather change. We're happily tucked away inside our flat at St Margaret, browsing the internet for new furniture and decor inspiration.

"What do you think of this one, H?" I ask, tilting my laptop screen so he can see it.

"A cream-coloured sofa? You really think that's a good idea?" He waves a chocolate-covered talon to emphasise his point.

I revise my search criteria and start scrolling when a knock sounds at the door. "Are you expecting someone?" I ask H. He shakes his head, looking bewildered.

It takes me a moment to untangle myself from my blanket on the sofa, long enough for the person knocking to rap again. I pull open the door to find Edward standing in the hall, barely visible behind the large gift-wrapped box in his arms.

"Oh, hi! Do you want to come in? That looks heavy." I hold the door open wide as he navigates through it. "Is that for me?"

"Erm, no," Edward mumbles. "It's actually for H. Is he here?"

H pops up from his seat on the sofa, flying over to hover above the box. "For me?" When Edward nods, H eyes the box skeptically. He circles above it before descending close enough to put an ear to against the top of it.

"What are you doing?" I ask.

"After all the time we've spent at the Ash, walkin' past the Greek statues, I want to make sure this isn't one of them Trojan 'orse situations." H lifts the box by the ribbon and gives it a good shake. Something heavy jostles inside, but what it is remains a mystery.

"It's not a Trojan Horse, H," Edward grumbles, rolling his eyes. He catches himself midway through, huffs out a breath and tries again. "It's a gift, from me to you. It's safe, I promise."

Annoyed, I grab the box and drag it closer to the sofa and tell H and Edward to have a seat. If they're going to stare suspiciously at one another, we might as well be comfortable. "Open it, H. If not, I'm going to lay claim to whatever is inside."

H raises a talon and slides it along the paper and ribbon to reveal a cardboard shipping box. He carefully slices through the taped sides and across the middle, and then opens the flaps.

The first thing I see is a dark, furry mass. Slightly worried and definitely confused, I lean over and help H pull the item from the box. Together, we tug it loose and set it on top of the coffee table.

I peer at the furry item. It takes me a moment to figure out what it is. "It's a cat bed!" I run my hands across the plush faux fur lining. "A really nice cat bed. This must have cost you a fortune, Edward."

Edward demurs, "Turn it around so you can see the front."

H flaps over to land at my side and we spin the cat bed so that the lowered side is facing us. H stares at it, then looks up at Edward, moving his head back and forth between the two. "It's got my name and a picture of a wyvern embroidered on the side," he says, his voice rough with emotion.

Edward shifts in his chair as he watches H's emotional reaction to the gift. "I thought we could keep it upstairs, in my front room."

Both H and I lift our heads to look at Edward, sure we must have misheard.

"It's a peace offering and an invitation. To you both, really." Edward takes my hand. "I don't want you to move across town and live in the shark house. I know H is important to you, and there is no way you'll go somewhere that he isn't welcome. I want you... both of you... to move upstairs with me."

I open my mouth to speak, but Edward holds up a finger. "Don't say no straightaway. At least think about it."

As lovely as the sentiment is, I can't help but wonder what brought on the sudden change. I narrow my eyes and ask, "Have you been talking to Mathilde?"

"No," Edward replies. "I've been talking to you. You've been telling me all this time what was important, but I was too busy being an arse to listen. It sounds ridiculous when I say it, but I was jealous of H and his connection with you and the magic. I didn't even realise how juvenile I was acting. I should never have treated H as nothing more than a pet."

"But you bought him a cat bed?" I raise my eyebrows, trying to square his words with his actions.

"I got H furniture." Edward turns. "H, I want you to know you are always welcome. You will always have a place. Hopefully, so will I." Edward turns his attention back to me. "You've been clear that there is space enough for us both. I was too stubborn to listen, but the thought of you moving away forced me to do some soul-searching."

I glance at H, unsure how to answer. "It's lovely, Edward. All of it — the gift for H and your heartfelt words. I want to say yes, but... well, we already have a house."

Edward's eyes grow wide. "Back out of the lease, Nat. If it costs you your deposit, I'll pay you back. It's my fault, anyway. I shouldn't have been so stubborn."

"No," I blurt without thinking, and I have to stop Edward from rising to his feet. "It isn't a lease. I own a house, a rather large one, a few streets from here."

Edward shakes his head, unable to make sense of my words. I explain about my grandfather's surprise visit this morning, our walk through the neighbourhood and his revelation that he left me the family home in Oxford. Soon enough, H and I are animatedly showing Edward the websites we've bookmarked and the paint colours we've selected.

Edward lets us carry on, nodding at the appropriate points, but his expression shifts from hopeful to stoic. When we run out of plans to share, Edward swallows and carefully picks his words. "That sounds amazing, Nat. Incredible, really." He nudges the cat bed. "I guess this can be a housewarming present instead."

He rises to his feet and stands awkwardly. "You and H are clearly busy with your planning. I'll leave you to it. Congrats on the house. At least you'll be close by, right?"

Before I can answer, H flies up from the sofa, landing on the back of Edward's chair. "You know, Edward... the 'ouse is plenty big. You could come along with us... iffen you wanted."

Edward freezes in place, his eyes focused on the floor.

"I was going to tell you all about it tonight over dinner," I add. "You beat me to it. I know it's a lot. You'd have to give up your flat here. It would be a big commitment."

Edward lifts his head, his expression unreadable. "Are you asking me to move in with you?"

"Yes, I guess I am." I stand up and move to stand in front of him. H nods his agreement, sending a stream of smoke curling from his nostrils.

I take Edward's hands in mine, look him in the eye and say, "Edward Thomas, will you move in with me?"

Edward answers me with a kiss deep enough to make my toes curl and to send H hiding his eyes beneath his wing.

Chapter Nineteen

W e're barely in our seats on a late Sunday morning train to London when H fights his way out of the large shopping bag I've hidden him in and tumbles across the carriage floor.

"Did you 'ave to stuff me in a bag, Nat?" H grumbles as he dusts himself off.

"We've been through this, H. Here in Oxford, the magic convinces people to accept all your crazy antics as completely normal. Once we get outside of Oxford's magical border, that won't be the case. Carrying you around in a big bag was the only solution I could throw together quickly. Would you have preferred a cat carrier?"

H shivers at the thought and then flies up onto the table, sitting on it to face me and Edward. Our train carriage is still parked at the station, practically empty, and fingers crossed, it will remain that way for the rest of our trip. I can't imagine bringing a magical wyvern onto a commuter-filled train.

"I don't know how long you'll be able to talk to us before you turn into a cat, H. Let's go over the plan one more time," I suggest as I distribute muffins and cheese croissants from the bakery bag. "When we get to Marylebone station, we'll switch to the Underground and head over to the neighbourhood where Beadle's museum is located. Once there, we should be able to see the real you — the wyvern you — because if our theory is right, Beadle has stretched Oxford's magic to include the museum."

"I've got a question," Edward says as he adds sugar to his coffee. "If Beadle has extended the magic all the way to London, why do you think H will get stuck in his cat form?"

"Think of it like a balloon, Edward. If you grab the tied end and stretch it out, what happens?"

Edward thinks for a second. "The oval shape gets distorted... oh, I get it. There is a band of magic stretching from Oxford to London, but it probably doesn't exactly match with the train line." He rubs his chin, adding, "I would guess it is pretty narrow as well. Now I see why you insisted on the bag, even if it isn't H's ideal mode of transportation."

"You can say that again, Edward," H mutters as he stretches his wings wide.

"I'm still undecided on whether you should come into the museum with us or wait outside, keeping watch." I eyeball H. "Do you have a preference?"

"I'm comin' in with you. We need to know exactly what we're up against. I'll be more use as an extra pair of eyes inside."

The carriage rumbles, signalling our departure from Oxford's central station. We relax into our seats, getting comfortable for the trip, which should be a little over an hour-long. Edward pulls a college newsletter out of his coat pocket. I entertain myself by watching the neighbourhoods blur past my window. When we stop at Oxford Parkway station, I keep a close eye on H, but for once, he behaves. I return to my new pastime, this time engrossed in spotting cows and sheep in the fields outside of Oxford.

"Oi, Nat!" H calls out. "Did you see that miaow?"

"Huh?" I shift my attention back to the table to find a black cat with white markings sitting where H had been. I whisper, "H?"

"Miaow. Miaaoowwww." H-the-cat paws the air and gives his whiskers a frustrated twitch.

Edward taps me on the hand, motioning to the other person in the carriage. The man is shifting around in his seat, trying to figure out where the cat noises are coming from.

"Hush, H. The magic isn't working. Someone is going to notice you." I worry as the train slows for the next station. "Sit in my lap and try to keep quiet!"

Edward and I exchange worried glances as a few more people enter the carriage. I unbutton my jacket and tuck H inside of it, relieved that his cat form is smaller than his wyvern one. Without the wings and ever-present threat of fire-breaths, H the cat is a lovely little cuddle buddy. I stroke his head as the carriage rocks back and forth, speeding its way to London.

H flickers back and forth several times on the trip as the train crisscrosses the magical boundary. Every time, he can barely get a word out before he blips back into his cat form. It is beyond bizarre to watch it happen. One moment he is an aggravated wyvern with fire shooting out of his mouth, the next he is a black cat grooming its face with a little paw.

All those times I wondered what the average person saw when they looked at H. Now I know and I wish I didn't. It must be terrible for him to be stuck in an animal's body, unable to communicate with us.

Finally, we arrive in Marylebone, the train announcer reminding us to gather our things and dispose of our trash before we leave. I coax H in cat form into the bag, promising to buy him a lifetime supply of his favourite Lincolnshire poacher cheese in repayment for the indignities this trip has forced upon him.

The station is full of departing and arriving passengers, causing a crush of people at the ticket gates. Edward shoulders the shopping bag and tucks it close against him with the suggestion, "You take the lead, and I'll keep H safe until we get onto the Underground."

I sigh in relief before squaring my shoulders and shoving my way through the crowd. For a country known for its love of the queue, for some bizarre reason, the order always transforms into mayhem at the ticket barriers.

We descend below ground on a giant escalator, one which I'm sure H would find endlessly fun. But the poor thing is trapped in a bag, his furry black head barely peeking over the edge. He loses interest as we cross through winding hallways, disappearing into the bag's depths.

Signs fill the platform, reminding us to *mind the gap*. I shudder at the thought of losing track of H down here. "Keep a tight hold of the bag, Edward," I command, not that Edward needs the reminder. His knuckles are white from the death grip he has on the strap. The underground arrives with a gust of wind that sends the bag swinging, nearly causing us all to have a heart attack. When the doors open, Edward and I stumble inside and collapse onto the hard plastic bench.

We don't get comfortable since we have to switch lines at Baker Street, which is the next stop. As we navigate the maze of platforms, searching for the Jubilee line, a burst of fire burns a hole in the bag, releasing H the wyvern. "Don't move!" I shout at Edward, stopping him in his tracks. "We don't know how much the magic covers here. You need to stay there long enough for the magic to repair the shopping bag."

To my dismay, H flies off, turning somersaults in the air. His excitement at being back to normal is overwhelming. "I'm freeeee!" he shouts, darting off, weaving his way between the line of columns dotted along the hallway. He's nearly out of sight when I hear a thud followed by a loud hiss and a worrisome miaow.

Edward and I lock eyes. He pushes me forward. "I've got the bag, you get H!"

So far from Oxford, the magical area is barely wide enough to cover the hallway, as H apparently discovered when he tried to leap onto an escalator. He had tumbled to the ground a few meters short of the first step, and that's where I had found him, sitting on his hind legs, practically spitting with frustration.

I scratch his ears as we wait for Edward to catch up, whispering, "Please behave yourself. We'll be at the Torture Museum in less than twenty minutes." When he hisses at me, I add, "I'll take you to that fish and chip shop."

Inside the Jubilee line train, Edward abandons his efforts to keep H inside the bag. As the train makes its way across London, crossing in and out of the magic's field, I watch with disbelief as my view alternates between a cat pretending to chase a mouse and a wyvern boomeranging around the poles in the aisles.

Any doubts I had about our suspect's London location dissipate when we arrive at the station nearest the Torture Museum. No longer flickering between forms, H the wyvern flies by my side as we climb the stairs and step onto a busy London street. The realisation of what we are about to do hits us all when the museum sign comes into view.

Looking fiercely determined, H mutters, "'Ere goes nothin'!"

"Hold on there, mate," I shout, grabbing his leg before he can fly off. "You can't go flying in there, hollering and making demands. This is supposed to be a reconnaissance mission."

Edward holds out the bag, giving H a look of sympathy. H

huffs a cloud of angry smoke and then flies above it, tucks his wings in tight and drops into it, nearly sending Edward stumbling.

"None of us have been here before," I remind them. "Our aim is to scope out the museum's exhibits to see if we spot any of Oxford's missing artwork and antiques. While we're doing so, we'll also have a chance to build an idea of what sort of Eternals might live there."

Edward tugs the bag up onto his shoulder, moving his arm so H can peer over the top of it.

"That won't work." I back up a step, considering our options. "H, can you use a talon to make two eye-sized holes in the side here? If so, you can look around without anyone spotting you."

H does as I ask, seeming content with the solution. Well, he's as content as he can be, given he's stuffed inside a large shopping tote. I do a quick last check and then declare us ready. There's no line at the ticket window, so we're inside within minutes. I elbow Edward as we enter, nodding my head towards the welcome poster.

It isn't the text which caught my eye, but the photograph on it. The man in the photo is sallow faced, his eyes squinting, and his mouth pulled back in a sneer. His dark hair is carefully combed over to disguise his bald spot. One might mistake him for a character in the museum except for the label sitting below it which reads *Oswald Beadle, Museum Director*.

"He looks like a cross between Professor Snape and Dr Evil. Which I guess is appropriate," I admit in a whisper. "I wouldn't expect him to be here, given it is a Sunday, but keep an eye out just in case. We do *not* want to bump into him."

We follow the hall into the first gallery. It takes my eyes a moment to adjust to the dim lighting. The walls are painted a deep grey colour, only a shade or two lighter than pure black. Red overhead lighting gives the room an eerie cast while spotlights shine on the exhibits. It is all I can do to control my shudder.

The torture devices alone would be horrible enough, but the museum has gone out of its way to remind visitors of exactly how they were used.

A male mannequin is stretched across the rack, his face moulded into an expression of perpetual pain. Nearby, another stuffed dummy is strapped into an old-fashioned electric chair, its head dropped to its chest so we can better see the metal cap and wires strapped on top of it.

Further ahead, the museum proves itself to be equal opportunity. Edward, H and I stop in front of a brightly lit scene of a medieval town. Two well-dressed medieval men look on as a woman, clothing in tatters, stands atop a burning pyre.

"Witches burning at the stake," I read from the nearby sign. "The background track with her screaming is a bit much, don't you think?"

Edward grimaces and takes me by the hand, pulling me away from the horror show. When a museum guide points us to the next room, it is almost a relief. Instead of reenactments, it is lined with glass display cases, filled with smaller torture instruments used throughout history. There are knives of every sort imaginable, tongs, scourges, and even nail-pullers.

We carry on into the third gallery to discover it is designed to look exactly like a medieval torture chamber. Animated dolls dressed as masked men, grinning fools, screaming subjects and villainous women bring the scene to life. I'm ready to move on as soon as we enter the room, but Edward drags his heels, scanning every inch of the scene.

"Look in the corner over there," he says under his breath, pointing across the room. "Can you see the edge of the painting sticking out from behind the desk?"

I slide over a couple of steps to get a better view. "Is that Iffley College's missing portrait? I can only see part of it, but it looks similar."

Edward nods and then draws my attention to other parts of the display. "The scales on the table look very similar to the ones Mathilde found at Barnard, they could easily be part of the same collection. And the little statues above the fireplace are identical to the ones stolen from the Ashmolean archives."

H pokes a talon through the bag, enlarging the eyeholes so he can get a better look. "The bloody tosser 'as 'idden it all in plain sight!"

"Let's get out of here," I groan. "I hope to goodness that nothing in here is an Eternal. I've seen enough to give me nightmares for a week."

"We can't go without photos. Kate and Mathilde will definitely want to have a look." Edward forces me to pose in front of the display, pretending to smile for the camera while he zooms in on the items of interest.

"Two rooms left," I say, looking at the pamphlet we picked up at the ticket office. We walk under a blood red curtain, entering a small movie theatre with a flickering black and white video showing on the screen. We don't even pause long enough to see what it is showing, hurrying past a group of teenage boys staring at the screens with their mouths hanging open.

The last room is blessedly free of torture devices. Life-size posters are dotted around the room, providing a virtual walk through famous faces from this history of torture and mayhem. We weave through them, slipping past the tourists who have willingly chosen to visit the place. I make a snide remark, but Edward quickly points out a truth. "It is important that people see it for what it is. Those who don't know history are doomed to repeat it, Nat."

One last monument to torture and death stands in the back of the room near the exit. Its golden surface shines under a perfectly positioned spotlight. I stumble to a halt before it, staring aghast.

Wings swept wide, the giant golden crow stands guard over a

pile of bones. Its beady, ebony eyes glitter with the promise of malevolence. Although it shows no signs of life, it sends a shiver down my spine.

Edward tightens his grip on the shopping tote, making sure H is safe inside. "Now I know why they call a group of crows a *murder*."

❖

After a subdued lunch of fish and chips at a nearby shop, we attempt to cheer ourselves up by proposing to take H on a tour of London.

"What do you mean you've never been to London?" Edward asks, looking scandalised. "You're four hundred years old."

"He was a gargoyle at the Bodleian for the first three hundred of those years," I remind Edward.

H throws his hands in the air. "And besides that, until recently, the magic of Oxford didn't reach London. Who was goin' to bring a cat on a tour of London?"

"Apparently, we are," Edward mutters, eyeing the shopping bag. "What do you want to do, H? Shall we stick to areas where you can be your wyvern self, or do you want to pack in as much as we can?"

H scoffs a chip as he considers the question. "Iffen we can work out a way for you two to understand me, even a little, I think I'd like to see as much as I can."

That's how Edward and I end up taking a small black cat (and sometimes wyvern) on a double-decker bus tour of London. We motor past Big Ben and the Houses of Parliament, circle around Piccadilly Circus, hop off at Hyde Park to stretch our legs and finish our day watching the changing of the guard at Buckingham Palace.

When my phone alarm signals it's time to proceed to my

parents' house for dinner, no one complains. We're all three tired and hungry, and the promise of a home-cooked Sunday roast proves irresistible. We pile into one of London's iconic black cabs and hurry over to avoid being late.

"Hullo darling," my mother greets me with a double kiss when I come in through the door. "How lovely that you brought Edward along... and the cat? You carried a cat into London?" She backs up a step, looking at me as though I've gone mad.

"What can I say? He's my baby!" I gush, waving behind my back for Edward to carry H into the front room and put him on the sofa to nap. I spin my mother towards the kitchen with an offer to help finish preparing the meal, hoping she'll forget about the strangeness of us carrying a cat around town in a shopping bag. Meanwhile, Edward wanders off to find my dad in his study.

Together, my mother and I carry dish after dish to the dining table. There is roasted chicken with a side of potatoes, mixed vegetables, gravy, and piping hot Yorkshire puddings. When my mother returns to the kitchen to get the drinks, I put together a plate for H and sneak it into the front room.

Eventually, my parents, Edward, and I seat ourselves, chatting merrily as we pass around the food. My mum is eager for an update on my plans for the Ashmolean exhibition grand opening. She beams with pleasure when I announce that I've set aside tickets for her and my dad to attend. It's a rare exception that they get to experience one of my events, as I rarely get the chance to add to the guest list.

I pop out to check on H when my mother mentions dessert, finding him curled up on the sofa, blissfully full, warm, and asleep.

Over coffee, my father asks, "How is your flat search progressing, Nat? Any luck?"

"Funny you should ask that," I say. "The short answer is no, none. However, visiting potential houses has given me plenty of opportunity to widen my knowledge of Oxford. It made me wonder... which part of Oxford did you grow up in, Dad?"

My dad gets that faraway look in his eyes as he casts his mind back to his youth. "Not too far from St Margaret, actually. My friends and I would ride our bikes over to Port Meadow and go swimming in the Thames in the summer. It's still a great neighbourhood, from what I hear."

"Yes, it is. I'd love to find a flat in the area, or, better yet, buy a place. But it is so expensive." I pick up my coffee mug and hold it in front of my mouth to cover my smile. "Whatever happened to my grandparents' house? Did they sell it?"

My father sits up straighter, suddenly paying more attention. "Not exactly... your grandfather sold the garden cottage you used to visit when you were little. The Oxford house, however..." his voice trails off as he shifts in his chair.

I pretend to be confused. "Don't tell me you held onto it? For all these years?"

"I wasn't trying to hide it from you, dear," my father clarifies, looking to my mother for help.

"What your father is trying to say, Nat, is that he's been holding onto the house for you."

Edward and I pull on our best shocked expressions. "What?" "How?"

My father grumbles under his breath, the words hardly audible although I pick out my grandfather's name. "Your mother and I both wanted to tell you when you took the job at Oxford, but my father insisted on a ridiculous set of constraints before we could do so. If you'd mentioned anything about buying a place, I would have told you sooner. As it was, I've been sitting uncomfortably on the information for six months now."

My poor parents look so distressed that I rush to reassure them I'm not angry. Edward and I take turns asking questions about the house, the location, its condition, and availability. My father disappears into his study, returning with the contact information for the estate agency which has been managing the property over the years. To my amusement, it is the same agency which managed the dream flat I lost out on in Summertown. Perhaps Oxford's magic was at work even then.

Genuinely excited, I rush over and give both my parents a tight hug, thanking them for taking such great care of the house over the years so that it could one day be mine. I make my mother promise to help me pick out furniture and drapes, knowing she'll enjoy it as much as I will.

With that matter settled, I turn my attention to my grandfather's parting instructions.

"Dad, whatever happened to your cousin Harold? I was telling Edward about our family and it dawned on me that I had no idea what he is doing now. Is he still working for the BBC?"

"Harold? You know, I bumped into him last week at a charity golf event. He's gone freelance and is directing a mini-series."

I glance at Edward, but he gives me a subtle shake of his head, no clearer than I am at why my grandfather would suggest I bring Harold up.

"What kind of mini-series? Something I'll recognise?"

"Eh? One of those period dramas which are so popular now. I think he mentioned the Great Fire of London."

My head snaps up. "Great Fire? The event itself or the rebuilding afterwards? Pepys or Wren?"

My father waves a hand, somewhat dismissing the question. "Wren maybe? I wasn't paying close attention. He said something about scouting locations in Oxford for an episode. I told him to look you up while he's there. Maybe he'll get in touch and you can ask him yourself."

A film about Sir Christopher Wren, shot in Oxford, and I have a family connection to the production?

Now I know why my grandfather dropped Harold's name. He

and the other Eternals must know that such an event would provide a tantalising lure for Beadle and his ancestor, Thomas Hobbes. There's no way they'll stand by while Wren, Wilkins and the rest of the group gain more glory.

If we play our cards right, this might be just the thing we need to catch Oswald Beadle, once and for all.

Chapter Twenty

It's the evening of the grand opening of the Ashmolean's new exhibition. After our trip to London a few weeks ago, time has flown by in a flurry of planning and preparation. I barely found time to move my belongings from St Margaret College to my new house. Now that the event is finally here, all that I have left to do is to be thankful the weather cooperated.

As I stand in front of the building, I can't help but admire how lovely it looks with its towering line of columns lit up with bright spotlights. An enormous banner stretches between the middle two, announcing the opening of the museum's new display. "Barnard College: Three Hundred Years of Hidden Secrets," I mumble under my breath, still hardly able to believe how much has happened since Mathilde and I stumbled across the open door to the secret chamber hidden in Barnard College's old library. This event to display the chamber's priceless contents feels surreal.

Satisfied with how everything looks, I stride down the front steps to wait on the pavement for my parents to arrive. They texted as soon as their train pulled into the station and should be here any minute. It isn't easy to keep the existence of Oxford's magic a secret from them, particularly the truth about my grandfather's return as a ghost. It almost slips out of my mouth all the time. Getting to share this evening with them, showing some of the wonders we uncovered at Barnard, is likely to be as close as I can come. To say that I am excited is an understatement.

I feel a tingle of nerves as a black cab pulls to a stop at the kerb. My father is the first to step out, waiting to hold the door open for my mother before coming over to say hello.

My mother pulls me into a warm embrace, brushing a kiss of hello against my cheek, and then steps back to inspect me. "You look wonderful, Nat. Oxford life certainly agrees with you."

"You look lovely too, mum!" I hug my father. "Shall we head inside? I cannot wait to show you what we've done."

At the front entrance, I introduce my parents to Jill, who is standing at the door, checking guests off the attendee list. My mother showers her in praise. "Natalie tells me you are responsible for the incredible illustration on the event invitations. You have an exceptional talent."

Jill blushes with well-deserved pride and waves us inside. "Will is getting ready to make his welcome speech and let the next group into the exhibition. If you hurry up, you can join in."

Once indoors, we join the ten other people waiting in a curtained lobby. Will stands in front, beside a giant wooden display. Taking great care, he designed and built it to be an exact — if oversized — replica of the library wall where the doorway to the secret chamber was discovered. To add an air of authenticity, there is a wooden backdrop painted to look like the library shelves positioned behind him.

He clears his throat, and a hush falls over the group.

"For three hundred years, a treasure trove of journals, books, artefacts, and paintings lay hidden inside a secret chamber, tucked within the walls of Barnard College's Old Library. For the first time, we are pleased to invite you to see inside." Will pauses to make sure he has everyone's attention. I glance over to see my parents staring raptly. "The items on display offer you a behind-the-scenes look at the imagination and explorations of some of Oxford's greatest minds in history. Although these particular items were hidden away for centuries, the knowledge itself was not lost. As you journey through the collection, you will have a chance to see for yourself how these works continue to influence today's innovations."

We all watch as he gives a gentle tap on the wooden door, causing it to spring open. He slides around to pull it wide, welcoming our group inside. My parents and I hang back, completing another round of introductions and effusive praise about the well-executed back drop. As my mother passes through the doorway, I hear her whisper to my father that she feels like Alice Through the Looking Glass and it makes me smile. Perfect!

As agreed during our planning session, we hung long curtains around the main entrance, directing our guests straight into the airy atrium where we've temporarily placed all the special exhibit items. Over the weekend, the staff will relocate them into the dedicated special exhibition room, but for tonight's event, the glass cases are dotted around in the open space.

I had originally envisioned turning Jill's illustration into signage, but she had a better idea. In the centre of the atrium, not far from the bottom of the winding staircase, sits a gigantic tree formed of wire and twinkling fairy lights. Guests watching the video screen placed in front of it are treated to footage of the real secret chamber and biographies of the famous intellectuals and artists whose work is featured in the exhibition.

From there, the fairy lights soar above our heads, creating a canopy of glittering arches, connecting all the display areas together. I guide my parents to the nearest one, where Edward is listening to the special guest speaker.

On the raised dais, one of the university's Architecture professors explains how Sir Christopher Wren took the known principles of architecture of his time and reimagined them time and again, to rebuild London following the great fire. The speaker captivates the audience, interjecting jokes and personal anecdotes as she explains how Wren's work, and specific items such as the early sketches discovered in Barnard's secret chamber, still inspire the students in her department.

The whole speech lasts no more than five minutes, freeing up the group to move on to another area within the room. Thanks to Mathilde's connections with the various departments, we've got physics, biology, mathematics, art and even medicine represented. The departments jumped at the chance to be involved in the event, recognising it as both an opportunity to showcase Oxford's legacy and a chance to connect with potential benefactors.

It takes us over an hour to visit all the display stations, stopping along the way for a glass of prosecco and to say hello to people I know. The interim Master of Barnard College gives me a warm hug. Kate frees herself long enough to pop over for a quick greeting. As the Director of the Ashmolean, she's expected to spend the evening chatting with all the high-profile guests. Every time I've seen her, she's been deep in conversation with someone new.

My parents are suitably impressed to make her acquaintance. Although I've mentioned Mathilde and Kate before, I don't think my parents realised how close our friendship is until tonight. My mother has always worried about whether I have a lovely group of friends around me.

"Terribly good event, Ms Underhill," my father says. "You must be happy with how it has turned out."

"I couldn't be more delighted," she replies with a smile. "Not that I ever had a moment of doubt. Knowing Nat's brilliance at organising events, and Mathilde's knowledge of the history and significance of the exhibition items, it was destined to be a success."

"Don't downplay your own role," I remind her. "You and Mathilde spent days at Barnard College identifying and cataloguing the items, some of which had never been seen before. This was definitely a team effort."

Kate's smile grows larger, her eyes twinkling as she gives me a nod. We hear someone calling her name, but before she goes, she adds one last remark. "Our trio can accomplish anything we put our minds to, and heaven help anyone who dares to stand in our way."

After a while I have to tear myself from my parents' side, leaving them in Edward's good hands. There are catering problems to resolve, misplaced coats in the coatroom, and other small hassles that always happen at events. With all my years of experience, I'd be more concerned if everything went perfectly.

I'm on my way back to the main atrium when I spot my father standing alone in one of the nearby galleries. "Have you got lost?" I call out. "Or has mum gone missing?"

My father twists around in surprise and then smiles when he sees it is me. "Your mum and Harry were deep into a conversation, so I thought I'd wander off on my own and look at the other open areas of the museum."

I glance at the nearest display. "I did not know you were interested in ancient African artwork."

"Neither did I," he says with a laugh. "Something compelled me to enter this room, so I came over to investigate."

"Something called to you, you say," I mumble, stepping away

from his side to cast my gaze around the room. Sure enough, I spot my grandfather standing, half-hidden, behind a nearby statue. I catch him wiping a tear from his eye before he sees me and quickly straightens up. Checking first to make sure my father is still focused on the display case, I subtly motion for my grandfather to come and join us. His eyes light up with happiness as he glides over to stand with us.

After a moment of silence, my father speaks up, his voice gruff. "Before you moved up here, I hadn't been back to Oxford for years. I thought maybe I'd outgrown the town of my youth, but I think the truth is that I wasn't ready to face it without my parents here."

I give my father a gentle pat on his arm. He takes a deep breath and turns to face me, his eyes bright with wetness. "Thank you for giving me a good reason to come back here. I worried for so long that coming here would make me feel the loss of my parents all over again. Instead, I somehow feel more connected to them than ever."

I throw my arms around my dad, squeezing him tight to hold back my own tears. My grandfather adds his arms to mine, letting me convey his love for his son on his behalf.

Thankfully, my mother and Harry enter the room, saving all of us from becoming blubbering messes. My dad and I exchange smiles as we pull apart and head off to rejoin the group, leaving my grandfather beaming with pride.

Before long, Edward and I escort my parents outside to a waiting taxi. The event is drawing to a close and they have a train to London to catch. We say our goodbyes, promising to meet up again next weekend for a furniture shopping expedition.

Taking advantage of our quiet moment together, Edward asks, "Did you notice that DCI Robinson was here?"

"I didn't see him, but I'm not surprised. Kate sent him a personal invitation."

Edward's eyebrows shoot up. "Really? Why did she do that? I wouldn't expect you, Mathilde, or Kate to be in his fan club."

I stop a few steps shy of the museum entrance. "I will admit that we've had our moments, but he did clear Francie of all charges. He was in a no-win situation. How could he have imagined that a magical crow committed the crime?"

Edward looks impressed by my explanation. "Yes, I can sympathise with him better than most. A few months ago, I was standing in his shoes."

"Exactly," I affirm. "If we want to bring Beadle to justice, we will need DCI Robinson to be on our side. I'm glad he accepted the invitation for the olive branch that it was. Did he give you any update on the investigation? It's been a few weeks since we showed him the interior footage."

"He did," Edward confirms. "The investigation uncovered that Andrei made several large cash deposits into his bank account, starting from a month before the fire."

"Around the same time he started dating Francie."

Edward cannot disguise the disgust on his face. "DCI Robinson believes Andrei used Francie as a cover-up, hiding stolen items in her flat so he could shift the blame in her direction. When the police reviewed more of the museum footage from the weeks prior to the fire, they discovered Andrei had been sneaking artefacts out during his night shifts."

"I'm relieved the investigation exonerated Francie completely." I spy Jill through the glass door, waving her hand to get my attention. "I need to help Jill wrap things up. Do you mind sticking around until we're done? I haven't seen H or Xavvie in hours and I may need help to look for them after everyone leaves."

"Of course I will," Edward promises, sealing it with a kiss. "I'll find Kate and Bartie to see if they can stay as well. Those two could be anywhere inside the museum." Edward checks his watch and adds, "We'll regroup under the big tree display in an hour."

I work as fast as I can over the next hour. With Jill and Will's help, it doesn't take us too long to send the last of our guests on their way. When the caterers and the A/V specialists pack up their last box, I tell my assistants I will stick around, passing them each a plate of desserts to carry home with them as they leave.

Back in the atrium, the towering wire tree still twinkles. Edward, Bartie, Kate and Xavvie are standing underneath its branches, looking decidedly worried.

"Where's H?" I ask, with a nervous feeling in my stomach.

"We were playing hide and seek," Xavvie admits, wringing his hands. "I've been hunting for H for ages, but I can't find him anywhere."

"Did you try shouting for him?" Bartie asks sensibly.

"But of course I did!" Xavvie replies, aghast. "I'm worried about the little beast. It isn't like him to disappear for so long. What if he is hurt?"

I look around at everyone, both exhaustion and concern clear on their faces. "We can't leave him here over the weekend, especially not if there is a chance he's hurt. Shall we split up, each taking a different part of the museum?"

Everyone nods their agreement and we divvy up the floors amongst us. Kate and Bartie take the basement, promising to stop by the security office to let them know we're hunting a stray cat. Xavvie offers to search the main floor. Edward volunteers us to start on the first floor. If we still can't find him, we'll all meet again and search the rest together.

Our plan in place, Edward and I climb the nearby flight of stairs, pausing for a moment at the top. From here, the view of the twinkling fairy lights is breathtaking. The tree branches twist and turn around one another before exploding across the room, sending rays of light to every corner.

I wrap my arm around Edward, leaning my head against his shoulder for a second of rest. "If we could see Oxford's magic, I bet it would look something like this."

As beautiful as the scene is, my worry about H takes precedence. I pull myself away from Edward's warm embrace and walk into the nearest gallery. "You take the left side of the room and I'll take the right."

We weave through the maze of galleries, calling out H's name and checking in every alcove, ceramic jug, 3-D model and display case. I make a last-ditch plea, cupping my hands together to make my voice carry across several rooms. "Aiitchh! My feet are killing me in these heels. If you're up here, please take pity on me and come out." We stand in silence, listening for the slightest sound. Nothing.

"I give up," I moan, feeling dejected.

"Maybe one of the others found him," Edward says, reminding me there is still hope. At the top of the stairwell, I slip my heels off, opting to pad around in my tights rather than risk another blister.

Xavvie, Kate and Bartie soon join us, all professing to have had the same poor luck.

"H is a trickster at heart, but he isn't mean-spirited. He'd never hide from us for this long. I'm really worried something bad has happened." I catch myself biting my fingernail, a sure sign of my nerves.

Kate straightens her shoulders with a determined look on her face. "We've covered most of the museum already, but there are plenty of hiding spots on the top two floors. I say we go all the way to the top and work our way back down again."

Kate looks at my stocking-covered feet and then leads us to the lift. We pile in and ride in silence until we reach the top. Room after room, we search in vain. Xavvie points out H's favourite hiding spots, but it's no help. They are all empty. Our heads are hanging as we reenter the lift and press the button for the second floor.

"He has to be here," I whisper to myself as we step out. The Renaissance galleries offer few hiding spaces. We check every case in the silver and ceramics galleries, but it is no hope. A scaly black wyvern would be immediately visible amidst the polished metal and gleaming white collections.

"Where could a wyvern go unnoticed?" I ask the group.

"We haven't searched the East Asian galleries yet!" Kate replies helpfully. "They are full of ebony statues and carved wood and would be a great place to hide."

With a surge of energy, we speed across the second floor until we spot the intricately beaded samurai suit which caught my eye on one of my first days at the museum.

"Nat, you and I can search this room," Kate instructs, turning to the men. "Xavvie, Edward, and Bartie, you three take the next."

I'm halfway through searching the room when I hear Edward shout, "I've found him! Over here!"

Aching feet forgotten, Kate and I practically sprint into the next room.

Edward, Bartie and Xavvie are standing in front of a giant glass display case which stretches from one end of the room to the other. Right smack in the middle, curled up in between a wooden flask and a black ceramic dish is a sleeping wyvern.

"How on earth did you spot him?" I ask Edward, genuinely impressed.

"One of the smoke curls from his snores caught my eye. Shall I wake him up?" Edward raps on the glass with his knuckles.

H opens one eye, squinting at us, still half asleep. He takes a minute to focus, but then his eyes open wide and he pushes himself to his feet.

"You scared us half to death!" I chastise him. "Come out of there so we can all go home."

Instead of following my instructions, H cocks his head sideways and motions that he can't hear me.

I look around, but it is clear that the others are leaving this problem to me. I do my best mime impression, asking whether he is stuck. He nods yes, looking embarrassed.

Kate rolls her eyes and then asks Bartie to fetch the display case keys from her office. He blinks out and is back again seconds later, with the keyring in hand.

Kate strides to the end of the case and unlocks a discrete opening at the far end. In his excitement, H wipes out an entire shelf of ceramic teapots. I flinch and then sigh when the magic steps in and repairs them.

As soon as he is free, H flies across the room and launches himself into my arms. "Thanks, Nat! You saved me! I thought I was goin' to be stuck in there forever!"

"How did you get inside there in the first place?" Kate asks as she locks the case up tight.

"I was 'untin' for a 'iding place when I ran into Alfred. It was 'is idea to 'ide in there. 'E said I'd blend right in and Xavvie would never find me."

"Alfred was right about that," Xavvie grumbles.

"Alfred picked me up and put me inside the case, sittin' on the bottom shelf where you found me. Xavvie passed by me, just like Alfred said 'e would." H lets go of me and swoops over to land Xavvie's lap. "When you came by the second time, I rapped on the window, but you couldn't 'ear me. I tried to push my way through, like Alfred did, but it didn't work. I was stuck! I waited so long, I guess I fell asleep."

"All's well that ends well," Edward says with a small chuckle. "Come on, H. I'll carry you home. It's really late."

Downstairs at the main entrance, Kate gives me one last hug before we say goodbye.

"Lunch tomorrow?" I ask, reconfirming our meet-up.

"Noon, and not a moment before then," she replies. "I'm looking forward to a long lie in tomorrow morning."

"Perfect! Get plenty of rest," I instruct her using my best mum voice. "We're all going to need to be at our best. Now that the Ashmolean event is behind us, we've got to finalise our plan for catching Beadle before he endangers someone else."

Chapter Twenty-One

The doorbell trills through the house, letting me know our first guests have arrived. "I'll get it!" I shout.

I open the door to find Mathilde, Kate, and Bartie standing at my new front doorstep. "Come in, come in! I can't wait to show you the place."

Edward arrives downstairs just in time to take a potted plant from Mathilde and a bottle of champers from Kate. "Housewarming gifts," Kate explains. "We could hardly show up empty-handed, even if this isn't your official housewarming party."

"You are all so thoughtful. We will definitely have a party to celebrate, but I want to wait until we finish the remodel and have proper furniture." As soon as they finish taking off their jackets and shoes, I hold my hand out and ask, "Would you like a tour?"

Mathilde and Kate leap at the opportunity. The pair have been excited to see the place since I got the keys. However, with all the event planning and preparation, this was the first chance they'd had.

"I'll stay down here and wait for Harry and the food delivery to arrive," Edward proposes, and Bartie generously offers to stay and keep him company. We leave the two men chatting as we move into the front room.

"Ignore all the furnishings. They are left over from when the place was rented out." I walk around the room, explaining our plans. "We're thinking of putting the sofa over here and then filling this wall with bookshelves. The television can go above the fireplace."

Mathilde seems dumbstruck. "All those flats we visited, Nat, and this is where you end up? It's a proper grown-up home. And it's gorgeous!"

"I know!" I can hardly contain my enthusiasm, still unable to believe my good fortune. We carry on through the dining room and the kitchen. I point out the brand-new shed standing in a corner of the garden. "It was Edward's suggestion. At first, I wasn't sure how H would take it, but he loved the idea. This way, he has his very own space out back, fully heated, but he can still come and go in the house whenever he wants."

"That explains the doggy door," Kate says with a snicker. "Do you think H will let us see his new space if I ask him for a tour?"

My face brightens with delight. "Oh, he would love that. He is fiercely proud of it, Kate. Please do!"

Upstairs, we look into each of the bedrooms and bathrooms. Here, the wear and tear from years of renting the place out is more evident. "Edward and I are going to do some of the surface work ourselves, such as painting and the like. But we're getting a contractor in for the big jobs."

Mathilde sizes up the built-in cupboard, filled with my clothing. "When is Edward moving in?"

"We're holding on to his flat at St Margaret until we're completely done with the building work." I give my friends a wry look. "Edward thinks the endless dust and paint smells will get to me eventually, and I'll appreciate having a place to escape."

Kate opens a nearby door, peeking into the guest bathroom.

She wrinkles her nose at the mould and lime stains and makes a swift exit. "Edward is a wise man... and a lucky one. You've got plenty of work on your hands, but I can't wait to see what you do with this place."

We make our descent when we hear Harry's voice calling up the stairs. She's already been around several times, helping me size up the work and determine which projects to tackle first. "Have you seen H's new garden shed? I'm on my way out back to see it. Anyone want to join me?"

Harry leads Kate, Mathilde and Bartie through the house while Edward and I remain in the front room, laying out an array of Greek food. I remember to hide one box of spanakopita. H will eat as many as he can get his talons into. Advance planning is required if anyone else wants a hope of getting one.

My grandfather is the last to arrive. He comes in through the garden with Harry, Kate, Mathilde, and H. I invite everyone to find a seat and help themselves. Sure enough, H lays claim to the feta and spinach pastries and everyone chuckles when I pull the other box out of hiding.

My grandfather settles comfortably on the window seat, beaming with delight, making me wonder if it was once his favourite place to rest. "While you all enjoy your meal, I'll recap the plans we need to put in place in the coming weeks."

"The floor is yours, Alfred," Harry mumbles, in between bites.

"Natalie, you met your Uncle Harold for lunch last week when he came up to Oxford to scout locations for his latest miniseries. It's set in London after the Great Fire, and Wren is one of the main characters."

"He told me all about it over lunch," I confirm. "It sounds amazing, definitely destined to be a hit."

"Harold always was full of imagination, even as a child." My grandfather shakes his head and returns his attention to the present. "One of the show's episodes is set in Oxford. Harold visited Somerset College, the Botanical Garden, and Christ Church Meadow. I asked the Eternals at each location to accompany him on his rounds."

Mathilde swallows a bite and interrupts with a question. "What were the Eternals doing? Did they observe anything of interest?"

"They weren't along as observers, but more as magical consultants, if you will." My grandfather winks. "They stayed by his side, whispering suggestions in his ear, to ensure he would demand they film locally rather than shoot on a soundstage in London."

Kate's eyebrows shoot up. "Very clever, Alfred! So, is the production coming to Oxford? Do we know yet?"

I jump in with the answer. "We do! Uncle Harold texted this morning with the news. They can't film until term ends, but the entire cast and crew are coming our way. That gives us about six weeks to organise everything before they arrive.'

"I'm so excited!" Harry gushes. "Rob and I are huge fans of the actor they've cast as Wren. He's brilliant!"

"You and your historical dramas," I exclaim with a knowing grin. "If they dress the characters in period costumes, you don't miss a single episode." Harry blushes as she nods, acknowledging the truth in my words.

My grandfather clears his throat, retaking control of the conversation. "They may not shoot until June, but we'll have no shortage of crew members coming to Oxford over the next six weeks. Based on the reports I got back from the Eternals, some of you should expect to be contacted in the next week or two with requests for help."

"Really?" Kate asks, intrigued.

"Yes, and we can start with you, if you like." My grandfather pulls his notes from his pocket. "From Nat's lunch with her uncle, we know that authenticity is of critical importance. The Head of

Eternal Affairs at Somerset College whispered a suggestion that the production could borrow original art and antiques from the Ashmolean. I wouldn't be surprised if the set decorator gets in touch."

Kate looks delighted at the thought. "I'll put Francie in charge of coordinating the request. She's due to return to work next week, and I am sure she would love to take on the project."

Harry has a particular soft spot for Francie. She brings her hand to her heart as she asks, "How is the poor dear?"

Kate gives Harry a grateful smile. "She's recovering well. Thanks for asking. I was worried she might not come back to work — too much trauma — but she is keen to get back to it."

Mathilde finishes her plate and sets it down with a clatter. "Anything for me, Alfred?"

"Yes, you're included as well. Let me see here..." He skims his finger along the paper, searching for the right line. "Ah, yes. Do you fancy acting as a technical expert?"

"Technical?" Mathilde scrunches her face up in confusion. "Like on lighting or equipment?"

"Based on your expression, I'd say no." My grandfather chuckles. "They'll need someone who knows the historical record backwards and forwards. Who better than the woman who spent weeks reviewing a secret treasure trove of journals and letters from the same time period?"

"Yes!" Mathilde pumps her fist, making us all dissolve into laughter. "That's brilliant!"

When the laughter dies down, my grandfather's gaze turns serious. "As fun as working on a film production may seem, we cannot forget that we have a very serious reason for being involved. It is almost certain that Thomas Hobbes has returned as an Eternal and is aiding his descendant, Oswald Beadle. We've seen in the archives footage just how far they will go in their efforts to steal Oxford's magic."

I glance at the others, noting the determination on their faces. H, in particular, looks fierce, with his mouth pulled back in a sneer and smoke trailing from his nostrils.

"What about me, Alfie? 'Ave you got a task only a wyvern can do?"

"You have one of the most critical tasks, H, if you are up for it." My grandfather pauses, waiting for H to signal his agreement. "All of our work will be for naught if Hobbes and Beadle don't take the bait."

"So you want me to go back to London? March in and challenge 'em to take us on? Let me at 'em!"

"No," my grandfather shakes his head furiously. "Nothing so obvious. We need you to use your magic to leak the filming news to the press. Sneak into the newsroom and whisper in the right ear. It's a big task, but we Eternals are confident you can do it."

H straightens with pride, declaring, "I always wanted to be a muse. Now's my chance."

My grandfather ticks an item off his list. "Nat, that brings us to you. Keep the communication lines open with your uncle. The more advance notice we can get on things, the easier it will be for the Eternals."

"I'm a step ahead of you, Grandfather. As the colleges will be closed for the summer, I don't have any projects in my diary. I offered my services as an expert on High Table dinners and other Oxonian ceremonies." I lean over, catching Harry's gaze. "If that isn't enough, I've also volunteered to organise the wrap party. Oxford will be their last filming location before they finish production."

"I'm going to need that date for my diary," Harry notes, only half-joking.

I notice Bartie and Edward exchanging looks. "What's up with the two of you? Do you have something else to add?"

Edward raises an eyebrow and then motions for Bartie to respond.

Bartie rises to his feet and begins pacing across the room. "Edward and I have been talking. It won't be enough to stop Hobbes, Beadle, and the Eternals they've created at the Torture Museum. They killed a man and nearly sent a young woman to jail for their crime."

My stomach turns over at the thought of their crimes. Burglary, arson and murder are already on the list. "What do you two suggest?"

"You can leave Hobbes and the Eternals to your grandfather and me. We will see an Eternal justice is meted out. But as for Beadle, he needs to be remanded into Her Majesty's custody." Bartie briefly looks at Edward before he finishes his statement. "We need DCI Robinson's full cooperation, and there is only one way we can get it."

All of us lean back in shock. My grandfather recovers first. "Are you suggesting what I think you are?"

Bartie's expression is grim. "We need to tell DCI Robinson about the magic of Oxford."

Sabotage at Somerset

OXFORD KEY MYSTERIES - BOOK FOUR

Nat has identified the evil menace stealing Oxford's magic. Can she and her friends stop them before it is too late?

Natalie, Kate and Mathilde know who is wreaking havoc on Oxford's magic. Now their challenge is to ensure they are brought to justice. When a film production comes to Oxford, it provides the group the chance to bait the perfect trap.

But the film set is plagued with problems from the moment it arrives. Equipment is damaged, scripts go missing and the lead actress is poisoned.

Nat and her friends will have to work fast if they want to salvage the production and trap the culprit.

There's just one problem: Has the evil menace caught onto their plans or is someone else trying to sabotage the show?

The Eternal Investigator
AN OXFORD KEY MYSTERIES NOVELLA

May 1941 - Money is missing from the coffers of St Margaret College.

Bartholomew Kingston is on the cusp of figuring out who is siphoning funds from St Margaret College when his friend Clark reminds him of their evening plans. He sets his work aside and travels to London for a night out on the town.

When he returns to work he makes a startling discovery: he's dead. Even worse, Bartie is horrified to learn he is being blamed for the theft.

As Oxford's newest Eternal, Bartie has some new tricks up his sleeve. With the help of the other Eternals, can Bartie find the real culprit? Or will his name be tarnished forever?

The Eternal Investigator is available on Amazon, order your copy now.

Acknowledgments

I was sure by book three I would have found my feet and flown through the writing. I was wrong. I vastly underestimated the impact of pandemic-related stress.

I owe a huge thanks to the amazing team who repeatedly picked me up and put me back on my feet. To Inga Kruse, Anne Radcliffe and Ken Morrison (aka my dad) - thank you for telling me time and again to keep going. I'd still be drafting chapter one if it weren't for your intervention.

Thanks to my husband and my kids for helping me find the time and space required to write. Thanks also to our schools for reopening. Absolute godsend!

Picking character names is my least favourite part of writing. I tossed a request for help in my Facebook group and got stellar suggestions! Special recognition to Monica Cobine, Gloria Thomas, and Medrith Loe for their help naming my potential suspects.

As always, a gigantic thanks to my cover designer, and friend, Emilie Yane Lopes. If you saw what I gave her as a brief, you would be amazed the covers turn out so well. Thanks for bringing my vision to life.

Thanks to Olga Mecking for being a cheerleader. When I lost the faith again, she read the first half of the book and shouted at me to send more straight away. I kept writing.

Thanks to my mom and my sister for moral support, keeping me entertained with group texts, and letting me vent when needed. Gifs are always appreciated. Thanks to my mother-in-law for hosting us this summer. We needed a break from our house and a small taste of normal life. Italy provided all that and more.

My online writing groups continue to play a huge role in my efforts to launch a writing career. Thank you to everyone who answers questions, shares information, commiserates, and cheers.

Last, but not least, thanks to the cats. Now get out of the refrigerator.

About the Author

Lynn Morrison lives in Oxford, England with her husband, two daughters and two cats. Originally from the US, she has also lived in Italy, France and the Netherlands. It's no surprise then that she loves to travel, with a never-ending wish list of destinations to visit. She is as passionate about reading as she is writing, and can almost always be found with a book in hand. You can find out more about her on her website LynnMorrisonWriter.com.

You can chat with her directly in her Facebook group - Lynn Morrison's Not a Book Club - where she talks about books, life and anything else that crosses her mind.

facebook.com/nomadmomdiary

twitter.com/nomadmomdiary

instagram.com/nomadmomdiary

bookbub.com/authors/lynn-morrison

goodreads.com/nomadmomdiary

Also by Lynn Morrison

The Oxford Key Mysteries

Murder at St Margaret

Burglary at Barnard

Arson at the Ashmolean

Sabotage at Somerset

The Eternal Investigator

Post Mortem at Padua (2022)

Midlife in Raven (Paranormal Women's Fiction)

Raven's Influence

Raven's Joy

Raven's Matriarch

Raven's Storm (2022)

Vampire Witch Mysteries

Stakes & Spells

Spells & Fangs

Fangs & Cauldrons (2022)

Nonfiction (published by Fairlight Books)

How to be Published

How to Market Your Book

Printed in Great Britain
by Amazon